"In *The Mother of Invention*, Claire Goldstein – mother, wife, university reporter – finds her comfortable life beginning to crumble. Her work assignment is borderline unethical, her teenage kids are secretive, her best friend is seriously ill, her marriage is showing cracks, her beloved grandfather is dying. Nina Miller writes with wisdom, honesty and humor of Claire's struggles to begin reinventing herself in the face of loss and betrayal."

–P.M. Carlson, author, *Murder in the Dog Days*

"This is a lovely, engaging novel of a woman confronting loss and change and what it means to be no longer young. Miller writes with a confident and elegant hand, covering momentous subject matter with a lightness of spirit and deep understanding. Well done!"

–Jeanne Mackin, author, *The Beautiful American*

"In this beautifully told novel, a woman in mid-life confronts the ultimate realities of aging and death. As she reevaluates her marriage, her relationship with her children, her work-life, and her commitment to social issues, she is helped by an older woman, a dear friend whose courage, humor, and wisdom sustain her in her journey."

–Miriam Schneir, author, *Feminism in Our Time*

The Mother of Invention

a novel by

Nina Miller

Wasteland Press

www.wastelandpress.net
Shelbyville, KY USA

First Printing – June 2015
ISBN: 978-1-68111-028-8
Library of Congress Control Number: 2015938132
Cover design by Dale Kaplan

Printed in the U.S.A.

0   1   2   3   4   5   6   7   8   9   10   11

For George, who will always occupy the deepest part of my heart

ACKNOWLEDGEMENTS

My heart is filled with gratitude to—

My insightful and patient friends who read the manuscript in its infancy and adolescence, especially Joan Brumberg, Carol Kammen, Jack Hopper and Gerard Cox, all thoughtful readers and critics.

Colum McCann, Alice Mattison and Julia Glass, whose workshops at the Fine Arts Work Center in Provincetown expanded my understanding of fiction.

Miriam Schneir, who, with patience and care, combed through and edited a mistake-ridden manuscript.

My brother Dale Kaplan, the artist who spent long, late nights transforming Michelangelo's famous hands into those of the women on the cover of this book.

Rachel Miller, who saved me from committing numerous anachronisms.

Christi and Jeff Cox, who brought their expertise in the world of publishing to my dining room table and walked me through an otherwise intimidating process.

The staff of Hospicare and Palliative Care Services of Tompkins County, NY, with whom I had the privilege of working for many years, and the patients and families whose courage, honesty and humor were a source of awe and inspiration.

All the compatriots of the several writing groups to which I have belonged over the years, especially those who spent hours reading this manuscript and making helpful suggestions.

Zee Zahava, whose supportive Writing Circle is my weekly Pilates writing workout.

David Gries, who came to the rescue of a bewildered novice Mac user on several occasions.

The Ithaca community I love so deeply, which has given me extraordinary opportunities to live a meaningful life.

And especially my children, Rachel, Ken and Jenny, who have supported and encouraged me throughout the years, and grandchildren Marni, Tessa and Georgia, who remind me that, even in the most difficult of times, there is still the possibility of joy.

Thank you all!

"I suppose there is one friend in the life of each of us who seems not a separate person, however dear and beloved, but an expansion, an interpretation of one's self, the very meaning of one's soul."

–Edith Wharton

CHAPTER ONE

ON TUESDAY MORNING, Claire Goldstein phoned the office of *Scholars,* where she was the editor of the newsletter for the faculty of Arts and Sciences, to remind her administrative assistant Marianne that she had a doctor's appointment and wouldn't be in until after lunch. It was probably an unnecessary precaution, but Marianne, usually so crisp and efficient, had been self-absorbed and distracted for the last few weeks.

Claire was long overdue for her gynecological checkup, something she regarded with dread. She hadn't minded the appointments when she was pregnant all those years ago, first with Stephen, then with Sarah. For those brief months she had been able to overlook what she was sure was the doctor's misogyny so long as she focused on the promised reward at the end of her tunnel. But after she had finished having children, the combination of dislike and anxiety kicked in and she would forget to schedule appointments, or would double-book with an important meeting at the university and apologetically call the doctor's office to cancel.

"Why don't you change goddam doctors?" Marco, her husband, would ask as she worked herself up before each visit, which became more widely spaced as the years went by. But Claire hated change.

She waited for almost an hour and a half in a reception room filled with big-bellied women whose faces reflected both the smug narcissism and the discomfort of the very pregnant. Hands atop their Buddha bellies, they chatted with each other about due dates, false labor, fluid retention. She seemed to be the only gynecological check-up on this morning's schedule, and the others eyed her as if she were a member of a different species. Well, at least this was one place where she felt slim, her hand on the less prominent bulge of her own stomach. Most of the young women wore tight-fitting tops over low-slung jeans or shorts, their basketball tummies proudly declaring themselves, so unlike the maternity outfits Claire and her peers had worn: pantsuits and simple sheaths with extra give in the middle. Things had certainly changed in twenty years.

The waiting room was pale yellow, with chairs covered in chilly green plastic and faux-wood tables topped with a tasteless supply of magazines. *Popular Mechanics* in a gynecologist's waiting room? Claire wondered if Dr. Jenkins was fascinated by the complex workings of everything, not just women. Nevertheless, when she finally entered the inner sanctum that led to the doctor's office, she wished she were back in the waiting area.

Millie, Dr. Jenkins' nurse, a woman in her late fifties with startlingly auburn hair combed unsuccessfully to cover bits of pink scalp, greeted Claire with a cool professional smile. She handed her a plastic cup. "Just a few drops," she called as Claire closed the door to the bathroom.

A few minutes later, blood pressure and temperature taken, pulse measured, dread scale confronted ("Hmmm, we've put on a little weight, haven't we!" from Millie) Claire sat on a molded plastic chair, waiting to hear Dr. Jenkins shuffle down the hall. When he entered, slightly stooped and beginning to soften in the jowls, she noticed how the years of midnight deliveries had worn on him. He looked as if he hadn't slept in weeks. Though his white coat crackled with starch, his posture exuded fatigue. His eyes were puffy and streaked. It had been nearly twenty years since Marco had summoned him to help wrinkled and goopy Stephen emerge from her womb; he had probably been in his early forties then. For a brief period during her first pregnancy she had thought him handsome, but now it was hard to imagine why. She remembered how Marco used to call it transference when she returned home from her early pre-natal visits waxing about Dr. Jenkins' encouragement of her progress toward motherhood.

"Good to see you, Claire. How've you been? And how's that husband of yours," he glanced at the computer, "Marcus?"

"Marco," she said, wondering why she was intimidated by the idea of calling Jenkins Dan, or even Doctor J, though he had always addressed her by her first name. Not that he had ever invited her to any greater degree of intimacy. Maybe it was a necessary attitude for physicians whose job it was to probe the most intimate areas of their patients.

Dr. Jenkins indulged her with neutral conversation for the requisite minute or two before she lost him to the computer. "Hmm." The sound made her more uneasy than she already was. Why is it, she wondered, that nobody ever says hmm you're terrific, or hmm, what a good job you've done, or hmm you look wonderful.

"You're overdue for your checkup by almost a full year. At your age that's not such a good idea."

The man was overflowing with tact and sensitivity. Claire's inner evolved voice said fuck off, it's my body. But her outer wimp mumbled, "It's been a busy year."

He seemed fascinated while he perused her electronic record, as if it was a mystery and he couldn't wait to find out whodunit. "Urine test's fine, no problems," he said. "Blood pressure's good, too."

Claire experienced a surge of kindergarten pride at her achievements. Maybe she could get a printout of the report and tape it to the refrigerator door where the kids' drawings used to hang.

"Well, why don't you put on a gown and we'll take a look inside." He offered a vague smile directed somewhere over her shoulder. She realized that he had not made true eye contact with her yet. Maybe Marco's right, it's time to change doctors, she thought, but knew she wouldn't. She was addicted to the familiar and avoided changes in everything possible: dentist, hairdresser, supermarket, internet service. Whatever she could hold constant, she did. And if she switched doctors, she'd have to transfer her records, and that would mean explaining why. No, she supposed she would suffer this fool, perhaps not gladly, until one or the other of them died. Some liberated woman you are, she scolded herself as she struggled to tie the short strings of the faded floral gown.

In a few minutes the nurse returned and helped her climb onto the examining table.

"Let's just slide our hips down a little further. That's the girl! Comfy?"

Her voice made Claire feel like she'd eaten too much sugar. Grunting, she inched her chilly buttocks toward the edge of the examining table. The nurse adjusted a white sheet on top of her as if she were a piece of sculpture to be hidden from an over-eager public.

"Doctor says you haven't been here for almost two years. Really important at your age."

Whatever happened to female solidarity, Claire wondered, as she stared at the drawings on the ceiling of an embryo in different stages of development. They were the same pictures she had pondered with great interest throughout both of her pregnancies, touched up over the years, she supposed. They showed the path from a squiggly mush of egg and sperm to a homunculus that resembled her bald Uncle Jacob at the end of his life, finally to a full-fledged baby. She used to watch the progression of pictures with delight when she came in for pre-natal visits all those years ago. She would lie in this same position, her fingers caressing the taut membrane of skin that covered her distended belly, and note the baby's progress along the guideposts of fetal development. "It looks like an anorexic shrimp," she reported to Marco after her eight-week exam, then later, "It's turned into a lobster." The first time she went into hard labor she imagined it had become a killer whale, but when Dr. Jenkins placed goop-covered Stephen on the deflated marshmallow of her stomach, she knew that he was indeed a baby, and that her heart would never be the same.

That was a long time ago. There should be different illustrations for women at mid-life who come in to make sure their internal organs were not in malignant decline. Pictures of – what? Old lace? A still life with teacups? The nurse was carefully laying out instruments as if they were the tools of an artist. Claire smiled at an image of herself, covered with only a sheet, lying on a scaffold close to the ceiling with the nurse handing her brushes so she could apply thick paint to wet plaster. The Michelangelo of the Middle Aged.

Like the technician at the Metropolitan Opera summoning James Levine with "Maestro to the pit," the nurse opened the door slightly and called, "Ready, Doctor."

Dr. Jenkins entered and pulled on a pair of thin white gloves. He moved to the side of the table and lifted the paper sheet away from Claire's chest. His fingers began to palpate her breasts and the area under her arms. His face was totally inscrutable as she examined it for any flicker of concern. She thought of the scar that had run across her mother's chest. She had been five years old when her mother had a mastectomy, and although her own chest was flat, she had fallen asleep for the next year with her hands on the place where one day her breasts would appear, as if to protect them from the intrusion that had invaded her mother's body.

"They seem fine, no lumps." The Lord giveth. "But of course we'll go ahead with the mammogram," he continued. "With your family history and at your age you should have one every year." The Lord taketh away.

When she had gone for her first mammogram nine years ago, obedient to the stricture that at forty a woman should start to have annual breast x-rays, her hands had trembled when she filled out the family history section of the information sheet. Mother: breast cancer. Recurrence six years later with metastasis to the lungs. Died age 49. Father's age at death 52. Cause of death: Accident.

The technician had tried to reassure her. "It's just routine, dear, it doesn't mean the doctor suspects anything. Just relax, there's nothing to it." But she'd been stiff with terror. Like a gourmet chef preparing pressed duck, the technician lay first her left breast on the cold glass plate and brought the top of the monster instrument down on her flesh, then backed out of the room to avoid the silent splash of radiation. When she returned a few seconds later she turned Claire as if she were on a spit, then repeated the process with her right breast.

Dr. Jenkins' voice brought her back from the memory of that isolation chamber where, in spite of her anxiety, the machine had regularly failed to find any sign of cells gone awry.

"Well, let's take a look inside," he said, as if he were about to lead a troop of boy scouts on a spelunking trip. He moved to the end of the table and perched on a low stool. The nurse, silent in the presence of The Master, hovered behind him.

Claire took deep breaths as first the icy speculum coated with thick lubricant, then Dr. Jenkins' gloved fingers prodded places inside her that were unaccustomed to strange visitors. After two successful pregnancies and God knows how many internal exams this should be easy. It never was.

The doctor's face, framed by her thighs, wore an expression of cool detachment. His eyes were focused on the wall behind her head as if a procedural diagram were taped there. She knew that nowadays medical training included touchy-feely sessions to help physicians tune in to their patients' emotional needs during the few minutes insurance companies allowed for a visit. But Jenkins was old school. He had already mastered Advanced Detachment when he was a young doctor delivering her first baby. She had wanted to strangle him when he calmly informed her that what she felt wasn't pain, only a little pressure. "Too soon for the epidural," he'd said, so she had alternately panted and moaned for the next four hours, Marco bringing her ice chips and trying to distract her with the Times crossword puzzle as he sweated by her side. Finally, like Moses delivering the tablets, Jenkins had brought in the anesthesiologist who rescued her from what felt like the jaws of hell prying open her body.

Now Jenkins' left hand pushed hard on her lower abdomen. "Little puffy there, having any trouble with fluid retention?" He glanced at her elevated ankles.

"No." Little balding there, she wanted to say, having any trouble with enzymes? She could have told him that in all likelihood the puffiness came from martinis with olives and Ben and Jerry's Chunky Monkey, but she wasn't up for a lecture on low-fat eating or the abstemious use of alcohol.

"Let's check the fit of your diaphragm," he said, opening the case she had given to the nurse earlier. He inserted the round disc and nodded. "No change." There was an embarrassing sucking sound when he retrieved it along with his Vaselined fingers, but he didn't register any reaction. Claire wondered if he thought she was trying to suction him back in. Removing the gloves, he scrubbed his hands. The nurse said, "Let's take our legs down."

Released from the stirrups, Claire was helped back into a sitting position, her legs dangling over the edge of the table like a child sitting in a grown-up's chair.

"Well," Jenkins said, "from the way your uterus looks, I'd guess that menopause is just around the corner. How old was your mother when she began?"

Look at my chart, dummy, it's all there. "She died before she started, I think. She was in her late forties."

Jenkins continued without any visible reaction. "There are a few things you should watch for. Any difficulty with lubrication?"

"No." Lubrication. It sounded more like something you did to a tired car, or applied to treat a skin rash. Her mother's form of sex education had specialized in euphemisms for body parts and intimate functions, words like tushy and wee wee and boom-booms. After her mother died, her grandmother, who had never raised a girl, had provided clinical reading material that seemed more like a plumbing manual. "Read it and then you'll ask me questions." She'd had dozens of questions that she never asked: why do people do it? What does it feel like? How does that big thing fit in? Even after all these years, the straightforward names of personal organs and activities still seemed detached and cool. She preferred pussy to vagina, cock to penis.

"Any hot flashes? Bouts of depression? Dry skin?"

No no no. He made a few keystrokes on the laptop as the nurse busied herself placing instruments in a wire basket. "Well, assuming the Pap smear comes back clean, I'll see you next year, unless you start to have any trouble with menopause." He tapped his nose. "Oh, and don't think you can't still get pregnant." On that cautionary note he rose and said, "Have a good year" to an indeterminate corner of the room, and vanished through the door, the nurse tripping behind him like an obedient wife.

The way things look inside. Menopause. Although he had been examining her nether regions, it was her unguarded heart he had located with the instinct of a born killer. Menopause. She was now an older woman. As she pulled on her slacks she pictured her interior space as a mysterious ancient cavern filled with hoar frost and cobwebs. A cavern which once housed two temporary tenants, never to be occupied again, except for Marco's decreasingly frequent visits to its entrance. She should be relieved that the exam was over, but instead she felt anxious and slightly depressed.

Driving home she noticed that a few trees were already beginning to turn. Too early, it's only the beginning of September, she thought. For most people in this town the calendar was established as much by the arrival and departure of students as it was by weather. You could tell they had landed by the stalled traffic at the intersection still known as the Octopus in spite of efforts to redesign it more efficiently, the longer lines at Wegmans and the bank, the difficulty getting into restaurants without reservations. But for the last couple of years the weather had been changing, and September was behaving oddly. Climate change, she supposed. What had Jenkins, that master of subtlety, said? The way things look inside. She imagined her internal organs turning dry and brown, as the leaves would before long.

THAT NIGHT CLAIRE HAD TROUBLE FALLING ASLEEP. Her stomach was cramping slightly in the aftermath of the examination. Marco snored quietly, his back to her, his buttocks companionably nudging her thigh. When she had turned forty-nine in March, she'd known that it was the age at which her mother had died, but she had buried that awareness. Today's examination had uncovered a feeling that combined gratitude and vulnerability. She lay in the darkness and began to calculate: her mother had died in August 1979. She was forty-nine and five months, fourteen days. Claire used her fingers to count out her own age: she had outlived her by fifteen days.

Claire didn't know if this was a gift of time, or a warning to use it differently. What did she want to change? What about her life wasn't working? What was around the corner and how much control would she have, anyway? Probably no more than her mother had had. Maybe the fact that she had lived longer than her mother didn't mean anything, was just happenstance. She lay still and checked to see if she felt different, the way a child does the morning of a birthday. She pushed away the approaching weepiness because she didn't want to wake Marco and try to explain why she was crying; she herself didn't understand why. Most of all, she wanted to talk to Maude. Marco once said, in that diagnostic tone of voice that made her want to scream, that because of the difference in their ages Maude was a surrogate mother. Claire hated that kind of simplification. "Why do you have to pathologize and label everything? Can't people of different generations be friends?"

But at that moment she longed to be wrapped in Maude's comforting arms with their soft, loose flesh. She'd have to wait for their regular visit on Sunday morning.

CHAPTER TWO

ON WEDNESDAY MORNING, Claire settled into her desk chair and checked the calendar: two articles that had to be edited by the end of the day, a staff meeting at eleven, an interview with a visiting scholar who was delivering a talk about recent Chinese political history. Sighing, she picked up the first article: a study that revisited gender discrimination in elementary school. The raised hands of boys are still recognized more than those of girls. Eye contact between teacher and boys is x times more frequent than with girls. She was about to cross out an awkwardly worded sentence when her inside line rang. She recognized the voice at the other end: cool, efficient Louise, personal assistant to the Vice President for Internal and External Communications. VPIEC.

"Jasper would like you to come over. Right away."

One didn't refuse Jasper's invitations. Or delay them.

"Call from command central," Claire said to Marianne, her assistant, who had been sitting at her desk twisting a rubber band around two fingers. It was unusual for Marianne to be a twiddler; she was usually a whirlwind of accomplishment. Claire grabbed her jacket and patted her hair in place. "I'm on my way."

"Your lipstick's smeared," Marianne said, handing her a tissue and a mirror from the top drawer of her desk. She watched closely as Claire blotted her lips.

"Much better. Good luck. When you get back can I talk to you for a few minutes?"

"Mmm," Claire mumbled, and started her rush across campus to the inner sanctum where the highest level administrators oversaw their academic fiefdoms. Why did Marianne feel that she had to wish her good luck? And why did she feel like she needed it? Damn Jasper anyway. He was several years younger than she, a hotshot the university had drafted away from Yale to take on the newly created position of Vice President for Internal and External Communications, one of several recently hired and highly paid administrators.

Jasper was the guru of spin. Whenever there was trouble he was called in to exercise his gift for reframing. Describing Jasper, Claire had told Maude that if the university had dropped a bomb in the middle of Calcutta, he would have claimed that they'd made inroads on solving the problem of homeless people sleeping on the street. Image was the controlling force in Jasper's life. He was acutely attuned to what kept donors happy and how to project the most positive impression of the university in the media. He schmoozed comfortably with the education editors of *The Times* (NY and London) and the *Wall Street Journal*, and had been interviewed on one of the Sunday morning news shows as a panelist discussing the future of higher education and justifying its exorbitant cost. Jasper loved the fast lane, was at ease with important people both on and off campus. But when it came to communicating with his staff of underlings, he had little time or use for casual conversation. She would have liked to believe that he was a Republican, but his name on sponsorship lists for Democratic fundraisers jarred her tendency to box people into stereotypes.

Claire wondered if she'd screwed up, done something egregious. She did a quick run-down on recent articles in the newsletter that might be the source of trouble, but all she could come up with was a piece on further evidence for climate change. Surely that couldn't be it; all but one or two of the scientists on campus were clear about the research findings. The icebergs were melting, no matter what the Tea Party said. The article on sighting a hawk thought to be extinct? Now who the hell could object to that? Awards announcements—had she overlooked someone whose ego was now bruised and would need to be soothed with an expensive lunch and a feature article? And why was she anxious, anyway? She'd been in her position longer than Jasper had. Neither of their jobs had the security of tenure, unlike the faculty who could probably perch naked on the library tower without fear of repercussion. But even without tenure, Jasper had the fast track to the President and the Provost, while both, whenever she encountered them, had trouble remembering her name and what she did.

The Administration Building was in the center of the campus, the perfect location for the student sit-ins which occurred every few years. The President's office occupied the entire top floor; Jasper and several other vice presidents were housed one floor below. Claire decided to take the elevator, in spite of her resolve to maximize every exercise opportunity during the work week. She didn't want to arrive breathless and sweating.

"He'll be with you in a minute," Louise said, barely looking up. Claire sat down in a comfortable purple and blue-flecked easy chair, and looked at the neatly arrayed magazines on the rosewood coffee table. *The Spectator. Vanity Fair. Country Life. The Atlantic Monthly.* It would be fun to slip in a copy of *The Nation*, she thought.

A buzzer sounded. "You can go in now," Louise said.

Jasper's office was luxuriously carpeted in dark blue. There were framed awards on the wall, as well as photographs of Jasper with the Clintons, with Condoleezza Rice, with Kofi Anan. And one Claire had never seen before, Jasper in a striped referee's uniform with two little boys barely visible beneath football padding. Maybe he was pissed about the article she'd written on football and concussions?

Jasper was sitting behind a glossy rosewood desk piled neatly with file folders, his huge computer monitor centered so that Claire could see only the top of his head until he swiveled sideways. He was a small man, not much above her five and a half feet, somewhere in his early forties. He was dressed in impeccably pressed trousers and a pale blue shirt, his tie diagonally striped in school colors. His shoe-polish black hair was neatly groomed, the part so straight that it could have been done with a ruler. Jasper looked as if he'd studied a manual on dressing for success. He reminded her of a stunted version of Mitt Romney. She wondered how much time he spent working out every day to keep that belly flat, though it was hard to imagine him with sweat running down his forehead.

"Good, you're here." He nodded her to one of the leather-covered chairs. "I've got something I want you to handle. Personally. Don't assign it."

No "how are you, did you have a nice weekend." Jasper didn't waste niceties on underlings. Still, Claire felt a rush of pleasure at what appeared to be a message of confidence, followed by an equally intense wave of anxiety. Before she could ask anything, he continued.

"This has to be completely confidential. I'm sure I can trust you," he said, his narrowed eyes undermining the certainty of his words. His chair squeaked as he leaned forward. "Of course you've been following this fracking business." He waited for her nod. "The university hasn't signed any leases with the drilling companies. But there are major donors—and I mean really major" – his index finger pointed at her for emphasis—"who are up to their asses in the industry, and they're putting pressure on us to lease some of the land we own out in the county. Of course we have no intention of doing that, though god knows we could use the money. But the issue is how and when to say a definitive no. We'll have to, eventually, but now is not the time.

"I'm sure you know we've got research going on in every part of the university," he continued. "They're looking at all the issues: safety, economy, chemical analysis, environmental impact. It looks like the results are coming in thumbs down on fracking, though of course you know that there are a few dissenting voice from pretty well-respected people."

That was one of Jasper's psychological tricks, acting as if you should be aware of something he hoped you didn't know anything about. Jasper paused as if his words had to reach across the chasm of her ignorance. The resisting chair squeaked again as he tilted back.

Fiddling with a paper clip he fished out of a small crystal bowl on his desk, he continued. "What we need is to buy a few weeks. A way to reassure both sides, for the time being. Passions are running pretty high on this thing in the community and around the state. So we want to get out a series of articles that summarize the latest findings on both sides, but wording it so it sounds like we're leaving the door open before we make a final determination."

"But we're not, are we? Everything I've read has seemed pretty conclusive. And you just said . . ."

He looked at her as if she had grease oozing down her chin. "Don't you get it? We have to say no in a way that sounds like it could be maybe, at least until the evidence is absolutely incontrovertible. Incontrovertible." He must like that word, Claire thought. How Jasperish.

"I'm not sure I'm the right person for this. I'm not a scientist. I never went beyond first year chemistry in college. And I practically flunked it." Ouch. She hadn't meant to show any vulnerability to Jasper. He liked winners.

"If I wanted a scientist they're a dime a dozen around here. What I need is a good P.R. writer. I'd do it myself, but my plate is already loaded." Jasper tilted forward to an upright position, the chair protesting again. "Got to get this fucking thing oiled," he muttered. He picked up the Cross pen that lay on the desk, caressing it as he continued. "You know what a hard hit the endowment's taken in the last couple of years. There's been a lot of pressure to get it back up—pressure from some pretty high places. The market is so fucking labile, knocked the shit out of my retirement fund, I can tell you. It's just beginning to come back."

That was the most intimate thing Jasper had ever said to her.

"Yeah, we've got all the development people breaking their asses, flying all over the country to dig up new money, but that won't make up for the losses. Anyway, you've got your assignment. Find a way to say no without saying no. You girls are good at that."

Claire wondered if that constituted sexual harassment but let it go by. "So what's the venue? The newsletter?"

Jasper narrowed his eyes. "Way bigger. This could be a career changer for you. Professionally, who knows where it could get you. I'm offering you a byline, wide distribution, not only on campus, but to the alums. But first you'll start with a letter from the President about how we're reviewing the latest research in all the relevant areas, and that we'll be reporting to the community in a balanced series of articles as we progress. We want it in comprehensible language, something that can go out to alumni, trustees, donors. That's your assignment. Run with it."

Claire's mind darted around trying to find the catch. There always was one, with Jasper.

He continued, "We have to be careful to keep this under wraps. We don't want to stir things up. You know these goddam students, any excuse to skip classes and demonstrate."

"Do I have a deadline?" Claire asked.

"I need the letter by the end of the day tomorrow."

Before Claire could register her dismay over the tight timetable, Jasper said, "You'll have more time for the series. There's a lot of information online, but a number of studies haven't been published yet. I've got some of them right here for you." He leaned down to retrieve a file box from beneath his desk. "Treat this like the family jewels. You'll have to scout around and see what else is cooking. And back burner whatever else is on your plate. Get someone else to take over the usual boring crap." Jesus, what a font of tact and kindness. That usual boring crap you're talking about is my life.

"After you get me the President's letter tomorrow I'll expect to have the first article in – let's say a week. Max. Do the first one on something where the evidence isn't absolute, like economics. Save the environmental stuff for later; it'll be harder to stay neutral on that." Jasper rose from his desk to dismiss her. "And don't forget, keep it under your hat. I don't want anything blowing up on campus."

WALKING BACK TO HER OFFICE, Claire thought about the years of demonstrations she'd read about or later witnessed. Maude had told her about the most dangerous one, the Black Power crisis in the sixties when a group of armed black students, feeling alienated and unsupported by the university, had taken over a campus building and issued a list of demands. The situation had escalated when it appeared that armed vigilante groups were heading in from all over the county. The students, some of whom would later go on to become trustees of the university or heads of large corporations, had made the cover of Newsweek with an iconic photograph that had, as her daughter Sarah would say, gone viral even before the widespread use of computers. The picture of angry young men draped with ammunition belts and holding automatic rifles had appeared in most newspapers and on magazine covers across the country. Maude said that for a few days it seemed as if Armageddon had arrived in their usually peaceful community. Fortunately the incident had ended without any injuries, but it had fractured friendships of many years as people took sides for and against the take-over with its potential for violence. Maude's husband Harry had told her that in those days you had to be careful about whom you invited to dinner because a perfectly nice evening could end up in a shouting match, or worse. Once he had come close to punching a history-professor friend who called the students fascists. The wives had pulled them apart, and although they were moderately cordial now, there was still a sense of unease when they encountered each other at a social gathering.

There had been the anti-Vietnam marches and sit-ins, then the anti-apartheid shanty village erected on the main quadrangle, where one night after a concert Pete Seeger had wandered from tent to cardboard box house to lean-to made of sheets and sticks, offering encouragement to the protesters and leading them in an emotional singing of "We Shall Overcome." Pro-choice demonstrations. Marches for increases in the paltry sums paid to teaching assistants. A clamorous protest when a popular woman professor was denied tenure. The most recent uproar had been over the razing of a small forest of redbud trees to construct a parking lot. That had enraged students and faculty alike, and some, including Harry, had handcuffed themselves to the chain-link fence the university had erected overnight surrounding the site. When Claire asked Harry why this was important enough to risk arrest at a time when the country was at war in Iraq, he'd responded that he was doing it mostly to support the students. "They feel so powerless about everything else going on, at least they can make some kind of a statement."

What the hell kind of statement am I making by taking this on, she asked herself. But she didn't feel as if she had a choice: she was forty-nine years old in a small community without lots of employment opportunities. Jasper had the power to make or break her; no one was going to demonstrate if she got canned.

WHEN SHE GOT BACK TO THE OFFICE, Claire instructed Marianne to cancel he staff meeting as well as all her appointments for the next week. "See if Terry will cover for me. I'm going to have to hunker down on a special assignment."

"What's up?"

"Can't say."

Marianne's eyes filled with tears. Claire knew Marianne was sensitive, but this was excessive.

"Look, I just got an assignment I can't talk about, I'm sorry."

"No, that's not it, I . . ."

"Not now, Marianne, I really have to dig in on this. Hold calls, please, and check in with me in a couple of hours."

Claire closed the door to her office and set the box down at her desk. It had been labeled "HYDROFRACKING" in thick black letters. The files inside had been neatly organized by one of Jasper's peons. The thickest file was labeled "Environmental Concerns", and contained a dozen folders: waste water, potential for increased earthquake activity, well contamination, on and on. Thumbing through, it looked to Claire like most of the studies focused on hazards in the chemical-infused water used to break up the shale, which hid pockets of gas. The wastewater was pumped out of the ground and stored in containment pools, which the industry insisted, were safe, but scientists pooh-poohed that. There had been methane seepage into nearby wells. An engineer was testing the long-term viability of the concrete used to line the wells. Some of the research was arcane and required more than her paltry understanding of science, but the summaries were helpful and almost comprehensible. She should probably contact someone at the medical school to see if anyone was working on disease implications of long-term exposure to increased amounts of methane.

There were folders on economic and social implications and the impact on the infrastructure. A sociologist speculated on the impact of young workers, mostly single males, living in temporary housing in unfamiliar communities, without enough to do after their shifts. An engineer in Operations Research had studied the potential deterioration of local roads due to extensive heavy truck traffic. The few reports that claimed positive outcomes for fracking looked almost lonely: one a study that projected improved air quality because of the reduction in fossil fuels, and another by an economist who outlined a boost to local economies during the initial period of drilling. But glancing through the material it seemed clear to her: fracking was a disaster in the making.

How the hell can I present this as anything else, Claire wondered. She opened a blank document and typed in "A Letter from the President." She was staring numbly at the words when Marianne knocked on the door. Claire tamped down her irritation when she noticed that for once Marianne didn't look like the model at a cosmetics counter. She had dark circles under her eyes, and one cheek had considerably more blush than the other.

"I really need to talk to you."

Claire stretched and nodded her in. "How was your weekend?" she asked automatically, then regretted the invitation.

"Not good at all. Terrible." The tears were threatening.

Oh Christ, not again. Claire was tired of being cast in the role of cheerleader for Marianne. Grow up, she wanted to say, pull up your socks and get on with your life. But of course Marianne didn't wear socks. Nor did she wear Birkenstocks over them. When she first showed up for her interview five years ago, Claire had tried not to react to the Fifth Avenue look of her perfectly fitting blue suit, ivory silk blouse, heels, understated jewelry. Christ, I hope these are just interview clothes, or the rest of us will look like bag ladies, she'd said to herself. Fortunately, the resume belied the look: Marianne had worked as assistant in the "Letters to the Editor" department of the *Times,* and her references were pitch-perfect.

It didn't take long to discover that masquerading beneath the chic clothing and exquisitely applied makeup was a bundle of insecurities. Marianne's work was excellent, but she needed constant reassurance. Yes Marianne, that's exactly what I wanted. No, Marianne, I wasn't annoyed when you corrected my grammatical error, I was grateful. The more support Claire provided, the more dependent Marianne became. At even the most delicately phrased hint of disapproval she would crumple, her wounded ego on ready display. But her prodigious work and devotion made Claire's life more manageable.

"Oh well, I seem to be stuck anyway. Maybe a lunch break will inspire me. Let's find a quiet spot," she said.

Marianne's face registered relief, and she turned, to reclaim what Claire guessed was her Manola Darghis pocketbook from the drawer of her desk.

The interruption was welcome. Claire felt as if her brain was stuck in thick mud. Her head was swimming with facts, her shoulders ached and she was pondering the indulgence of making an appointment for a massage. She stacked the papers, replaced them in the box and locked her office door, something she rarely did.

They decided to have lunch at the Union, a short walk across the quad, which was filled with students warding off the approach of chilly autumn by their refusal to dress for the weather. Even though the temperature today was only in the mid-fifties, many wore sleeveless shirts and shorts. Some threw Frisbees with self-consciously dramatic swoops; others lay on the grass studying. Several couples were locked in clinches with partners of the opposite or same sex. Claire stepped around a grad student who sat cross-legged, drinking coffee and pecking at his laptop. Probably tweeting or twerping or whatever the hell they do. Another leaned against a tree mumbling a meditation phrase, like a poor imitation of Buddha beneath the cobra.

The cafeteria, with its old wooden tables into which years of graffiti had been scratched, reeked permanently of French fries. After she and Marianne had been through the line and gotten their lunch, they carried their trays to a table in a far corner.

"So what's happening?" Claire asked. "You look like something's very wrong." She spooned some yogurt into her mouth and waited for Marianne's reply.

"It's Chet." Chet was Marianne's graduate student husband. He had been working on his doctorate in musicology for five years. "He's stuck, he says he can't go on, he's got to get out of here. He says he hates Sibelius, he hates Finland and the Finnish. He hates all the music Sibelius ever wrote. He says he can't think about the violin concerto without wanting to vomit." She picked delicately at a corner of lettuce sticking out of her untouched egg salad sandwich.

"He's been wrestling with his dissertation for, god, I don't know how many years, and he's just not making progress. And now he says he wants to bag it. After all this time. I gave up everything to come here. But he's trying to convince me that quitting is a rational decision, it's for our future, blah blah blah." Marianne's beautifully manicured hands began to shred the edge of her foam coffee cup. "And the worst part is that he wants to move back to Cincinnati and work for his father in the auto parts business until he figures out what's next. Or maybe teach five year olds how to play cymbals. He wants to leave now, says he can't cope with any more failure. He says he can't face the blank computer screen; he can't turn his ideas into words." She paused to blow her nose on a recycled napkin. "I don't know what to do. We had so many plans, and now . . . I can't stand it--Cincinnati!" She said it with her face puckered as if she'd just witnessed a cat bringing up a hairball.

Marianne's green eyes spilled tears onto her plate. Claire reached across the table and touched her arm, trying not to notice the egg salad swimming in a thousand calories of mayonnaise.

"Do you know what I've given up to get him through this damned degree? I left a job I loved in New York to come to this boring grey place so he could finish."

Claire had a flash of anger. You're talking about my town, babe, then recalled her own unhappiness when she and Marco had first arrived here.

"And I moved away from all my friends, and he's at the music library all day and half the night. And we're broke. He's had a teaching assistantship, but basically I've been supporting us. We've used up most of our savings. I haven't even bought a scarf in four years. When we came here he promised me that I would have the right of refusal on the next move, and now he's saying it has to be Cincinnati."

"I'm sorry, Marianne, this has to be tough for you. I know you've been looking forward to the next part of your life. Do you think he'd stay if he could get through the dissertation?"

She did feel genuinely sorry for Marianne, but she also knew that it would take time to find someone half as good to fill her job.

"I know he would. He's just doing this because he can't stand feeling like a failure any more. And . . ." Marianne's face crumpled, "I'm beginning to think of him as a failure, too."

Claire finished the last drops of her yogurt. "Well, I don't know if this would help, but I know a writing coach who has worked with faculty and grad students." Claire poked around in her pocketbook and pulled out her cellphone. She scrolled through until she found the name she was looking for, then wrote it on a napkin which she handed to Marianne. "She's very good. Last year, even though he'd already published a lot, Marco hit a time when suddenly he couldn't write. He just totally blocked. He was so depressed I thought he was going to crawl into a hole and stay there. I was confiding in a friend, and she told me about this woman." Claire remembered that at first Marco had been too embarrassed to call her; he'd acted as if she were recommending a sex therapist. "He was a little reluctant—you know how guys are about asking for help--but once he got started with her, she showed him ways to work through the block. It might be worth a try."

Marianne grasped the napkin and folded it carefully. "I'll try anything. Can I tell him that your husband used her and it worked?"

"Why don't you say it was someone in the history department?" Claire wasn't sure why she was being protective; maybe she too thought of it as a form of erectile dysfunction.

BACK AT THE OFFICE, Claire turned over the editing work out to one of her staff so that she could spend the remainder of the afternoon drafting the president's letter. She finished the two-page document just before five. It wasn't very good, but she would polish it in the morning. At least it would go out under the president's name, not hers. She was nonplused at the idea of her byline on a series of neutral articles about fracking; maybe she could talk Jasper into taking authorial credit.

On the way home Claire drove through town to pick up something for dinner. She thought about Marianne, and about how unchanged women's lives were. Yes, you could get into Rotary meetings, wear trousers to anything, even be the president of an Ivy League University or Secretary of State. But for most women the culture still dictated the same old standards: stand by your man, whither thou goest, all the old values still ruling their lives.

As she passed Planned Parenthood she saw a group of seven or eight people standing across the street holding signs with pictures of mutilated fetuses. One older couple stood in a position of exaggerated prayer. Claire had a fleeting desire to swerve and plow them all down. When does this ever end? All the battles her generation had thought they'd won had resurfaced and were threatening to explode again. She tapped the car horn and waved at two women, about her age, who were sitting on the porch of the Clinic. They wore bright orange vests that said Escort, a job that involved helping women safely into the Clinic, away from the taunts of protesters. She longed to open her window and give a finger to the protesters, but she drove on, promising herself that as soon as she could carve out some time she'd volunteer at

Planned Parenthood. What a fucking crazy world, she said aloud as she pulled the car into the supermarket parking lot, and in a minute her attention was riveted on the tantalizing bowls set behind glass in the carry-out section, where she couldn't decide between a roasted chicken and lamb Korma.

CHAPTER THREE

C LAIRE IMMERSED HERSELF in the fracking literature all day Thursday, with time out for a call to Maude's house to say she'd stop by at the end of the work day. She found herself tapping frequently into her search engine and the dictionary to wrestle with unfamiliar terms and concepts. The deeper she got, the more uncomfortable she became with her assignment. After a dozen revisions, she completed what she hoped was an adequate fence-sitting statement to go out over the President's name, and emailed it to Jasper with a sense of both relief and fatigue. He needn't have issued the injunction against discussing it with anyone; she would have been too embarrassed. Still, she felt a strong need to see Maude, and decided to deliver the family compost to her after work.

Stopping at home, Claire left a note for Marco and Sarah saying she'd be late. She picked up the container of food scraps they'd saved and placed it carefully on the floor of the Prius, though if it had tipped, other than the stench, it would hardly have been discernible among the jumble of unopened ads, charge slips, notices from Sarah's school, and the other detritus of daily life that had accumulated. Marco used to complain that Claire used the car like a pocketbook, and often repeated how he'd once lectured with a lollypop hanging from the back of his jacket, much to the delight of his otherwise laconic students.

CLAIRE PULLED INTO MAUDE AND HARRY'S DRIVEWAY and got out of her car, carefully lifting the covered bucket of food scraps

"Maude?" Claire called, still outside. "Garbage delivery!"

There was no answer, so she pushed open the screen door and walked through the cluttered living room, through the kitchen to the back door and out into the garden.

Walking through the vibrant colors of the back yard, Claire thought about how much she hated gardening. That was a radical and slightly embarrassing confession in a town where people, mostly expats from big cities, took such pleasure in growing their own food. They loved to talk about how they made catsup from their own tomatoes, and that they had discovered yet another recipe for zucchini, which was so abundant that you had to lock your car at harvest time or someone would place a bushel of it in the front seat with a note urging you to enjoy the fruits of their labor.

When Claire and Marco had bought their house two years after coming to town, Maude helped them design a perennial border along the driveway. But it didn't take long for Claire to realize that all she got out digging in the earth was dirt under her fingernails and an aching back. Her throat would constrict if she accidentally touched snail slime, and garter snakes with their swishing sly movements made her retreat to the house in panic, yielding to what Marco called her childish phobia. Before she went out to cut the few flowers that had survived her inattention, she would bang on an empty can to frighten away the unwanted slithery creatures. Much as she trusted Maude, she found it hard to believe her reassurance that they were harmless and actually beneficial. "How do I know they read the same manual you did?" Claire had demanded. Marco wasn't much more of an enthusiast for maintaining their little piece of greenery. He hired their neighbor's son to come once a week to drive his bucking mower around their lawn as if he were in search of cattle rustlers.

MAUDE WAS SQUATTING DOWN inspecting a leaf with a magnifying glass. The pads she wore strapped around her knees made her look like an aging hockey player. Looking at her from above, Claire noticed for the first time that her beautiful white hair, pulled back with a green stretchy hairband, had begun to thin.

"Hey. You look like Sherlock Holmes with that glass."

Maude looked up and grinned her broad toothy smile.

"Something's chewing on what's left of my phlox and I'm going to get the little bastard. I just have to figure out what he is so I can mix the right poison." She slowly rose to her feet, biting her upper lip.

"Hurt?" Claire asked.

Maude made a dismissive gesture. "I just need an oil can for these creaky joints."

She stuck the magnifying glass in her apron pocket, which she wore over her standard uniform: denim skirt, plaid shirt with sleeves rolled to the elbow, white sneakers stained with grass. Claire noted a certain tautness in her face, a caution in the way she moved.

"Hello, dearie. I'm so glad to see you! I'm ready for someone to bring a little laughter into my life," Maude said.

"You look like you're still in pain."

"Nothing to worry about. What goodies do I get today?"

Maude lifted the lid of the container Claire was carrying and peeked inside at the mess of fruit and vegetable scraps, egg shells, moldy bread, leftover rice. She grimaced as the smell rose to her nostrils. "Looks like you had ratatouille this week," she said. "Watermelon for dessert."

"What are you, one of those detectives who reconstruct people's lives by examining their garbage?"

"I just like to make sure you're getting proper nutrition."

Claire set the bucket on the grass and hugged Maude. She smelled like newly turned soil.

"Let's get rid of this and go inside. I'll tackle the enemy later. I need a drink," Maude said.

Claire followed her along a stone path leading to the compost pile hidden behind the garden shed. She emptied the smelly mess, then looked around while Maude covered it with some of the decaying matter from the bottom of the pile.

Maude and Harry's yard was bordered with roses, their fragrance almost concealing the rotten-food smell of the bucket. Perpendicular to the rose bushes a bed of zinnias still blazed red and orange and pink. Curved yellow squash lay bright against a swarm of green leaves. The last of the tomatoes waited to be picked, pulling against the tall stakes where Maude had tied their branches with old stockings. Maude was a purist about tomatoes "Heirloom shmeirloom, give me a Big Boy any day," she said.

The tomato plants were interspersed with perky yellow marigolds. "Keeps the tomato pests off," Maude had told Claire on her first visit to the garden. "That and the ladybugs." Maude's mail-order ladybugs arrived every spring in a plain brown wrapper like a collection of pornographic books. She stowed them in her refrigerator where they lay dormant until she took them out. Then, as the warm air kissed them back to life, they stirred and began to scoot around like tiny liberated Volkswagens.

Maude read garden catalogs as if they were racy Gothic novels. She studied what she called the juicy parts, and then, after sketching and planning, she would send in her order and wait for the seeds and seedlings to arrive the way a child waits for a birthday. In early March her sun porch was filled with trays of tiny pots bearing sprouts, which she set out at the end of April in the cold frames Harry had built for her. She placed them in their new enclosures with the tenderness of a mother leaving her children on the first day of nursery school. By the time spring bulbs were fading to crisp brown—the very moment Claire's yard turned into a morass of early chickweed, thistle and crabgrass—Maude's flared with summer flowers and the bright blossoms that would soon become vegetables. And by early fall, like now, when most people's gardens showed signs of their owners' fatigue, Maude's was still glorious with fruition. Everything she touched flourished, even plants the catalogs caution would not grow in their harsh northern climate. "Bosh," she said. "They're just protecting themselves in this age of litigation." Maude was the only person Claire knew who said bosh.

"I should have called to make sure Harry told you I was coming," Claire said as they scrubbed at the kitchen sink.

"Bosh, you're always welcome. And I'm not cooking tonight because Harry's off at some kind of meeting. I think this is the living wage group. You know Harry and his meetings." She half-filled two juice glasses with red wine and followed Claire into the living room, the bottle tucked under her arm. They shifted piles of *New Yorkers* and *Nations* to make room on the blue tweed sofa with its squishy cushions. One long wall was filled with bookshelves. The room was a clutter of artifacts from Maude and Harry's travels: a bright, multi-tiered Mexican candelabra, vividly painted animalitas from Oaxaca, a cracked German beer stein, a Renaissance etching of the town hall in Siena, an onyx bust of Karl Marx that had belonged to Harry's father. The walls were covered with whimsical framed posters put out by the London Transit Authority, a reproduction of Rivera's peasant woman bending beneath a basket of calla lilies, and paintings done by local artists.

Maude leaned back on the sofa and put her sneakered feet on a stack of newspapers on the battered pine coffee table.. "Well, dearie, you've been on my mind. Didn't you have an overdue checkup with your gynecologist this week? How did it go?"

"Flying colors. And I got a little bonus. Jenkins told me that menopause is lurking around the corner. Like a stalker." Claire pulled a thread that hung from the bottom of her white shirt and watched as part of the hem unraveled.

Maude smiled and patted her hand. "Just the thought of a hot flash fills me with nostalgia." She took a deep swallow of her drink. "I can't believe that my seventy-ninth birthday is just around the corner. How did this happen?" She sighed and shook her head. "Almost eighty. Sometimes I catch sight of myself in a store window and I ask myself who that old broad with white hair and wrinkles could be."

Claire touched her cheek. "You don't have that many wrinkles."

Maude laughed. "I think you saw the wrong doctor. You need an ophthalmologist, not a gynecologist."

"What's the big deal about eighty, anyway? Decade birthdays are just snapshots that tell us is which wars we've lived through."

Claire traced the top of the glass with her index finger, noticing the snippet of nail that was about to chip off. Tucking her legs under, she shifted to face Maude. "The most extraordinary thing happened to me the night after I saw the doctor and heard that the menopausal axe was about to fall."

"Marco would be flattered that you still think it's extraordinary, after all these years."

"I should be so lucky. No, I was lying there thinking about what Jenkins had said, and about my mother, and all of a sudden I found myself counting and I realized that I've made it a few days past the age she was when she died. I felt like I'd been reprieved from a death sentence I didn't even know I was under." She wrapped her arms around her knees and continued. "I woke up with this feeling that I'm at some kind of turning point, as if something has to change. It's, I don't know, sort of ominous. Like a tsunami might sneak up on me and sweep me off into unknown territory." As she said it, she thought about the fracking assignment and wondered if that heralded an approaching typhoon.

"You know," Maude said, her fingers tracing a stain on the sleeve of her shirt, "I've often caught myself thinking well, my dear, you have x more years to get done the things you want to do. And it's always the number of years left up to the age my mother was when she died. I would guess that lots of people carry that around. I suppose it's one of our residual beliefs in magic. Marco would probably be able to explain it."

Maude thought because Marco was a psychologist he understood the underlying causes for everything, even though Claire had told her many times that he had switched out of clinical to social psychology after only a year and that his specialty was peer pressure. Marco could be as dense as anyone about other aspects of human behavior.

"You wouldn't believe how much he doesn't get," Claire said. "How old was your mother when she died?"

"She was eighty four."

"You had her for a long time."

"Weren't we lucky, we had all those years to dislike each other. It never changed." She shook her head, then patted the green hair band back into place. "We used to go at each other over every damned thing until I was finally able to get out of the house. I worked my butt off to get a scholarship, mostly so I could leave it all behind. Leave her behind. If I'd stayed I might have been arrested for matricide." Maude's smile was humorless. "I know I've told you all this before, haven't I? I'm getting so forgetful these days."

Claire had heard about Maude's childhood many times, but she sensed the older woman's need to tell it again and sat back quietly.

"She was a piece of work, my mother. She thought it was a waste of time and money for girls to go to college. And what's worse, they might encounter Jews. Blacks were so out of her frame of reference that she hardly even worried about them. When I called to tell her I was marrying Harry Cohen, well, you can imagine how that went over. She damn near fainted."

"Actually, you never told me about the first time you brought Harry home."

"Consider yourself lucky. I guess it's the power of repression. Sometimes Harry brings it up, but there are some things that are better staying buried. Though I suppose Marco wouldn't agree with that."

Who knows what Marco's thinking these days, Claire mused. "I bet your mother would have gotten along well with Marco's," she said. "Even though he left the church years before we met, she's always blamed me for his lapsed faith. Saint Marco. I think he was her ticket to heaven. She always hoped he'd become a priest."

"Oy," Maude said. Claire laughed at the Midwestern inflection Maude managed to give the word.

"Marco never says outright that he's quit the church," Claire continued. "He's calls himself a Lapsed Catholic, capital L capital C. When I first went away to college I met so many people who described themselves that way I thought it was a branch of the church, like Franciscans." She rolled her shoulders and stretched.

Maude smiled. "There was nothing lapsed about my mother, she was pure Missouri-Synod Lutheran. She was a true believer right up to the end." She shook her head. "When somebody died, there was no room for tears at the funeral. For her it was a reason to celebrate because they'd gone to the arms of Jesus—assuming, of course, they were abstemious in all things and had sex for procreation rather than pleasure." She sighed and shook her head. "And her politics! McCarthy was a hero, school desegregation was a communist plot, I could go on forever. If she were alive today she'd be squawking about how liberal the Republican Party has become and how the Tea Party is the only hope for America. I used to lie awake imagining what it would be like to belong to a different family. There were so many times I wished she would just disappear through a hole in the floor, though I didn't say it out loud. One didn't, in those days."

"In all the years I've known you, you've never said much about your father."

"I hardly knew him. He worked his butt off on the farm. He pretty much ate dinner and went to bed so he could get up early in the morning. Seven days a week, didn't even go to church with us, which gave my mother an excuse to rag at him every Sunday. She hated that he came in dirty, made him take off his overalls in the back hall. He mostly let her do the heavy lifting with my sister and me, went along with whatever she said. I've often wondered if he really had to work that hard, or if it was his way of getting the hell away from her." She paused and took a sip of wine. "He made his grand escape when he was only fifty years old, just keeled over in the barn one morning when he was milking. When I think of him all I see are those stained denim overalls and his old work boots. I have no idea what he thought about, what kind of person he was. I suppose he must have been a masochist to live with her all those years. It's sad, isn't it?"

"You and your mother never worked things out?"

Maude shook her head. "After Alice died I put in my years in a therapist's office, I know I've told you about that. Not that it helped." Alice was the daughter Maude and Harry had lost when she was seven years old. "After a few months the therapist pushed me to talk about my mother. I suppose she thought it would be good for me to forgive her. But I never really got to where I could. Especially because she didn't come to Alice's funeral. She was so angry that we weren't going to have a church service that she flat out refused to come. And it was probably just as well, because if she'd talked about how joyful it was that Alice was with the Lord I probably would have decked her."

She was quiet for a moment, then continued, staring at her empty glass. "When mama died I went to her funeral. Harry wouldn't come. Who could blame him? I didn't get up and say anything; I left that to my sister. I couldn't think of anything good to say about her. I'm not even sure why I went." She seemed to make a decision and grinned. "Are you going to bill me for this session? That's enough of my wallowing in the past."

"Did Harry's parents care that you weren't Jewish?"

Maude laughed. "David—that was Harry's father—he saw religion as one of the world's great deceptions. So long as I wasn't a churchy type he was okay. And Rose—well, she wasn't a believer, but she held on to some of the traditions she'd grown up with. Like lighting candles a couple of times a year, or when someone important to her died. David used to tease her that she was taking out heaven insurance, just in case. His religion was pure socialism."

"I'm sorry I never met them. I remember when you and Harry flew to Israel to visit them," Claire said. Harry's parents had moved to a left-wing kibbutz a few years after Alice's death.

"The work must have agreed with them," Maude said. "They were healthy until just before the end. They learned Hebrew, worked in the day care center, took an active role in running the kibbutz. Very special people. When they died David was in his mid-nineties, Rose was ninety-one." Maude sighed. "I'm glad they didn't live to see what's happening today with the settlements and the ultra-Orthodox running the country. They would have felt like their lives were wasted. They had such hopes for the possibility of socialism in Israel."

Maude stretched her arms out in front of her and squeezed her fingers open and closed. "How on earth did we get here? Enough of living in the past, I want to hear about you. Tell me about work. And aren't you going to visit your grandfather soon?"

"Saturday. Work is the same old," Claire said, looking away from Maude's face to her glass. "I'm restless. I wish I could think of something else I could do."

"Is this part of your mid-life reprieve from the Grim Reaper?" Maude asked, leaning forward to pour more wine into their glasses.

"You tell me, that's what I'm here for. Your job description says you have to be my source of inspiration and unqualified support."

"I wouldn't worry too much. Maybe it's just a midlife crisis."

Claire had never before felt trivialized by Maude. She felt tears start, and lowered her head to hide them. Maude seemed unaware and continued. "Is there something you've been wanting to do? Some fascinating man you've had your eye on?" She grinned. "Now there's an idea!"

"Another time."

Maude lifted Claire's chin and dabbed at a spilled tear with her thumb. "I'm sorry, I didn't realize how upset you are. See what happens when I talk about my mother? I lose any trace of humanity."

Claire regained her composure and said, "It's complicated. But maybe I'm just premenstrual. I guess I should cherish my ebbing and flowing, so little of it left." She drained her glass and said "Hey, when I called this morning Harry told me you'd had another bad night and were still sleeping in. It was after eleven. More back pain?"

"It came on last night when I went to bed so I took one of those damned sleeping pills. You know how they affect my memory, which is no great shakes these days anyway. For all I know I might have gotten up in the middle of the night and eaten a quart of ice cream and a jar of olives." She patted her stomach. "Anyway, I woke up at noon with a chilly hot water bottle. But I suppose at my age you're lucky to go to bed with anything, even a hot water bottle." Her croaky laugh came from way back in her throat. When Claire's children were little they called her the lady with the frog laugh.

"This has been going on for too long, Maude. I wish you'd take it seriously. And maybe you ought to ease off the gardening for a while."

"I keep telling you, it's just old bones and creaky joints. Everybody my age has arthritis."

"Even so, maybe you ought to see a specialist."

Maude leaned forward to put her glass down and winced for a millisecond. "No wonder Harry loves you, you're as much of an old fusspot as he is. Anyway, just to get you both off my back I made an appointment with a neurosurgeon. Someone our family doctor recommended. I'm seeing him tomorrow."

Claire was startled, but Maude's tone changed, signaling that the topic of backaches was concluded. 'What's the latest with the kids?"

Maude loved children and young people, though Claire liked to think that hers were special favorites. Maude had been a librarian at one of the town's middle schools. She remembered not only every kid's name, but also what they liked to read. She would put notes in their mailboxes to let them know about a new book she thought they might enjoy. As a way of keeping in touch after she retired, she ran a book club at her home for any student who wanted to attend. Claire's daughter Sarah was a regular, even though at fifteen she was one of the oldest kids.

"Sarah have any new piercings?" Maude asked.

"She doesn't let me get close enough to see anything more than the most obvious ones. I'm not sure I want to know about the others. I've told her no tattoos until she's at least eighteen. Her friend Joline came over with a tattoo of a cell phone on her shoulder. Jesus."

"Well, better than drugs."

Claire frowned. "Who knows what's going on in that department? I must bore you to tears with my Sarah complaints. But dammit, everything I say turns into a fight. She makes me feel like a complete failure. I'm conventional, I don't act on my convictions, I don't understand anything, I think I'm some big deal feminist because I once went to a pro-choice rally. Yadda yadda yadda."

Maude patted her hand. "Did I tell you what she said at our last book group meeting? But don't let on that I shared this with you."

"It's a book club, not a psychotherapy group. I don't think the rules of confidentiality apply."

"Anyway, we were talking about *Catcher in the Rye*. I was curious to see what it means to kids today, if it has the impact it had when I was a teenager, probably you, too. Sarah said, and I quote, 'Salinger was a self-involved asshole.' Two of the kids who loved the book got really belligerent, as if she'd committed treason. But our Sarah held her ground. She insisted that Salinger doesn't deserve to be read any more because, and I quote again, 'anyone who had that much influence didn't have a right to live like a hermit.' She said he should have been on the front lines for political change instead of hiding on a farm someplace in New England."

"I have to remember to tell that to Zayde. He'll be so proud," Claire said. Zayde was the Yiddish word for grandfather.

"She'll get past being awful to you, you just have to live through it. Sarah is basically a solid, wonderful kid. They both are. The next time she hasn't stopped talking to you tell her to stop by. I have a book I think she'll like. And tell her she can complain about you and I won't repeat it. How's Stephen?"

"He came over for dinner with Nora a couple of nights ago. With laundry, of course. I think I'm going to run for President of the Old Fart Society. You'd think that sleeping together at his place would be enough. I can't get used to them feeling each other up under the table in the middle of dessert."

Maude laughed. "Would you like it better during the soup course? It's hormones, dearie. Yours may be starting to decline but he's firing on all cylinders."

"He's working part-time at the job he had this summer. I hope he can manage it with his classes and all the other things he gets into. He's organized a committee to work on something he won't talk about, some kind of political action." She shook her head. "I swear that kid thinks he the world's first radical. I made the mistake of telling him about the demonstration in Washington when we still thought we had a shot at getting the ERA passed. You know what he did, my revolutionary, child of my loins? He sneered at me and gave me this self-righteous spiel about how you can't change the hard economic order by burning bras. The little snot."

Claire was often the victim of her children's judgments. It seemed to her that Stephen and Sarah wore their weighty sense of injustice like body armor. They were also, unfortunately, sure they had most of the answers, and that she and Marco were fundamentally antediluvian. They held Claire to a higher standard because she had lived with her grandparents during her adolescence, and her grandfather had been a card-carrying communist until the 20th party congress, when Khrushchev blew the whistle on Stalin's atrocities. Marco, on the other hand, they saw as a Catholic in recovery, and expected less from him. During one of their arguments when she was asserting that a third party would weaken the Democrats, Stephen had looked at her with contempt and said "Didn't you learn anything from Zayde?" The kids thought of her as passive and arcane, like a Victorian antimacassar. "You think that writing letters to politicians and signing email petitions will produce change," Stephen said. Stephen and Sarah both considered it charming and slightly daffy when they learned from an old classmate of Claire's that she had smoked pot when she was in high school. She never let on about the other drugs she'd tried.

Sometimes Claire wondered if there was a political gene passed down from her grandfather that had hidden out in her DNA and seeped into the souls of her embryonic children. Even as toddlers they had shared their toys and had an intuitive sense of fairness. When Stephen was seven he wrote a story about a group of people who refused to accept Baby New Year because he was black. Wise old Father New Year delivered a potent lecture about racism to the assembled masses, who then, humbled and enlightened, embraced the dark baby as their own. Claire put Stephen on the phone to read the story to her grandfather. Across the miles he wept for his lost faith.

MAUDE AND CLAIRE TALKED ABOUT THE KIDS for a while. Over the years, Maude had demonstrated infinitely more patience for their antics than Claire, from Sarah's three months of spiky purple hair to Stephen's numerous boycotts and dietary shifts (vegan, raw food, the brown-and-green diet, among others). When she had become pregnant for the first time, Claire had hesitated to tell Maude because of Alice, Maude and Harry's only child, who had died of leukemia. Maude rarely talked about her; nor had she ever said whether they'd tried to have another baby.

After Alice's death Maude had taken a job at the middle school library, and Harry had assumed additional responsibilities at the university. Twice a year, on Alice's birthday and the anniversary of her death, Maude would disappear for a couple of hours. At first Claire thought she must be visiting the cemetery, but Harry told her that Alice had been cremated and that they had spaded her ashes into the rich soil of the rose garden. "She just drives somewhere and sits in the car by herself," he said. "Then she comes home and we light a candle and go on with our lives."

When Claire's pregnancy was about to become visible, she had told Maude. Without a trace of hesitation Maude had let out a whoop. In fact, she'd been almost as excited about the coming birth as Claire was. She'd monitored Claire's increasing girth with interest and delight. She was the first person Claire called after she was wheeled back from the delivery room, Marco holding her hand and beaming about what he called her magnificent performance, though she didn't see what choice she'd had; if there had been a way to get an understudy to fill in, she would have grabbed it. She had drifted off to sleep with Maude's words dancing in her mind: "Think of how much fun we'll have raising him, dearie!"

CLAIRE FILLED MAUDE IN ON NEWS gleaned from her job as editor of the arts college newsletter, some of it undocumented rumors, but avoided any mention of the fracking assignment. Maude loved to hear the latest gossip from campus—who was retiring, who was coming up for tenure and likely to get it or not, who was leaving his or her spouse and for whom, other local trivia. One of Maude's most endearing qualities was the way she listened; it made Claire feel like Scheherazade.

Turning to politics, they shared their contempt over the Republican's willingness to shut down the country. "I've stopped watching the news before I go to sleep," Maude said. "I don't know what this country's coming to. Except for our town." This was spoken with the smug self-satisfaction of many local liberals. It was not uncommon to see cars which proudly bore a bumper sticker that bore the name of their town, followed by "Ten Square Miles Surrounded by Reality."

Claire checked her watch and was shocked to see that it was almost 6:30. She often lost track of time when she was with Maude. "Marco's going to start eating cookies out of the freezer if I don't get home soon. After all these years it still doesn't occur to him to start making dinner without me. Can I drive you to the doctor tomorrow? I can take a few hours off."

"No, Harry wants to go with me. You know Harry, he would never miss a chance to rat me out. Can't you hear him?" Her voice cascaded into a whine. "'Maude ate hot peppers last week. Maude drank two martinis Friday. Maude stayed up all night reading the new P.D. James.' "

"I'll call you to find out how your appointment went."

Maude rubbed her lower back as they walked to the door. "Take the mums, I put them on the front porch for you. But plant them as soon as you get home, they're getting pretty dry."

"Are you sure you want to give them to me? You know I'm a hazard to all things that grow. Even my children."

Claire hugged Maude. She felt brittle, like the stalk of a dried weed.

CHAPTER FOUR

O N THE WAY HOME, Claire she stopped at Wegmans to pick up flounder fillets. The lines were long, and by the time she checked out she was irritable and tired. Even the normally light traffic was heavier than usual, and it took fifteen minutes to make a trip that generally took half that time. Marco was standing at the kitchen counter reading the local newspaper and drinking the rest of last night's wine out of the bottle.

"Hey," he said without looking up. "This paper is total crap."

"Hey yourself. You used to at least make eye contact when I came in."

"And you used to iron my pajamas. "

"That's bullshit. I wouldn't have been caught dead ironing your pajamas."

"I guess we're not the people we once were. Besides, blame this fascinating newspaper of ours. Big story: 8 year old boy wins frog-hopping contest." He turned to brush her cheek with his lips.

"You smell like a tavern."

"Same to you. Anyway I don't go to bars, I get quietly tanked at home. Must be your Jewish influence: don't do nasty things in public—what's that phrase —something about not being shamed in front of the goyim. Whatever you do, don't embarrass the Jews."

"You're such a goddam anti-Semite."

"Right" he said, and made the sign of the cross. He sniffed the bag. "Fish?" His eyes moved back to the newspaper, and in a few minutes he asked, "How're Harry and Maude?"

"I'm worried about her," Claire said, her voice muted by the refrigerator where she was foraging for the salad greens she'd bought last week. When she pulled the package from the crisper it dripped green slime on her foot.

"Crap. There goes the salad." She tore a piece of paper towel off and began to sponge the mess.

"What are you worried about?"

"She's still having trouble with her back. She has an appointment with a neurosurgeon on Friday. That doesn't sound good.' Claire glanced at the empty cooktop. "How come you didn't start the rice?"

"You didn't leave me a note or I would have. I didn't know what you wanted to serve."

"All you have to do is pick up the phone and call. Maybe once in a while you could open the fridge and see what I defrosted in the morning. Or better yet, once in a while you could even take over and decide what we're going to have, you know, thaw it out, cook it. I'm not even talking about shopping or putting groceries away. Show me where it's written that I have executive authority over the kitchen."

Marco's voice remained mild, which only made her angrier. "If you want me to make dinner once a week, three times a week, every night, all you have to do is say so."

"Goddam, can't you take a little initiative around here?"

He ducked as if she'd hurled a frying pan at him. Then he began to rabbit punch the air near her face. "You want to fight? Put up your dukes. I'm not good for more than three rounds, but I'll give you a fight if you want." He bobbed and wove, then snapped his head back as if she'd landed a powerful blow.

"Cut it out, damn you. I'm not in the mood."

"Listen, babe, every time you're getting ready to visit your grandfather you pick a fight a few days ahead of time."

"Don't call me babe. And don't analyze me, that has nothing to do with it."

"No? So what is it, you expecting your period?"

He must have realized that he'd gone too far as soon as the words were out. Before she could scald him with a reply he grabbed the newspaper and wine bottle and scooted toward the living room. Claire watched his retreating back, noticing once again that the way he walked reminded her of Groucho Marx, shuffling his feet, a little scrunched down as if he'd never learned to live in his six-foot body. "Pick up your goddam feet," she muttered, loud enough for him to hear. He switched to an exaggerated goose step as he turned into the living room.

Marco's walk had always irritated her. Their rugs had flattened traffic patterns from the way he shuffled. There were lots of things that bothered her, small things, but they accumulated into periodic eruptions. She was annoyed by the way he went off to floss his teeth after every meal, even in a restaurant. And balled up his underwear on the back of the toilet at night, waiting until morning to put it in the hamper. "Why the hell can't you put it in the hamper as soon as you take it off?" she would ask, and he would shrug and say, "What's the big deal?" And he loved boxing. Boxing. "Don't complain," he said, "it's the way I handle my bottled up aggression. Keeps me from beating on you."

She didn't remember those things bothering her the year they lived together before they got married, but maybe they were habits he developed later, or maybe, in her twenties, her own hormones were kicking up enough heat to blot out anything else. Sometimes she wondered if she and Marco were to meet now, at the midpoint in their lives, would they get together? Would she, foraging through Match Dot Com or one of those web sites, pick out this man if his personal description included his irritating habits even though he was, by objective standards, still pleasant looking, well-educated and responsible, a good father? She imagined the ad: Six foot tall psychologist, adequate lover, full head of graying hair, slight paunch, leaves underwear in bathroom, doesn't lift feet when he walks, is a compulsive flosser, is obsessive about work. What would he write in an ad about her? Almost fifty year old woman, fifteen pounds heavier than when she married, unwilling to spend money, complains endlessly about her job, worries about things over which she had no control, refuses to accept partner's personal quirks but has plenty of her own.

Still, in the category of husbands, she supposed Marco was at least an 8. He had never been unfaithful, as far as she knew. Never given in to the stereotypical professor-leaves-wife-for-beautiful-young-graduate-student. If anything, she was the one who had "sinned," as his mother called it when she talked about the movie stars whose reprobate lives she read about while waiting in supermarket lines or doctors' offices. Claire's extra-marital activity was mostly the stuff of fantasy and curiosity; she sowed the real oats before she'd met Marco. After the marriage, there was the architect who remodeled their kitchen (a quick grope in what would become the pantry), and the neighbor who taught linguistics and wrote scholarly articles about medieval Bulgarian with whom she had rolled around one time on his Bukhara carpet when his wife was away, but she'd pulled away before he entered her, and there had not been a recurrence What the two men had in common was a sophisticated sense of humor that Claire found sexy. She'd never felt anything more than a brief flush of excitement, never been tempted to pursue anything further.

In fact, sex with Marco was still pretty good, though less frequent as time went by. Over the years they had learned each other's bodies, enjoyed the comfort of that knowledge, with occasional bursts of passion that left them amazed and humming the next day. She supposed that slowing down was normal; it was one of the few things Claire didn't discuss with Maude, who usually served as her reality barometer. Although they gossiped about other people's affairs, there was a wordless agreement that their sexual lives were off limits. She couldn't imagine Maude and Harry being part of the swinging sixties, going to swapping parties, throwing their keys into a fishbowl for haphazard retrieval of the night's sexual partner, all the other pre-AIDS revelry she'd read about with interest and maybe just a touch of envy. She'd heard rumors about Maude having an affair with a poet visiting in the creative writing program. That subject, too, was untouchable. Occasionally she wondered if Maude and Harry still made love. It was hard to imagine their age-speckled bodies rubbing against each other. But then their kids probably thought about her and Marco that way.

MARCO AND CLAIRE HAD MET IN 1985 when she was sharing a small apartment with Rivka, still a close friend, who had been a casual acquaintance in her dorm a few years earlier. Rivka had transferred to Penn after commuting from Crown Point to Yeshiva University for one semester, having persuaded her parents that the finest teacher of biblical studies was on the Penn faculty. But as soon as she arrived, she was in full flight from the restrictions of the Orthodox world in which she'd grown up. For the remainder of her time at Penn Rivka was in catch-up mode, preoccupied with fitting as many males as she could into her schedule and her pants. She had little time for the women in the dorm, and Claire remembered her as a girl who would glide through the hall wearing jeans that looked like they'd been glued on and slinky shirts without a bra.

A few years after graduation they had run into each other at a film about the abuse of women in middle-eastern countries. Afterward, sitting in a in a café that smelled of freshly ground coffee and stale smoke, Rivka had talked about her mother and the community of Orthodox women who were always pregnant and lived by rules that men set for them. "It's like the Middle Ages. And the worst part is they don't have any idea that they're slaves."

For Rivka, nothing less than being forced to wear a burka approached the insult of religious laws with their arranged marriages, sexual taboos around menstruation, and relegation of women to the upper tier of the synagogue where an iron screen prevented them from tempting the devoutly praying men below. She hated that they were barricaded inside long sleeves and high necks. The prospect of being deflowered in an arranged marriage, followed by life under a wig and one pregnancy after another, threw her into a fit of rage. Well, she'd solved the deflowering problem two weeks after she arrived at Penn, and evaded the pregnancy bullet with yearly visits to Planned Parenthood.

A few months after they reconnected, Claire and Rivka decided to share a tiny apartment in the Society Hill section of Philadelphia. Although they had become friends, it was mostly an arrangement of convenience; neither of them could afford her own place. They aspired to be part of the crowd of young and hip twenty-somethings who hung out in cafes and bars after work, most of them sporting Mondale/Ferraro buttons. Claire was free-lancing, doing mostly technical writing and periodically submitting articles to *The Atlantic* and the *New York Times*, for which she received pre-printed rejection slips. She experienced a brief surge of victory if, when opening a self-addressed stamped envelope (SASE in the Times crossword puzzles to which she was addicted), some underling, probably a 21 year old graduate of Williams, had penned a two word note on the edge of a rejection slip that said, "Nice writing."

Rivka, who continued her one hundred eighty degree path away from her Orthodox upbringing, was a graduate student in women's studies, living on a Spartan fellowship. She was immersed in a new kind of orthodoxy, analyzing the writings of early feminists like Simone de Beauvoir, Shulamith Firestone and Betty Friedan.

One evening when Claire returned from interviewing the head of a computer company, a young hot shot so full of himself that he was offended when she'd moved his hand off her thigh, she walked in on

Rivka pumping up and down on a man on the living room floor, her large breasts bouncing rhythmically.

"Whoops," the guy said, breaking the motion of his hips.

"Hey, I'm sorry," Claire said, standing in the archway entrance to the room, unable to escape to the bedroom without stepping over them. Rivka climbed off and sat with her naked buttocks on the uncarpeted floor. She was unfazed, and introduced them while the guy stood, his back to Claire, and pulled on a pair of boxers with pictures of Mohammed Ali when he was a young fighter, his gloved fists ready to strike.

"Marco, this is my housemate, Claire."

"Nice to meet you," Claire said, trying to keep her eyes on the wall over his shoulder. She wondered what Rivka's parents would do if they walked in on a scene like this. Sex was bad enough, but she was having it with someone named Marco, probably the owner of an uncircumcised penis and wearing underpants with pictures of a self-proclaimed Muslim.

Claire offered to go out for a sandwich, but Marco, pulling on his chinos, said he wouldn't hear of it. They settled for sharing a supper of leftover meatloaf and rice on trays in the tiny living room. It was an awkward meal, and Claire excused herself to go to bed as soon as they had cleared away the dishes. It occurred to her that if he needed to use the bathroom Marco would have to come through the twin-bedded room that she and Rivka shared. Although she'd had a glimpse of his ass, she didn't particularly want to hear him peeing, and was relieved when she heard Rivka call "Goodnight, babe" and the sound of the door closing.

At breakfast the next morning Claire asked Rivka if he was someone special.

"Who knows? He's a smart guy, good looking, too. And I love the idea of introducing him to my parents: Shmuel, Chanala, meet Marco Capobianco, my latest fuck."

A few days later when Marco came to collect Rivka on their way to a poetry reading, he grinned at Claire. "I've got dinosaur ones on tonight. Wanna see?" he asked, fingering his belt buckle, but before Claire could come up with a funny answer Rivka emerged from the bedroom, gave him a quick kiss and they left. Claire settled into her narrow bed with a copy of *The Name of the Rose*, but she kept flashing onto the image of Marco, grinning as he teased her about his underwear.

IN THE NEXT WEEKS, Marco and Claire found themselves conversing while he waited for Rivka, who was usually late, to finish applying kohl to her eyes and compress her mane of black curls into some sort of order. They shared their despair about Bhopal, worried about the identity of the Unabomber, their outrage when the mayor of Philadelphia, after an armed standoff, ordered the bombing of the MOVE headquarters, killing more than a dozen people and destroying surrounding homes.

But within a few months Rivka had grown bored with Marco and he abruptly stopped appearing in the small flat. Claire thought about him a few times, but she had just started dating Carl, a law student she'd met at a vigil to observe the fortieth anniversary of the bombing of Hiroshima. Rivka, meanwhile, had moved on to Ravi, nee Herschel. Ravi was an aspiring guru who had lived in an ashram in the

Catskills for two years before returning to Philadelphia to set up his own meditation and chanting center. Claire imagined his parents staring at a picture of their Bar Mitzvah boy on the grand piano and moaning "What did we do wrong?"

Marco called Claire a few weeks after the split to ask if she'd come out for a drink. "I need to talk to someone," he said. When she told Rivka, not wanting to be disloyal or secretive, she said, "Go for it, why should I care? He's a nice guy," and added "He's not bad in the sack."

"That's not going to happen," Claire said, words which Rivka would later quote with delight.

MARCO'S FACE REGISTERED HURT AND DISAPPOINTMENT as he talked about Rivka. "What's with her? I thought we had something going. Then bang, out of the blue she just calls it quits, said it was over and wouldn't tell me why. I thought maybe she talked to you about it."

Claire tried not to be irritated; she restrained a condescending desire to pat his head as if he were a disappointed child. "It's not you, she's just searching for, I don't know, I guess she's breaking loose from that crazy oppressive family."

Marco frowned. "You want to know about crazy families? You should see mine. Mass every day, twice on Sunday. My mother 's still in mourning because I didn't become a priest."

"You?" Claire had an image of the Mohammed Ali underpants. "Did you ever consider it?"

"Oh, maybe for a while. Then half way through high school I discovered girls and it all fell apart. I stopped believing in god and started believing in gonads. God didn't stand a chance."

Encouraged by her laughter, he went on telling funny stories about slipping away from the constraints of his Catholic boyhood. Claire noticed, not for the first time, that he was great looking: tall and solid, the kind of guy you could lean into without feeling as if you'd knock him over. He had dark hair and eyes and a smile that curved one side of his mouth higher than the other.

After a false start in clinical psychology, Marco was getting his doctorate in social psych, and was excited, even a little obsessed, about his dissertation research on peer pressure among Italian street gangs in South Philadelphia. At the moment he was interviewing mothers of gang members. "I can't believe how willing these women are to talk to me. We sit at their kitchen tables and they just pour it out."

"Yeah, well, they probably see in you what they always wanted their boys to be. At least the ones who didn't become priests."

"I bet I've gained ten pounds. Every time I take a questionnaire into a house they sit me down and feed me rigatoni, spaghetti, sausage, ravioli, cannoli, you name it."

He told her about some of his encounters in the neighborhood. He was clearly proud of his ability to navigate the tough streets; maybe that accounted for the boxer-covered underwear. He's got Mohammed Ali covering his ass, Claire thought.

They shared a joint in his car that first night, and when he dropped her at the door he kissed her cheek in a brotherly way. "I'll give you a call. And thanks for letting me sound off about Rivka. I still don't understand what happened, but I had a good time tonight and I feel better."

He called a few days later. "I just want to thank you for getting me over a tough hump." Claire smiled at the unintended double entendre.

Marco told her that the wound was closing, thanks to her listening to him whine, and asked to take her out for dinner on Saturday to show his appreciation for her help.

"I'm busy Saturday, but I could do it the following week." She already had a date with Carl, and even though she was glad not to seem immediately available, another week seemed like a long way off. When Carl asked her to come to his place for a drink after dinner on Saturday, she faked a headache and told him she'd call in a few days.

Marco was waiting in the small coffee bar where they'd agreed to meet. He greeted her with a friendly hug. "After we have some coffee I want to show you a little of my world," he said. "My favorite places in South Philadelphia."

"I'm not anxious to get stabbed. Or grabbed," she said.

"You're safe with me," he said with a slight swagger she found appealing. "They pretty much know me. I won't let anything happen to you."

They took a bus through streets with row houses, their gleaming wooden doors polished to a mirrored finish, with short flights of steps leading up from tiny squares of clipped grass. "These folks take a lot of pride in their homes. They work their asses off to buy them and then they treat them like museums," he said, as they looked out of the bus window. They got off and walked several blocks along a lively street filled with grocery stores, barber shops and beauty salons, pizza parlors. The store fronts with their fat salamis dripping with grease, bowls of olives and tantalizing displays of cheese made Claire nostalgic for parts of New York she had walked through as a kid.

They stopped at a delicatessen where the owner, wiping his hands on a stained white apron, greeted Marco as if he were a returning war hero. They left the store a few minutes later after admiring his inventory, and continued their walk gnawing the chunk of Asiago and anise-flavored crackers he had insisted they take. In a few minutes they reached Marco's favorite wine bar. Inside it was dark, with small candles dripping down empty Chianti bottles on the red-checkered tablecloths. Sinatra was crooning from the jukebox.

Marco ordered a bottle of Chianti classico and a large platter of antipasti, over which the waiter dribbled fruity olive oil. For the next two hours they talked without pausing. He told her more about his family and growing up in Carroll Gardens, the Italian section of Brooklyn. He was the only son and youngest of five children, burdened by the expectations generated by that status. "It's like having five mothers," he said. He attended Catholic school until high school, when, to his parents' dismay, he had insisted on transferring to Stuyvesant, for which he had secretly taken the admissions test and been accepted. Even the commute was a welcome escape from the claustrophobic world of his childhood. "I was probably the only person on that subway who liked it, liked swaying up against all kinds of people, liked hearing all those languages I couldn't understand. I liked imagining what people did, where they were going, what their lives were like." That was when his world began to change, to open up. He'd won a full scholarship to Swarthmore, where he'd first discovered psychology. His sisters were all married to good Catholics and two of them were reproducing at a rate that he called downright irresponsible.

"Listen to me, I haven't stopped talking," he said, pouring their third glass of wine. "I want to know about you."

Claire told him about her mother's cancer and her parents' deaths, though she wasn't ready to say anything about the mystery surrounding her father's accident. Marco rested his chin on his hand as he listened to her description of grandfather's days of radical politics. They both talked briefly about disappointing relationships they'd had.

Finally she looked at her watch. "Whew. I've got to get home."

He insisted on taking the bus back with her. At the door he gave her a brotherly hug, and she was aware of the muscular bigness of him underneath his windbreaker.

"See you soon," she said.

BUT TWO WEEKS WENT BY, and he didn't call. Claire felt more than a vague sense of disappointment. She found herself looking for him when she went out with friends. She had a date with Carl, but by the end of the evening she told him that she was sorry, she'd met someone else and wouldn't be seeing him again.

Thoughts about Marco often intruded when she tried to work. She doodled his name on the margin of notes she'd taken for her latest assignment. Finally, she dialed his number.

"Hey, it's Claire."

"Hey," he said. Silence.

"I was just wondering how you're doing. I mean, Rivka and all."

"I'm so over her. Listen, you're probably wondering why I haven't called. Can you come out for a drink?"

Claire lied that she was busy right then; she didn't want to appear too eager. They agreed to meet the next night. She was annoyed with herself for not holding out longer, but then told herself she was too mature to play games. "That's so old," she said aloud.

The next evening she tried on and rejected first a black dress (too dressy), her green slacks (made her butt look too big) and finally settled on a black wool skirt and red sweater, then applied makeup that she seldom wore, swearing as she wiped a smudge of mascara away from her lower lid. She pulled her hair into a bun, then shook it loose, tried a low ponytail, then shook it loose again.

As soon as she saw him sitting at a table in the back of Tony's, the neighborhood bar where they had arranged to meet, her breathing quickened. He rose and took her hand, then pulled out a chair. Maybe not politically correct, but she liked the gesture.

"Look," he said, skipping pleasantries and speaking in a rush of words, "I want to tell you why I haven't called. You must think I'm a total shit. After I took you home, what was it, about a month ago?"

"Almost three weeks but who's counting," she said.

"Okay, almost three weeks. It felt like a year. Anyway I realized that something's happening here. I mean between us, that you were, I mean you are . . ." He stammered and searched for words. "Jesus, listen to me, I sound like some teenage asshole. Anyway, it seemed crazy, because the thing with Rivka had just ended and I figured maybe I was rebounding off that. And I didn't want to hurt you if that's all it was, so I figured I'd take some time to be sure that she was off my radar. But I've been thinking about you the whole time, sort of counting down until I thought it would be okay to call you. And then you called, and here you are, and I can't talk straight."

He sighed and leaned back.

"Wow," Claire said. "That's a lot to take in."

"I'm so glad to see you I feel like shouting it to everyone in the bar. I just want to be with you. I want to get to know you."

"Biblically or otherwise?"

"Every way there is. Any time you're ready, no pressure. Though now would be great."

They sat in the café talking for two hours. It wasn't the usual conversation she'd so often had with guys, both of them straining to show how smart and witty they were. It was as if they had already done the introductory dance. They talked about their aspirations, their self-doubt, past heartaches. Claire shared her uncertainty about how her father had died. Marco's eyes flashed with anger. "Sure, he was depressed, but I don't see how you can do that to your kid."

"If that's what happened. It's the not knowing that makes me crazy sometimes."

Around ten Marco put his hand on Claire's arm. "What say we get out of here?" he asked. She felt a sense of physical urgency that made her almost breathless.

Marco's apartment was a few blocks from the café, on the second floor above a dry cleaner in a run-down brick building. The apartment smelled of chemicals. It was filled with board-and-brick bookshelves. A single bed that also served as a sofa was covered with a bright green quilt and several pillows, and there was an unframed Maigret poster taped to the wall, along with photographs of Martin Luther King and Bobby Kennedy. Almost a quarter of the faded kitchen linoleum was filled with empty soda bottles. "That's my pension plan," he said. "An investment for the future, if I ever get around to returning them."

With the palm of his hand he tilted her head upward. "You're beautiful."

"No, I'm not."

"Shut up," he said, and kissed her. It was a tender kiss, almost chaste. He pulled back and looked at her again. "You ARE beautiful," he said, his hands raking gently through what she had always thought of as the jungle of her hair. The next kiss was different, passionate and exploratory as he tasted the inside of her mouth, probing, withdrawing, licking her lips. She didn't resist when he led her to the bed and undressed her slowly, luxuriously, so unlike the anxious and impatient guys she'd been with before. His erection was strong, and he seemed to know just where to touch her, how slowly to move until she came twice; then he surrendered to the force of his own need.

"Wow," he said afterward. "Double wow."

"Did you learn your technique in catechism class?"

"You're not going to hold my Catholic boyhood against me, are you?"

"That's not what I want to hold against you," she said, pressing into him. She felt a kind of happiness she had never experienced before: a crazy mix of joy and excitement and peace.

They saw each other almost every evening, and spent weekends at his apartment. Rivka had moved on from her Guru-in-training to a Nigerian tribal chieftain spending a year at Penn studying business administration. She and Marco seemed perfectly comfortable when he came to the apartment to pick Claire up.

In July they decided it was time to live together and found an apartment in West Philadelphia. "I'll miss you," Rivka said, hugging Claire. "Watch out for those Catholics, they never get it fully out of their systems. Think of James Joyce. And for god's sake, don't marry him, he'll hide your diaphragm and keep your belly bulging. They're as bad as the Orthodox."

A year later they were married, Zayde, Rivka and a few other friends standing with them in a judge's chamber. Marco's parents and sisters had declined to attend because the ceremony was not being conducted by a priest, but a few months later, his mother and father relented and came to visit the newlyweds in their third-floor walk-up apartment in West Philadelphia. They greeted Claire, if not with enthusiasm, at least with a minimal level of civility.

"Don't fall for it," Marco warned. "They figure if they win you over you'll raise our kids Catholic. Baptism, mass every Sunday, the whole shmear."

"You speak gorgeous Yiddish," she said, nuzzling his neck.

Now, all these years later, Claire found herself considering their marriage as if she were Minerva holding a scale. The kids adored him. Why not, she thought; he was always the good cop. They mostly liked the same people, were nostalgic about "The Rocky Horror Picture Show" and Woody Allen's early movies, and could recite whole scenes from "The Big Chill". They had similar political views most of the time: they agreed about immigration policy, gun control, the evils of the death penalty, the threat of Citizens United. But Marco had retained dollops of conservatism that infuriated her when they surfaced. Like last week when he'd become irritated as she railed about pedophile priests, insisting that it happened "because of the church's dumbass policy that doesn't let priests marry."

"I didn't realize priests had the patent on child molesting. What about all the other offenders? Including Orthodox rabbis?"

The argument flared until Marco turned retreated to his study. Claire had shouted after him, "You can take the boy out of the church but you…" as the door slammed.

"Fish again? Yech," Sarah said, inspecting the fillet on her plate as if it were a cadaver being readied for autopsy. "I hate fish. Besides, we're depleting the oceans."

"It's good for your aging parents' cholesterol."

"Why can't we like go veggie, like the Morrisons? That's, like, low cholesterol."

"Stop saying like twelve times in every sentence, you're murdering the language I love. And if you want a straight answer, it's because you don't eat broccoli, I don't eat cauliflower and beans make your father fart."

"Jesus, you're in fine form tonight," Marco said.

It was true. Claire felt like a dragon looking for something to toast with her breath, and her family was in the line of fire. Take it easy, she told herself. She remembered the course she had taken in Breathing and Relaxation with Anna Weintraub, the wife of a physics professor who looked and sounded like a member of old German royalty. She had been trained in autogenic breathing techniques. Six women lay on yoga mats listening to her heavily accented voice: "Tongue at the top of the mouth, ladies, donggg donggg donggg, feel the vibrations." When Claire was rushing the kids to music lessons, dentist appointments and soccer practice she used to chant donggg donggg donggg as she hurried from one place to another, fretting over when she would have time to complete a work assignment. Donggg donggg dongg. The kids would moan with embarrassment, and once she heard Stephen say to a friend buckled in next to him in the back seat, "Don't mind my mother, she's a little crazy."

This didn't seem like a good time or place to start dongggging. They got through the rest of dinner in silence. Sarah managed a few mouthfuls of fish, hiding the rest under a pile of peas. Claire and Marco avoided eye contact as they cleared the table and loaded the dishwasher.

"I'm meeting Joline for an early movie," Sarah said.

"Since when do you go to movies on a school night?"

"Teacher conferences tomorrow. No school. I already told you."

"What are you going to see?" Claire asked.

"Why, you want to start censoring what I watch? Like what are you, the Queen of the Catholic Church?"

"I'm just asking. It might surprise you to know that I'm interested in what you do." And what you're smoking or swallowing, Claire added silently.

"The King's Speech. PG rating. English accents. No sex, no drugs. Very Masterpiece Theater. You'd approve."

"Sounds like fun. Say hello to Joline."

Sarah grabbed a sweatshirt from the closet, "Later," she said, raising her hand without turning to look at them. Behind her the door slammed in a way that said, "Don't think you're forgiven."

Another night in Paradise.

CHAPTER FIVE

NORA LAY ON HER STOMACH ON STEPHEN'S BED, her dark hair falling almost to the textbook that lay propped on a pillow between her elbows. She was wearing a tee shirt and floral bikini underpants. Stephen was at his desk, reading notes he'd entered into his computer.

"Jesus, look at the time, I gotta get out of here," he said.

"What about your bio exam?" she asked.

"I'll finish studying when I get back. I'm late already. Big decisions tonight. You saw the paper, governor just came out saying he may not support continuing the ban on fracking. Except for near the area that supplies New York City's water and maybe one other place. Like the rest of us don't mean shit. If something doesn't happen to stop them it'll be too late." His words were muffled by the grey sweatshirt he was pulling over his head.

"It's okay if I don't go, isn't it?" she asked. "I've got an exam on Gothic cathedrals tomorrow morning."

"It's okay, it's a planning meeting. Stay here and study, I'll fill you in when I get back." He stooped down and rubbed her barely covered bottom. She turned her head to look at him.

"You're too skinny," she said.

"And you're just right." He felt himself getting hard again, even though it had only been an hour since they'd done it.

She pulled up onto her knees and wiggled.

"Don't do that to me, you witch. It's time to deal with fracking, not fucking," he said, "I'm late already. Have a great time with your totalitarian architecture. Power to the Pope."

She twisted her neck to kiss him, but reached his chin instead of his cheek. "Have a good meeting."

"Don't go back to the dorm, wait for me. I'll walk you home—maybe."

OUTSIDE THE SKY WAS DARKENING, a reminder that in a few weeks it would be time to turn the clocks back. Stephen checked his watch, then lengthened his stride as he hurried toward one of the steep hills that separated the campus from the city. He passed once grand Victorian houses that had been carved into student digs, their untended gardens vanished under the weeds of early fall, their fire escapes piled with cartons of empty beer bottles. He could probably traverse this town with his eyes closed. Sometimes he chafed at having grown up in such a small place where just about everyone agreed with each other on the big issues. Part of him longed to be a leader, to change hearts and minds, but there weren't many that needed changing in this cloistered college town.

"You should think about law school," his father had told him when he made the debating team.

"Or god forbid, politics," his mother said.

He'd stood on street corners downtown waving signs that said "Out of Afghanistan" and "Gun Control Now," but most of the pedestrians and passing cars gave him the thumbs up sign or honked their approval, when what he really wanted was to argue people into changing their minds.

But hydrofracking, or fracking as it was known, was different. There was heated disagreement about whether it should be slowed or stopped altogether. Their town was located on the Marcellus Shale, a geological area rich in deeply buried natural gas. At first there had been a lot of interest in mining the gas as a clean alternative to coal—until the facts about the problems and risks involved in the process started to emerge. By now the issue of fracking had split communities apart. The city was pretty solid in its negative reaction to fracking. But in some of the more rural areas where farmers were struggling to hold on to their land, land that might have been in the family for generations, the situation was different. The gas drilling companies had surged in with promises of quick wealth in return for signing leases that would allow them to drill and inject chemical-laced water deep underground to break up the soft shale, releasing gas which they assured everyone would be contained in concrete wells. Many landowners had already signed leases and were vocal in their support for drilling. But as environmental problems began to emerge, the opposition had grown quickly. The activists were increasingly strident, and insisted that industry and government needed to develop truly clean energy as well as policies for conservation. Fracking was being argued at every level of government. Clearly it was time to act, and Stephen was ready.

The NFH (No Fracking Here, though in private they called it the NFFH—No Fucking Fracking Here) Committee, which he'd organized, had been meeting every Thursday night for the past several months. They gathered in the basement of a church overseen by a sympathetic pastor who had managed to retain his job even though he had been outspoken in his opposition to Bush's foreign policy and continued to demonstrate for the closing of Guantanamo.

Stephen thought about the bumper sticker he'd seen on dozens of cars claiming that their town was ten square miles surrounded by reality. How many towns could brag about a socialist mayor in the recent past? About an all-Democratic Common Council? About a liberal African American mayor in his twenties who had once been a homeless kid? But reality was intruding on this smug little corner of the world.

Halfway down the steep hill Stephen thought about his last visit with his parents. They'd been yelling at each other again in that sort of tamped down way of theirs. He couldn't even remember what it was about. It seemed like they were at each other almost every time he came home, which wasn't all that often. Mostly it was to do his laundry or get something from his old room, sometimes bringing Nora with him and they would stay for dinner. Sarah, his sister, wouldn't say much about what was going on, except to complain that mom was always on her case, and that she seemed edgier than usual.

Stephen didn't quite get his parents' marriage. He wondered if they still turned each other on. What else could have held them together all these years, besides Sarah and him? They didn't have that much in common. His father was always working and up to his ass in all the crap politics of the university. He'd get pissed about stupid departmental stuff that didn't mean shit. He didn't seem to care much about anything else. Oh, yeah, he voted the right way, and once in a while he'd pick up his old banjo and strum a few old protest songs even though he'd forgotten half the words. But mostly he was a model of what Stephen didn't want to become.

His mother was more out there, kind of a people person. She'd get all hot about what was going on in the world and go off on a tirade about stuff like minimum wage or some stupid fucker in Washington who got caught with his hand in the till. Though she didn't do much about any of it besides sign email petitions or write a few checks. Once in a while she'd write a letter to the editor, but they were pretty mild, compared to what she said at home. When he called her on it, she said she had to be careful because of her job. Too bad, if she wanted she could have made more of her life than that dumb newsletter. She was actually pretty smart, though he wondered if it bothered her that she hadn't gone to graduate school, living in this town where even the people who flipped burgers had goddam doctorates. She could have gone back to school if she'd wanted to. Why the hell didn't she?

WHEN HE ARRIVED AT THE CHURCH there were about a dozen people seated at a conference table. They were passing a bowl of sunflower seeds in one direction, a bag of tortilla chips in the other, and drinking cheap boxed wine from small paper cups they'd found in a dispenser in the men's room.

"Our fearless leader, late as ever," George Gordon said.

"Sorry, guys. I was making a quick pass at my bio notes before the exam tomorrow and I lost track of the time.'

"Bullshit, I bet you were making a quick pass at Nora," George said.

Stephen ignored him. "Let's get right to it. I think we've done enough talking about this thing. We're all on the same page. We need to come out of this meeting with an action plan, what we're going to do, who's going to do it, when it has to be done by, you know the drill. And we have to move, because the other side is gaining momentum. If we don't act soon we won't be able to stop the bastards."

The next hour was filled with suggestions, some totally off the wall, as far as Stephen was concerned. Like spray painting barns on farms that had signed leases, or pouring chemicals into a farm pond that would smoke and give people an idea of what could happen.

"Come on, guys," Stephen said, "we don't want to alienate the farmers. You know that half the growers who sign are struggling to hang on to their farms. They've probably lived all their lives on their piece of land and now they're making less money and the taxes are shooting up and they might lose it. And along come the gas companies and they put on this hard sell, and hey, these guys are desperate, if they lose their farms they lose their whole way of life. As if it weren't enough that these huge mega-companies like Monsanto squeeze the shit out of them with their genetically modified seeds and their teams of lawyers."

One of the other committee members nodded and said, "You have to aim at stopping those fucking corporate liars, not hitting the little guys."

The sunflower seeds made the rounds as they continued to brainstorm possible courses of action.

"You're right, but let's stay focused," Stephen said. "I think the only way to stop the gas corporations is to get to the people who make the laws—if they're not already on the take. We need new legislation and a way to enforce it. And we've got to get the public lined up on our side, cut through their fucking complacency. There's no point hitting the people who have already signed, those are a done deal, unless the good-guy lawyers can figure a way to get out of them. We have to work on Cuomo and the Albany crowd to ban it, make it permanently illegal, at least until the scientists come up with a way to solve the problems and make it safe And then it has to be regulated and monitored."

"Yeah," Terrence said, "nice try. With all the budget cuts you think the government will spend money on monitors to make sure it's safe?"

"If we can get the state to ban drilling there won't be much to monitor. And then the lease is just a piece of paper," Stephen continued. "No one's going to sign a new one if there's no profit in it."

Carl Watson rocked onto the back legs of his chair and picked at a sunflower seed caught between his front teeth as he spoke. "I think we have to find a way to get people up off their asses. They have to show they care enough about this shit to put pressure on the legislature."

"That'll take a hydrogen bomb or a fucking miracle," George Goldberg said.

"The gas companies are pouring millions of dollars into advertising and lobbying. And now they're threatening to sue local governments that ban fracking," Ellen Zabarsky said. "All the stuff we've done--petitions, emails, letters in the paper—we haven't accomplished a damned thing." She picked up her pen and started to doodle on the margins of the newspaper in front of her. "And if the big guys sue, who's going to come up with the money to fight them?"

"We've accomplished something, at least," Stephen said. "We got the temporary ban. Let's not get discouraged; we have to keep going."

He suggested that they brainstorm a list of possible actions they could implement quickly. He asked George to take notes using a thick black marker and a pad of newsprint. He was careful not to assign that role to any of the five women on the committee. He remembered their family friend Maude telling him about activist meetings when she was young, probably back in the seventies, when even in meetings of radical groups women were relegated to bringing coffee and taking notes. They had been the free help, the unpaid clerks who were supposed to be grateful to be allowed into the room. "We had a place at the table," Maude had told him. "Clearing it."

Gertrude MacKenzie, her fingers playing with her long feathered earrings, suggested crossing the Pennsylvania border and defacing some of the concrete pads already in place. Aerial views showed the extent to which a once pristine landscape of rolling farmland and a winding river had already been defaced.

But Stephen thought that might be too risky. "I hear they're pretty heavily guarded," he said. "Let's try not to get anyone beaten up or arrested. The gas companies probably have the local cops in their pockets."

Gabe Winter thought they were being too easy on the large landowners who had already signed leases. He agreed that they didn't want to hurt the little guys, but suggested tapping into a water well of one of the people who were in it just to make a killing. "We could pipe in some gas so it would come out when they turned the faucet on. That'll get people's attention." He reminded them of the documentary on drilling in Pennsylvania, where a homeowner was able to light the water coming out of his kitchen faucet.

In black marker, under where he had written, "spray paint well pads," George wrote, "tap into water well."

Someone started to argue but Stephen interrupted. "We'll talk about feasibility later," he said. "Let's just generate a list of possibilities. Anyone else?"

They agreed that there was no point approaching their local legislators, who were already on board and doing whatever they could to strengthen anti-fracking regulations.

They had to carry this higher, join up with environmental and other organizations that were planning to make a big splash at the state level in November. George listened, then wrote "Organize big crowd to attend demonstration in Albany." Stephen said that if they were successful, it might be effective enough to force the Governor and the legislature not only to agree to continuing the ban but to making it permanent. "So come on, guys, let's have some more ideas."

Mia McHenry proposed that they make a recording of heavy trucks on the highway and blast it over loudspeakers, with signs that let people know what their quiet country roads would sound like when drilling started. "People don't have a clue about the truck traffic and the noise," she said. "And the impact on the roads. We have enough trouble filling potholes now, can you imagine what will happen with hundreds of trucks grinding up the concrete?"

As he wrote, "truck noise and infrastructure damage," George said, "Yeah, remember the hysteria about the noise windmills would make? They're a fucking lullaby by comparison."

They floated a few more ideas around, some bizarre, some impractical. Then George put down the marker he'd been using. "Listen guys, this is getting a little crazy. I know I'm only the secretary around here, but how about this? You remember hearing about what happened in the Vietnam protests? The monks who burned themselves to death in front of crowds of people? People who burned their draft cards? Fire gets people's attention."

"Are your volunteering to immolate yourself?" Stephen asked. Everyone laughed, and Alison offered to light the first match.

"No, assholes, listen. Suppose we created a dummy that looked like – hey, I don't know, maybe the governor—we'd have to figure it out—and take it to the demonstration in Albany and find a way to burn it? We could hand out flyers with the facts and what we're demanding. The media will all be there for the protest; they'll love this."

There was a murmur around the table. "I could get into that," Gertrude said. "It has, like, resonance. It'll make people our parents' age think of Vietnam and all the shit that went down there. Suppose we made a map of New York State, something that would burn slowly. We could have, like, dummies of two little kids holding it. Like they represent the future. We'd have to figure out the technical shit, but I bet it could be done." Gertrude was studying theater.

"Yeah, and one of us could wear a mask of the governor—you can order one online---and set fire to the state, and it would spread to the dummy kids."

"Well, nothing hidden in that agenda. But maybe we have to hit people over the head with it," Stephen said.

"Subtlety's not going to get us anywhere. I like it. I really like it," said Alison.

"We have to have something to hand out to the crowd and a press release. You think we can be ready to go to Albany in the next few weeks?" Carl asked. "It's coming up soon."

"I think we should start locally, build up support so we take busloads of people with us when we go to the Capital. Let's think about doing it here first, in the quad," Stephen said. "Besides, even though the university hasn't signed any leases, they still haven't come out with a definitive statement against fracking. It's about time they put their money where their mouth is."

Gabe laughed. "Maybe it's because their money tells their mouth what it can say."

"Isn't Parent's Weekend coming up in two weeks?" Alison asked. "There will be a mob on campus, great time to get a lot of attention."

For the first time the committee was unanimous in its enthusiasm.

"It'll be like a dress rehearsal for Albany, get people on board and put the squeeze on the university to take a stand," Gertrude said.

They spent the next hour planning details, and agreed that they needed a dry run to make sure they had everything in place. They set a date to rehearse the action before parents would start to arrive in town. Stephen indicated that he knew someone who might be able to help them get the media there; maybe it would even go national.

NORA WAS STILL STUDYING when Stephen came back to his room two hours later. His face was flushed with excitement, and he was high from the joint they'd smoked outside the church after the meeting.

"How'd it go, babe?" she asked, sitting up.

"It was so cool, best meeting we've had since we started. We've got a plan; I think it's really going to work. I'll tell you about it tomorrow, I have to get ready for this damned bio exam."

Nora rolled onto her back and stretched. "Ooh, I'm stiff. I haven't moved since you left. But I can tell you all about the differences between the Romanesque and the early Gothic arch. I can see you're dying to know."

Stephen leaned over and brushed her neck with his lips. "Mmm," he said, sliding his hand along her thigh.

"I thought you had to study."

"I'm doing biology," he said. "This is field work."

"You're stoned," she said.

"And you're hot." He lay down next to her, the pages of her notebook crumpling beneath his weight.

SARAH CALLED STEPHEN THE NEXT EVENING. "What's up?" he asked.

"Mom's acting all weird again, being a real pain in the butt. Can I come over?"

"Not a good time, I'm working on something. "

"Come on, Stephen, I gotta get out of here and Joline's at her grandmother's. Please please please?"

"Well, maybe you can help. Bring your laptop."

Why not, he thought after he hung up. She's a smart kid and she's knows how to do stuff. She can help with the flyer. He'd volunteered to do too much of the work for the demonstration, so Sarah's assistance would be welcome.

When she arrived he filled her in on their plans and swore her to secrecy. "Wow," she said. "That's awesome. What can I do? I want to be in on it."

Stephen outlined the points he wanted to cover in a one-page flyer. "Come up with a catchy design and bullet it: fracking is bad because . . ."

"But I don't know enough about it," she said.

"Jesus, don't you read the paper?"

"Don't yell at me, I've been working on pro-choice after school."

"All right, look at some of this stuff." He handed her a folder with a dozen or so articles in it. She curled up on his bed, switched on the light and started reading. Stephen worked at his desk, checking the legislative calendar in Albany, and looking up campus permit requirements for demonstrations.

"Wow. This is heavy stuff," Sarah said.

She read on, puzzling over some of the scientific words. "What's methane?" she asked.

Stephen swiveled around. "Look it up on Wikipedia, I don't have time."

Sarah searched and read the definition. She began to make notes, and in the next hour she had put together a one-page document, with major points bold and bulleted, underneath a picture of a smoky polluted pond she'd clipped from the internet.

"Would you look at this?" she asked her brother. He came over and perched on the bed, looking over her shoulder.

"You're something else, kiddo, that's better than most of the guys on the committee could do. Just a few minor changes and it'll be ready. Great job. I have to run it by the others, but I think they'll be good with it."

"When's it happening? I want to go with you."

Stephen was cautious and warned her that it could get a little heated. "I don't know if they'll send in the cops or what. Mom would kill me if you got busted or suspended from school."

"And I'll kill you if you don't let me come. Besides, may be some of my friends might want to take part, too." She glared at him. "Even high schoolers care about the environment, shithead."

"Okay, for starters you can come to the dress rehearsal. We're doing a dry run to make sure we've covered all the bases. And bring enough copies of the flyer for everyone on the committee so we can get their approval."

THE NEXT DAYS WERE FILLED WITH ACTIVITY. Alison went online and found a mask of the governor, which would be delivered federal express from a store in Buffalo. Dominick and Gertrude drew a map of the state on two pieces of board which they hinged together. Once that was done, they filled the space between the boards with a flammable substance that would ignite and burn slowly but dramatically. Nora went to Wal-Mart to buy a pair of large Raggedy Ann and Andy dolls. She said it was against her principles to shop there, but she couldn't find them anywhere else. She and Terence spent hours figuring out how to assemble the whole thing, using tomato stakes and duct tape so that when the whole thing was assembled, the dolls were holding the map between them. Stephen was elected to be the governor. "Yeah, asshole, and when you've got this fixed you can raise the minimum wage," Gabe said. He and Stephen argued over the best time during Parents' Weekend to carry out their plan, and about which end of the quad would provide the most dramatic setting. They finished late Tuesday night, a few days before parents were due to arrive on campus, and high-fived each other on how well it had come together. Several of the guys loaded the assemblage onto Carl's pick-up truck and covered it with a tarp, ready to take its place in the long and respectable history of campus demonstrations.

CHAPTER SIX

ON SATURDAY MORNING, Claire made the two-hour drive to Scranton to visit her grandfather. She tried to go at least once a month, except in the worst of winter. The road wound through beautiful countryside in the southern tier of New York and northern Pennsylvania. She usually enjoyed the quiet drive, feeling a surge of competence as she steered the Subaru into the curves of Route 81. But today, as she passed gas-drilling wells set on their concrete pads, she was filled with recrimination about the letter she had composed for Jasper, and the work still waiting for her. She knew that she would not tell Zayde about it.

Claire's grandparents had taken her in after both her parents died. When she was eleven, only six years after her mother's disfiguring mastectomy, the cancer that had been hiding in the remaining breast had erupted to destroy her lungs. After her death, Claire and her father had endured a year of barely spoken grief, moving shadow-like around each other, as if to speak of it would destroy what little equilibrium they had managed to create. She became frantic every time he was a few minutes later than she expected him. Then, one day, as she waited for him to come home so they could assemble a rudimentary supper, a police officer had arrived, looking as if he wished he were somewhere else. Claire would learn later, when her stunned grandparents came to get her, that her father's car had veered off a bridge on his way home from work. There was no note, no sign of alcohol, nothing other than his profound sadness to indicate that it might have been intentional, but the cause remained inconclusive. She would never know what happened on that dark road, what pulled his car over the side of the bridge. She would spend years wondering why she wasn't enough to keep him from that desperate act, if indeed that's what it was.

She had moved into the Riverdale apartment with her grandparents, who had struggled to hide their own grief as they tried to help her cope with the double disaster. They did everything they could to provide her with a normal life, whatever that meant. As she began to recover over the next few years, they tolerated loud rock music, fed the insatiable appetites of serial boyfriends, stepped around tangled nests of dirty clothes on the floor of her room. All without complaining. She was, she knew, their only remaining hold on the future, and she absorbed their love without the *sturm und drang* her teenage friends experienced with their parents, though sometimes she was embarrassed by the Yiddish expressions that crept into their conversation when she brought friends to the house. She was even more uncomfortable with her grandfather's loudly expressed radical opinions as he tried to persuade her teenage peers to his point of view. When she graduated from Stuyvesant with high honors and a full scholarship to Penn, they were in the front row, their faces lit with pride and gratitude. After the ceremony, she averted her eyes from the tears that traced lines through her grandmother's rarely applied makeup.

Claire was living at home for the summer before her senior year in college when her grandmother died of a heart attack. It was early July when Zayde called her at the small newspaper office where she was interning to say that she should come home right away without telling her why. She rushed out of the office, and when she arrived he was waiting for her in the downstairs foyer. He held out his arms without saying anything, and she fell into them, choking back sobs she could not allow herself to release. The funeral directors had agreed not to take the body away until Claire had a chance to say goodbye. Upstairs, she leaned over the bed where her grandmother lay. Claire kissed her cool forehead and tried to understand what had happened. Her grandmother was still wearing her shoes on top of the white chenille bedspread. Claire had an impulse to take them off. Grandma would never have worn them to lie down on the bed. "Who knows what germs you pick up on the bottom of your shoes," she used to say.

The next weeks were filled with the activity that follows a death: visitors, paperwork, arrangements. They didn't talk about their grief. She would sometime stand outside her grandfather's bedroom door and hear him curse the god he didn't believe in. She buried her own profound sadness in working on the final report she had to write at the end of her internship. As the summer wound down, she offered to transfer to a school in New York so that she could live at home, but Zayde insisted that she needed to have her own life. He was still working part time for the union, mostly work he could do from home since she'd helped him master the use of "that farkokteh computer," as he called it. He had his Mets games on television and his weekly pinochle cronies, all of them munching chocolate-covered raisins with their false teeth and slugging Dr. Peppers or shot glasses of Jim Beam. They used the card game as a foil for proclamations about suicide bombers, the Thatcher government, whether Argentina would be able to maintain a democracy, Jesse Jackson's presidential bid, occasionally breaking into Yiddish curses directed at that farshtunkene actor who thought he knew how to be president.

AFTER ZAYDE'S STROKE SOME YEARS LATER, Claire and Aunt Helen, his only sister, had selected the Center because it was a few blocks away from Helen's house, and two hours closer to Claire and her family. Helen was eight years younger than Zayde, and visited him several times a week. But last year, as Aunt Helen's' own health declined, she had moved to North Carolina to be near her daughter. Claire explored transferring Zayde to one of several facilities in her town, but the staff at the Center persuaded her it would be too disruptive to move him again.

Claire spent most of the ride getting ready for the visit, preparing mental lists of things she could talk about in their one-sided communication. She searched for anything that might seem funny to him, but came up empty, except for a couple of anecdotes about the kids. The latest books she'd read. Maybe a television program, probably a documentary. News about relatives, Marco's latest research, their vacation plans. She hoped he'd be pleased to learn about their friend Harry's efforts to unionize the non-academic staff.

Not her work. Definitely not her work.

What did they talk about at home, besides Sarah's comments on the disgusting food her mother served and how antiquated they were?

Pillow talk but that was off limits, and besides there hadn't been a lot of it lately. The political situation in the US and overseas, yes, lots of heated talk about that. But with Zayde that was a hotbed of uncertainty. Until years after the 20th Party Congress he had been an unrepentant Bolshevik, calling Khrushchev a capitalist tool. Finally, when it became impossible to deny the irrefutable evidence of the slaughter of millions, the anti-Semitic Doctor's Plot, Stalin's gulags and other well-documented horrors, Zayde had slumped into a worrisome depression that lasted for a long year. When he emerged, drawn back by values that had been the core of his commitment to the Communist vision, he redirected his energies to civil rights and the union movement. The subject of communism was off limits, as if it had never happened. All of that before the stroke. Now she didn't know what he thought, or if he even cared, but she clung to the idea of the Zayde of her childhood. She remembered the arguments he used to have with her grandmother in the years before his faith in the Party was destroyed. "Please, Duvidl, tonight no politics," she would say before they visited their more conservative relatives, some of whom had remained observant Jews. "Okay, okay," he would mutter, but his agreement would vaporize within minutes. If Claire sided with her grandmother, both of them anxious about the tensions that arose when he began to lecture, he would silence her by saying affectionately, "Pisher, what do you know?" There were more than a few evenings with relatives that ended in shouting matches. Zayde would point an accusing finger at whoever deigned to challenge him and say, "You'll see, comes the revolution I'll eat strawberries and cream and you they'll shoot." If a visiting relative talked about God, he would smile as if they'd walked into a pre-set trap: So where was your precious God when they killed the Scottsboro boys? When people were starving on breadlines and jumping off rooftops? When Hitler was murdering your relatives all over Europe? Could be maybe your God was in Florida playing golf? Or maybe having a shvitz down at the baths?"

Claire missed the booming voice in which he pronounced his absolute solutions to the world's problems: it's the class struggle, he used to say, his finger poking the air between him and his listener. She missed the Yiddish endearments he reserved for her, the music they sang together, Woody Guthrie and Pete Seeger songs, Yiddish folk tunes, Negro spirituals. What must it be like for him, locked in a useless body, without the ability to communicate? Sometimes as she drove home she had fantasies of putting a pillow over his head, or powdering Seconal into his tea. She thought about that man in Florida who was in jail for shooting his long-suffering wife in the hospital, and resolved again to write him a letter, though she knew she probably wouldn't.

THE RESIDENTIAL CENTER WHERE HER GRANDFATHER LIVED was not unpleasant, at least not on the side where ambulatory residents spent their time. It was housed in a two-story brick building with two wings surrounding the central area where the cafeteria, lounge and offices were located. The left wing where her grandfather lived was for ambulatory patients. The right wing housed people who were immobilized in crib-like beds. The first time Claire came to visit she turned down the wrong hall. She entered what she thought was her grandfather's room and found herself looking into the frightened eyes of a woman whose arms trembled under a maze of tubes attached to her body.

The cafeteria walls were papered with bouquets of red poppies on a white background. The day's schedule of events was posted on a bulletin board near the entrance: visiting dogs at one, pinochle and canasta in the lounge at three, a sing-along before supper, a karate demonstration by the local self-defense club in the evening. There was an empty sign-up sheet for an upcoming trip to a casino in New York State.

Cafeteria tables, each covered with red plastic, seated four and were designed to accommodate wheelchairs. There were lots of windows, and the sun poured in to augment the already steamy temperature, kept at eighty degrees because residents usually felt cold. The hallways smelled of disinfectant and boiled chicken, and resounded with the tap-tapping of walkers and canes. Outside, a wheelchair ramp led to a small grassy area with stone benches and picnic tables, which only the staff appeared to use.

Residents' rooms, with their white walls and faded red bedspreads, carried out the decorating scheme. The admissions office encouraged residents to bring small personal items from home, so dresser tops were hidden by photographs of smiling brides and grooms, babies in ancient smocked dresses, fat-cheeked bar mitzvah boys in stiffly starched shirts and grown-up suits, high school and college students smiling like young wizards underneath their mortarboards. The wall next to her grandfather's bed had pictures of Claire's parents in their casual wedding clothes, Marco and her, and of course the grandchildren. The family photographs were arranged around an autographed glossy of Gil Hodges and a framed letter signed by Henry Wallace.

The center had a social director who looked like a plump middle-aged cheerleader and scolded if anyone said patient instead of resident;

a social worker who knew the ins and outs of Medicare and Medicaid and offered workshops with titles like Anticipatory Grief and Attending to Unfinished Business with Your Aging Parent. There was also an exercise therapist who coaxed movement from limbs that ached with distended joints; an occupational therapist with a wagon full of jigsaw puzzles, paint-by-number outlines of Grandma Moses pictures, and crocheting supplies to keep arthritic fingers in motion. There were numerous aides whose first language was Spanish or something Asian, she didn't know if it was Thai or Tagalog.

CLAIRE SIGNED THE VISITORS' LOG at the nursing home desk and chatted briefly with the social worker, Mrs. Lincoln, who wore a smock the color of tomato soup. "Your grandfather is doing very well. His level of participation in the activity program has improved substantially." Claire forced herself to smile. Where the hell did she learn to talk that way? A self-improvement program?

"I hope you'll stay for lunch," Mrs. Lincoln continued. "I know your grandfather would be very pleased."

"Let's play it by ear, "Claire said. Meals at the nursing home reminded her of the annual PTA Open House she and Marco used to attend at the kids' elementary school: progress reports followed by a meal of soggy lasagna and pastel-frosted cupcakes.

Zayde was sitting in a green vinyl armchair looking at a quiz show on television. He was wearing the slippers she had brought on her last visit. His wavy white hair was neatly combed and Claire was struck once again by what a beautiful old man he was, with his dark eyes beneath thick white eyebrows, a strong jaw, large ears tucked flat against his head. He wore a neatly pressed flannel shirt, one she'd gotten him last year, and khaki pants. She averted her eyes from the stains around the crotch.

"Hello, Zayde." He looked up at her with a crooked smile of recognition and said "Son of a bitch." It was the one phrase he had retained after the stroke that had left half of his body paralyzed and destroyed his speech. The doctor assured Claire that this sometimes happened with stroke patients.

Abe Greenberg, her grandfather's latest roommate, was perched on the edge of the other bed reading aloud from the *Daily News*, a paper that Zayde used to denounce as "*dreck*" when he saw someone reading it on the subway. "Filthy capitalist press." Sometimes the victim of his disdain would shout at him to take his crappy *Daily Worker* and go back to Russia, and Claire would want to hide under the woven train seat.

"Claire!" Abe said, pushing the newspaper aside and rising to hug her as if she had come to visit him. "They didn't tell us you were coming. But then why should they, it's not like we'd be out dancing at the Copacabana." He began to laugh, but it turned into a barking cough.

She greeted Abe quickly and went to her grandfather. When she pressed her cheek against his white stubble he smelled like prune juice. "How are you, Zayde?"

He shrugged his left shoulder, the one he could still move, and nodded. "He's doing fine," Abe said. "He's eating real good these days. You should see how he handles a fork with his left hand, it's a miracle what they can teach you these day, even, you should excuse me, *alte kockkers* like us. By the way, those cookies you sent? They were so good, we finished them in a few days."

Claire wondered how many her grandfather had actually gotten to eat. "Sarah made them. My daughter."

Zayde used his good hand to lift the deadened limb from his lap to the arm of the chair.

"He's doing real good, don't you worry. Remember how when I first moved in here, he wouldn't do anything? They even had a hard time getting him to go for his exercises, doctor's order or no. I used to tell him you got to move or your bones will stick to that chair, Duvidl." Claire swallowed the impulse to tell him that only her grandmother had a right to call him by that name.

Zayde's face darkened with irritation, but, oblivious, Abe went on to tell Claire how her grandfather now watched Wheel of Fortune every night after supper and wrote down the answers on a pad with his left hand. And Oprah reruns, and Judge Judy. Then, winking, he said "Not that I can take all the credit. He's got himself a new friend. A lady friend."

Zayde's eyes drifted back to the television.

"A nice lady, she came in last month. Since she got here I hardly see him no more. Yesterday we had a treat; they brought in a singer from the city. An old timer, he used to be some big shot, played all the big hotels in the borscht belt. You should have heard him, Bye Bye Blackbird, My Gal Sal, all the old songs. Probably you don't even remember them, you're too young."

Menopausal me? Claire thought. Who would say those words to her when Abe and Zayde were gone?

"Anyway, it was some terrific show, your grandfather and his lady friend could hardly sit still. I said to myself watch out, they're going to get up and start singing."

Not my grandfather, Claire thought. Maybe if they coaxed Pete Seeger or Paul Robeson to come in and sing *Los Cuatro Generales* or the Peat Bog Soldiers, but old show songs? No way.

"I brought you some food, Zayde, and some books. I've got something for you too, Abe."

"What a sweetheart! But you didn't have to bring me nothing," Abe said, eyeing her shopping bag. He seldom had company. Both his children and their kids lived on the west coast. They sent birthday and father's day cards, and once a month UPS delivered a box of perfect Valencia oranges or red delicious apples or Bartlett pears from Harry and David.

Claire started to unpack the bag: dried apricots, raspberry sucking candy with chocolate centers, Hershey bars without almonds. A quart of Johnny Walker Red disguised in a brown apple juice jar. A box of chocolate-covered matzos for Abe, who still had his own teeth, rare as Turkish coins in this setting. She used to bring small cans of juice until she realized that her grandfather couldn't open them with one hand, and that Abe was probably drinking them all. Zayde watched carefully as she removed each item and showed it to him. "Son of a bitch," he said, nodding.

An aide with skin the color of creamy coffee appeared at the door. "Hello, Ms. Goldstein, good to see you," he said with a warm smile. "Your grandpa's doin' just fine, better'n when he got here, I can tell you. I gotta take Mister Abraham here for a sitz bath."

Abe tucked the box of matzos into the cabinet next to his bed. "Such a treat! Thank you, sweetheart," he said. "I'll be back in a while, I have to take my treatment." He shielded his mouth and whispered to Claire as if he were revealing a state secret,

"Hemorrhoids." The aide pushed a walker at Abe. Claire and Zayde were left alone in a room that seemed suddenly very quiet.

Zayde pointed to the door after Abe had left. "Son of a bitch."

"Yup," Claire said, laughing. The twisted corner of her grandfather's mouth made her heart ache.

"Marco sends his love, he'll come with me next time. He's in the middle of reviewing some films for his latest project. You'd like them, they're from the old Candid Camera show. He's using them as part of a project on peer pressure. There's one that gave me a stomachache, I was laughing so hard. This guy gets on an elevator and there's this look of surprise on his face because everyone is facing the back. He stands there for a while, facing front, but he keeps checking out the other people, and the expression on his face is so funny! And sure enough, by the time the elevator lands, he's turned around facing the back like all the others."

The functioning side of Zayde's mouth turned up slightly, encouraging her to go on, even though her own voice sounded hollow and slightly frantic to her. "The kids are great. I brought you some new pictures." She took out a packet of photos she'd printed from her computer just before she left: Sarah and Stephen clowning for the camera, Marco lying in a hammock reading the *Times*, Stephen pumping his muscles. "Just like the old Charles Atlas ads, Zayde, remember them?" He nodded at each picture. "Son of a bitch," he said.

"You look good, better than last time I was here."

His left shoulder moved up in a little shrug. Claire told him about the article she'd written a week ago—before the fracking assignment took over her agenda-- describing an Eskimo art exhibit at the

University museum. He nodded, but his eyes kept shifting back to the television. Watching him, she wondered if she would like to be an Eskimo, to sit on an ice floe and quietly, quickly die.

"Speaking of art reminds me, Zayde, Maude and Harry send their love. Harry's all involved in unionizing the teaching assistants. The Trustees aren't very pleased, you can bet. And Sarah told me that Stephen's up to his ears in planning some kind of demonstration, but she won't tell us what it's about. Top secret. Apparently he's working with a group to organize some sort of protest and they don't want the administration to know about it in advance. I guess he's got your genes, Zayde. They must have skipped a generation."

There. She'd played her ace, given him the best gift she'd brought. Too soon? Her grandfather nodded and smiled vaguely, as if he'd barely noted her words.

"I brought you some more books, I hope you'll like them." One of the aides had rigged up a bookstand with a sliding arm to keep the pages open so that Zayde could manage with one hand. Mostly he read books from a cart wheeled through the halls by a volunteer: travel books about train rides across Asia, a mule trip through the Andes, white-water rafting in New Zealand.

"I brought you a novel about Peekskill. I'd forgotten all about it, then I saw it in a used bookstore. Some of it's about the Robeson concert." No reaction. Claire put a slightly tattered copy of *World's End* on the table next to him. "I remember the stories you used to tell about how the goons of Westchester County were waiting after the concert, and how they ambushed people with stones and clubs as they came out. And the cops just stood by. Grandma told me how you went back to help more people get out after you got her and daddy to the bus safely. Daddy used to talk about how the next morning he went outside and saw the smashed windshield on your car."

Claire pulled out three more books: a recent analysis of the Rosenberg case—"there's new information, it shows for sure that Ethel was innocent." Now she wondered if these were bad choices, if she should have resisted her need to see even a glimpse of the old passion in his expression. She showed him a slightly tattered book of essays by Molly Ivins—"she's so right on and so funny about Bush, you'll love it. I was looking at it before I went to sleep last night and I woke Marco up. I was howling with laughter." She wished she could pull the words back; if he were to howl it would be with pain and anger, and it might never stop. She was grateful that the last book was neutral, a collection of Sholem Aleichem's short stories. She piled the books on the table next to him. He pointed at World's End, shook his head, and drew the forefinger of his left hand across his throat. The top book fell off the pile and crashed to the floor. "Son of a bitch," her grandfather said.

Claire excused herself and hurried to the empty visitor's lounge. The social worker had said it's not good to let them see their visitors cry. She sat down on the cracked vinyl sofa and stopped fighting the tears that had been clogging her throat as she babbled on to fill the silence. There was a half-full box of Kleenex on the small table next to her. Clearly she was not the only visitor who mourned the living dead.

THEY WENT TO LUNCH, her grandfather leaning into his walker as he pulled the deadened leg along. Abe chattered on, indifferent to whether anyone was listening. Claire tried not to see how Zayde struggled with his fork, but he managed to get most of the food into his mouth.

They were spooning the last drops of sugary lemon meringue pie off their plates when a plump elderly woman approached, using a walker that she had decorated with a bright green bow to match her polyester pants suit. Her hair was dyed a carroty color, and had been sprayed into a bouffant that looked as if it would scratch your fingers. Her grandfather looked up and smiled, the broadest smile she'd seen since he had his stroke. He pointed at Claire.

"This is your granddaughter? The one you raised?" she asked.

He nodded, still grinning that crooked smile of his. His cheeks were suddenly pink under the white stubble.

"This is Bessie, the lady friend I was telling you about." Abe winked at Claire again.

"You wouldn't believe how much your grandfather has told me about you."

Damned right I wouldn't, Bessie, Claire wanted to say, my grandfather hasn't said anything besides son of a bitch for three years. "Pleased to meet you," she said.

"I've seen pictures of your children. Beautiful. Myself, I have six grandchildren, nine great grandchildren. You mind if I sit down? Arthritis," she said, pointing to her knees. Claire pulled out the fourth chair at their table.

"Some card shark you have for a grandfather!" she said, and he grinned again. When he smiled his false teeth looked like they need to be adjusted. "I made him this box that holds his cards, and we play every game you can think of—canasta, gin, casino. He always wins," she said, and then, by damn, she giggled. The woman must have been eight-five years old and she giggled.

CLAIRE LEFT SOON AFTER LUNCH, the sweetness of the lemon pie clinging to the back of her throat. She could still feel the bristle of her grandfather's cheek when she kissed him goodbye. The drive was long and dull and she was grateful for the silence in the car.

That night she dreamed that she was walking past her grandfather's bedroom in the house she and her father moved to after her mother died. She heard Zayde's voice on the other side of the door, not the raspy sound of the old man who smoked Camels until he was seventy-five, but the strong, absolute voice she used to hear through the door of her childhood bedroom, arguing dialectical materialism with visitors. In the dream she opened the door and saw that he was sleeping soundly on one side of the bed, the way he did after her grandmother died. But the voice kept talking. It seemed to come from the glass bowl on the night table next to him where his false teeth, set in their Pepto-Bismol colored gums were soaking. Claire drew closer and saw that the teeth were moving rapidly, like those wind-up choppers people used to bring to parties to break the ice. They were delivering a lecture about the exploitation of the working class and about what lay in store when the proletariat rose up in revolution. Her grandfather opened his eyes, reached out with his right hand and hurled the bowl against the wall. "Son of a bitch," he shouted.

THE NEXT MORNING, Claire couldn't shake the mood of the dream. She wished she could simply be happy that her grandfather was finding some pleasure at this late point in his life. But the image of Bessie—her badly dyed hair, her shallow conversation, everything about her—it all seemed so remote from the world her grandfather had cared about.

Marco had closeted himself in his study after breakfast. Claire sat at the kitchen table, staring out the window, the unread newspaper opened in front of her. Her index finger traced circles around the chipped coffee cup. Outside a mother deer and her fawn nibbled on a spirea bush. Claire banged on the window. "Read the book, stupid," she shouted, "you're not supposed to like spirea." Oblivious, the deer munched on. "Okay, but don't come to me for sympathy if you get a bellyache, you little bastards." That was another battle people were pressuring her to join: how to deal with the overpopulation of deer. Deer. Won't you put this lawn sign out? Come to the hearing on fracking. Help us get out the vote. Join the march against hunger, poverty, AIDS, breast cancer. It was all too much to think about. And then there were the emails and phone calls. And the letters! Piles of requests from needy organizations that the poor letter carrier deposited in her box every day. She had stopped reading them, ignoring the effort that had gone into composing letters to touch the heart and open the checkbook. What did they call it? Compassion fatigue. Or was it compassion overload. And who will have compassion for me? Enough. What happened to your sense of humor? You used to be able to laugh; it was your primary survival mechanism.

Sarah had already left for lacrosse practice. The house was eerily quiet. She used to welcome the silence as a reprieve from the demands of her life; now it felt like a pronouncement of failure. She looked at the Sunday crossword puzzle, penciled in a few words, then decided that a walk might improve her mood. She showered and washed her hair, wondering as she did so if she should cover the grey that had started to thread through the dark curls she had never been quite able to control.

The morning walk didn't help. She wandered through the hills of the Plantations, past the duck pond and back to the car, without really registering the pleasure she usually took in the landscape. Sunday had always been her favorite day, but today it dragged into evening and the usual routine of "60 Minutes" followed by a British costume-drama. At midnight, Marco snoring peacefully beside her, she fell into a dreamless sleep until the clock rang seven hours later and Monday promised a fresh start.

CHAPTER SEVEN

C LAIRE OFTEN SAID that if not for Maude she would never have agreed to stay in this town she had come to love. She hadn't wanted to come all those years ago. She and Marco had been married for almost two years, living in Philadelphia near the University, in an old house, which might have been elegant before it was carved into primitively equipped apartments occupied mostly by graduate students. They rented a third-floor walk-up apartment— "good cardio workout," Marco said as they trudged up the long flights of scratched wooden steps hauling suitcases and cartons of books. For that privilege they paid five hundred dollars a month, with no additional charge for the waterbugs that scurried like tiny runaway shopping carts whenever someone put the lights on in the middle of the night. Claire had stretched her bladder almost beyond capacity to avoid the possibility of stepping on one in the darkness, with the accompanying scrunch and splat that forced whatever she had eaten for dinner to the back of her throat.

An honors major in journalism at Penn, the only job Claire had been able to find was part time, three days a week without benefits, screening letters to the editor of one of the city's newspapers. She spent the rest of her time looking for free-lance work and a better job. Her current gig involved writing and recording cassette summaries of articles on gingivitis and other oral diseases for a dentist who, as he commuted in his BMW to and from a wealthy suburb, listened to them to earn continuing education credits. The pictures of rotting gums accompanying the articles made her stomach lurch, but the work helped pay the bills. The academic job market was in a slump, and Marco wound up commuting an hour each way to a temporary position teaching at a small college in the state system. Most of their friends had moved on to high tech firms in the west, law offices in New York City, clinics on Indian reservations. But Claire and Marco stayed where they were and felt as if they were on hold, waiting for real life to begin, though she hoped it would begin in Philadelphia. Claire hated change. Marco spent hours each week perusing employment notices in his professional journals and sending out resumes.

When he first got an invitation to apply for the job at a major university in upstate New York, Claire immediately began to construct a wall of resistance. But Marco worked at scaling it with fierce determination.

"How many chances do you think I'll get at a tenure track job at an Ivy League school?" he asked. He took a bottle of Dos Equis, one of their few indulgences, out of the small refrigerator. Claire sat at the kitchen table, her fingers splayed, and twisted her wedding ring around.

"Jesus, hon, how many good jobs do you think are out there?" He sat down opposite her and held out the bottle. She shook her head.

"But it's so far," she said. "Is there even an airport? If I get a better job here or even in New York we'd never see each other. It's further than the commuting limit we set." They had agreed before the wedding that they would, if necessary, manage a commuting marriage for a couple of years while each built a resume.

Marco put the bottle down and reached across the table for her hand. "Claire, if I get it—and we both know it's a long shot—come with me."

She withdrew her hand and sat back in her chair, her fingers twisting a strand of brown hair. "You're kidding. What on earth would I do there? It's a small town, isn't it?"

"I'm not kidding. It's a big school, they probably have some kind of journalism job you could do. And Syracuse is only an hour away"

"Syracuse!"

"Yeah, Syracuse. It's a real city. And Rochester is only a little further."

"The hotbed centers of journalistic America."

"Don't be like that. Come on, you'll find something, maybe something better than what you've got here. I don't want us to be away from each other." Marco emptied the bottle of beer. "It's not like you're so happy with what you're doing. Anyway, we're jumping the gun. It's just an invitation to interview, they're probably looking at a dozen people." He stood up and walked behind her chair. His fingers begin to caress the back of her neck. "I really don't want us to be away from each other," he said. He leaned forward and nuzzled just under her left ear.

"No fair using erogenous zones," she said, and then, as he pulled her shirt over her head, she mumbled "Okay, but we'll talk about it right after we both come."

"I accept the challenge," he said, his hands moving to circle her breasts, his thumbs stroking her nipples.

IN SPITE OF HER ANXIETY, Claire had to agree that it was too good an opportunity for Marco to ignore. Maybe he was right, if he got it she might have a better chance at getting a real journalism job on a smaller paper, although she'd probably wind up covering county fairs and Easter egg hunts. They both acknowledged that the idea of being separated was unappealing. They knew several couples who were in long-distance relationships, some of whom appeared to manage quite well. But one commuting couple had divorced, after struggling with a Boston-Washington arrangement for a year. Claire and Marco were still in the sexual flush of people in their twenties, and the idea of weeks of deprivation was dismal. And although it pained her to admit it to herself, she suspected that they both knew she was the kind of woman who would follow her man.

CLAIRE HELPED MARCO PICK OUT HIS INTERVIEW CLOTHES: not a suit, too formal, she said, extracting a pair of almost new blue slacks from the press of clothing in their shared closet. Tweed jacket. Shirt: light blue. Tie? She thumbed through Marco's few ties; most of them were too vibrant or sported silly designs, like the one with Rorschach blots she'd given him for his birthday last year. They settled on his one solid tie, maroon. He pulled on a pair of jeans while she arranged the whole outfit carefully on a hanger.

"Do you have your good shoes?" she asked. And stop looking so worried, you'll get it on looks alone," Claire said as he turned to hug her. "Call me as soon as you finish the interview." She watched as he pulled on his sweatshirt and was filled again with awareness of how much she liked the way he looked: clear brown eyes as dark as his thick hair, a dimple in his chin, ears that rested flat against his head, a narrow straight nose. Olive skin that he got from his Sicilian ancestors. My own Mafioso, she called him. There was something solid about him, something in his body, his posture that communicated reliability.

She spent the day in a mood of unproductive restlessness. Finally, in the middle of the afternoon she ordered herself to her desk, where in a few minutes she was engrossed in summarizing a dental article on increased migration of leukocytes into junctional epithelium. When the phone rang she glanced at her watch and saw that it was after six.

Marco's voice was louder than usual, as if he were countering the distance between them through sheer volume. "Wait until you see it, babe," he said, "I mean, if I get invited back. The campus looks like one of those old English universities you see in guidebooks. One of the guys in the department took me for a drive. We just got back, and he's picking me up for dinner with a few other people in a few minutes. Sweetie, the countryside will knock you out! Waterfalls, hills, sunsets you can actually see. And everyone says it's safe." That was for her; she'd been anxious about the increase in crime in their neighborhood. Just a few weeks ago a student had been raped coming home from an evening class.

Marco rushed on, telling her about the interview and the people he'd met, the teaching and research expectations, the interest people on the search committee showed in his work. "They had a lot of good comments about my book. They actually read the damned thing!" She hadn't heard him talk with that much enthusiasm about anything besides the year the Phillies won the World Series in 1980.

Three weeks later the call came, inviting him for a second visit. This time Claire joined him for the five-hour trip north. Half way there he asked her to take the wheel so he could rehearse his presentation to the psychology faculty on the use of adolescent peer pressure in television advertising. The ride seemed very long, though the road was easy with only a few trucks zooming past. Once she settled into steering their rusted Escort, she was able to listen to Marco's recitation.

"There. That's where the first slide goes," he said. "Shit, this stuff must sound really boring."

"It won't be to them. You'll knock their socks off."

His voice droned on and Claire stopped listening, enjoying the ride through rolling hills, groomed farms with red barns and silos, small towns with green squares surrounding white bandstands. "America," Marco said, looking out the window. "It's prettier than Philadelphia."

"What about Bucks County? The Arboretum? The Art Museum?"

"I'm trying to concentrate here."

"You started."

Claire hummed softly as she drove, until they passed a billboard. "Oh my god, did you see that?"

Marco looked up. "Jesus, Claire. What's so important?"

"A billboard. 'Abortion kills' in huge letters, with a disgusting picture of a bloody fetus. What kind of place is this? The middle of the Ozarks?"

"We're still at least half an hour away," he said. "There won't be anything like that where we're going, you'll see."

"Yeah, but nice neighbors we'd have if we wanted to take a ride in the country."

Marco went back to his notes.

As they reached the top of the hill approaching town, Claire had a view of the sparkling blue lake, dappled with the reflection of cottony clouds and dotted with the white triangles of sailboats. The lake was framed by tree-covered slopes with cottages peeking out along the shore. It was so beautiful that it looked contrived, as if a photographer had set it up.

They were early, so after they drove down a steep hill, they parked on a side street and walked to the pedestrian commons to have a snack before checking into their hotel on the campus. The commons had a dozen empty stores, their windows plastered with political posters and meeting announcements. There was one visible movie theater showing "Ferris Bueller's Day Off." Several head shops sported fancifully twisted tubes and arrays of incense burners. The one department store occupied two floors of a brick building and featured polyester leisure suits and Vera for Women in its windows. They passed a dingy Chinese restaurant and settled on a bakery-luncheonette where the only temptations were half-moon cookies. After a reviving cup of coffee and injection of sugar, they returned to their weary car, which noisily chugged up the long Buffalo Street hill and turned toward the campus.

Claire saw what Marco had been describing: oak and maple trees, broad expanses of green, neo-Gothic stone buildings interspersed with cotemporary structures that didn't quite fit in but had their own architectural pleasures. It was like someone's fantasy of what a university should look like.

They checked into the hotel, where a spacious, well-appointed room had been reserved for them. Hotel school trainees were obsequious in their desire to please, as if Claire and Marco were going to grade their efforts. They toted luggage, turned down blankets, handed over keys and waited politely for their tips.

"Whee!" Claire shouted, when the last of the students departed. She kicked off her shoes and dropped onto the mattress. "If you get the job can we live here? I love hotels."

Marco lay down next to her. "You know you'd miss the waterbugs," he said, nuzzling her neck and running bug-like fingers under her tee shirt.

"Mmm, I like being felt up by a professor," she said. "Even a professor in waiting."

THAT NIGHT THEY HAD DINNER at the Faculty Club with Frank Thomas, the chair of the search committee, and his wife Elaine. Both were in their late forties and had lived in town for twenty years. Elaine was trim and looked like she'd just escaped from the Talbot's catalog. She talked about the Campus Wives' book club (*"The Closing of the American Mind,* you have to admire Alan Bloom, whether or not you agree with him,"), the golf tournament she was playing next weekend, the dozens of college visits they were making with their daughter who, as a junior in high school, had amassed several equestrian trophies. With an attentive smile frozen on her face, Claire's mind wandered through academic novels she'd read: Lucky *Jim,* what was that David

Lodge book, *Stepping Westward*—something by Alison Lurie. Maybe she'd write one . . .

She was more interested in the snippets of Frank and Marco's conversation that she could overhear: the conflict between experimental and clinical psychologists for control of the department and the balance social psychology could bring; whether it was appropriate to increase the numbers of graduate students, given the job market; the potential candidates for the provost's position, opening in a few months. She noticed that Elaine didn't ask her a single question about her.

Later they lay in the king size bed with its 600 count cotton sheets and down quilt, imagining what it would be like to live and work in this community. To Claire it felt like a foreign country, a place one visits for a long weekend before returning to the real world.

"Alan Bloom!" she said. "Maybe she'll invite me to the campus Republican Club. Can't you hear my old Bolshevik grandfather on that one! And golf tournaments! Did you see the way she was dressed, everything perfectly coordinated, little gold earrings, the works? I thought we promised each other we were not going to fall into all that suburban crap!"

"We won't, babe. I'm sure she's not representative. Probably most of the people here are more like us. And I bet most of the women have careers. I think we could really make a good life here. Anyway, this is premature. They haven't offered me the job yet."

"They'd be crazy not to," I said. "I'd hire you in a minute."

"Yeah, but they're not like you, they're not looking for a stud," he said, his hand moving under the tee shirt Claire wore to sleep. She sighed and opened her legs to his exploring fingers.

"Aren't hotel rooms great!" she mumbled into his neck. "Like eating oysters."

"Good luck," Claire said the next morning when she dropped Marco in front of one of the few modern buildings on campus, a rusty structure that looked like it had been left out in the rain too long. "You look handsome. Very professorial."

"You really think I should have worn a suit?" he said, adjusting his tie and flicking an invisible dust mote off one dark sleeve. He was too preoccupied to wish her good luck back, or even to comment on her appearance. Oh well, this is his party, Claire thought.

The chair of the psychology department had arranged an interview for her with the editor of the weekly Arts College faculty newspaper, modestly called *Scholars*. She had dressed more conservatively than usual in navy slacks and a red blazer, not realizing that she was donning school colors. None of the flamboyant ethnic jewelry she usually wore, just a pair of small gold hoops that had been her grandmother's. She found a parking lot and got directions from the attendant. As she walked across the campus, she was astonished by how young the students looked, even though it didn't seem so long ago that she had walked from Penn's College Hall to Smoky Joe's where over pitchers of beer she and her friends had argued about the draft, nuclear disarmament and about how the Reagan budget cuts would affect education.

The office of *Scholars* was in the basement of a building at the far edge of the quadrangle. It was poorly lit, which was just as well since it looked as if it hadn't been painted for years. She wrinkled her nose at the musty basement smell. Looking through the glass door, she saw a short, owlish man stooping over a steel desk that looked as if been reclaimed from a defunct army post. He looked up from the magazine he had been reading when she knocked and waved her in.

She introduced herself and he shook her hand with his pudgy one.

"I'm Hal Cantor, the editor." He was in his late fifties; everything about him was round, including his horn-rimmed glasses. His light blue shirt drooped over his khakis like an extra stomach.

"One minute. Yeah, here we are," he said, shuffling through a pile of papers, picking out one which she recognized as her resume. She saw that there was a bright green sticky on top of it with writing she couldn't make out.

"I have you down as Claire Capobianco," he said

"I use my own name. Goldstein."

Hal glanced at her resume. "Oh yeah. Goldstein."

He led her into his windowless office. There was a huge bulletin board with clipped articles tacked to it, a framed picture of a boy in a cap and gown, a painting that made her think of the paint-by-numbers pictures people in old-age homes were given for occupational therapy. This one was a painting of the stone tower she had noticed when they drove onto the campus.

"Sit down, sit down," he said and smiled. "Glad to meet you. I read the stuff you sent." He pursed his lips and nodded. "Good writing. I know good writing when I see it. You got a nice edge there. I was a journalism major, too. Long time ago. University of Chicago." He spent the next half hour talking about his early career covering political corruption for the *Chicago Sun Times*. Then, after asking a few superficial questions, he said, "We don't usually hire people without a backlog of experience, but I think we can make an exception in your case."

He filled her in on details of the job: benefits, salary (not much, but better than she'd managed to piece together in her hodge-podge of jobs). "We do some damned good work here, but we're not a high priority. You can probably tell that from the office," he said, his hand sweeping the air. "Our job is to stay on top of what's going on in the Arts College, what's happening in research, awards people get, changes in policy. I like to think of us as having an ear on the University's pulse." He smiled, pleased with a metaphor Claire would have given a D minus.

"So," he said, leaning back in a wooden chair that protested with a squeak, "you planning to have kids?"

The question seemed abrupt and maybe even illegal. Wasn't there a law about not discriminating against pregnant women? Not that she was expecting, or even expecting to expect for a few more years. But the question rankled her. Was he worried that she'd start the job and then vomit for nine months?

He seemed to notice her discomfort and said quickly, "That didn't come out right. You could probably sue me. I was just asking because if you do have kids, you get a good break on tuition." He pointed at the photograph of the graduate on his wall. "My son. Went here, worth thousands. Sort of a golden handcuff situation."

She began to like Hal, and thought he was probably the kind of person who had a well-meaning way of blundering into things.

"So, when do you think you'll be ready to start?" he asked.

Claire explained that she couldn't make a decision until they knew whether Marco had gotten the job, and that then they'd have to talk it over. She didn't add that she wasn't at all sure she wanted to move to this remote place, or spend her days laboring in this dungeon.

"Oh, he'll get it," Hal said. "I understand your hotshot husband has a future here. It's my business to know what's happening with faculty, and I know that they want to upgrade social psych."

Hal introduced her to Mary Watson, who occupied the next office. Her desk was on the other side of a partial Plexiglas divider that separated all of the working spaces Claire could see. She was aware of people sneaking looks at her.

Mary was in her early sixties. She wore her glasses on a braided black cord that hung over an unbuttoned grey cardigan. She'd been with the paper for twenty years and was planning to retire in three more. "Mary's in charge of the staff that covers news about all the non-sciences. That's where I'll put you," Hal said. "You'll learn a lot from her. And it'll give you a chance to meet a lot of interesting people."

Charlie, who covered the sciences, looked like a lanky grown-up fraternity boy. He had dark glossy hair and wore Clark Kent glasses; Claire had an image of him ducking beneath the glass wall to change into his superman outfit before flying from one building to another. They moved along the corridor that divided the glass boxes as Hal introduced her to the rest of the staff, ending with Louisa, the department secretary who proudly announced that her husband was working on his Ph.D. in microbiology and that they would be moving in another year.

"Trouble with a campus, you get good help and they move on," Hal said. "That's why I like to hire faculty wives."

"What if the faculty is the wife, do you hire the husband?" Claire asked, then regretted the snotty tone of her question. Hal looked like he hadn't understood what she was asking.

"We're not a high priority here as you can see from our space," Mary said, echoing Hal's words when she showed Claire to the ladies room at the end of a long hallway. "But Hal's a good guy, and we do get the inside scoop on what's happening on campus. Even if we're not always allowed to print it."

When Claire left the interview she understood that the job was hers if she wanted it. Word had evidently come from above that she was to be wrapped into the Marco package. Years later, even when she had moved into Hal's job, she would still feel that she hadn't gotten there on her own merits.

TWO WEEKS LATER THE FORMAL OFFER ARRIVED. Marco couldn't stop grinning, and insisted that they celebrate with a dinner that cost half a week's salary. But Claire's ambivalence went into full throttle. She couldn't get excited about the newsletter job, which seemed less than challenging. Even their miserable apartment in a run-down part of west Philadelphia appeared endearingly quaint rather than shabby when she thought about relocating. Although most of their friends had left the city, she didn't look forward to finding new ones in a strange community.

Claire was especially concerned about being so far from her grandfather whom she used to visit every second Saturday. At the time, Zayde still lived in the same Riverdale apartment to which she had moved when she was twelve years old. It was only a couple of hours away by Pennsylvania Railroad. She was all the family he had left, except for his sister Helen, who lived in Scranton. Claire knew that her bi-weekly visits were the highlight of his life since her grandmother's death a few years ago. He would put his newspaper on the arm of the battered recliner and rise, his smile almost as wide as his open arms.

But it was clear that Marco wanted the job as much as he'd ever wanted anything. He began working Claire with a sales pitch worthy of Madison Avenue, calling on every complaint she had ever uttered about Philadelphia and their current living situation: you're always whining about how much it costs to live in the city. We can't afford to go to the theater or a club to hear music. You've been afraid to walk to the corner mailbox at night since the rape happened. Once we have kids, what kind of crazy place is this to raise them, we'd probably have to send them to private school. And who can afford that, and anyway you always say you don't believe in private school. He was unrelenting. At breakfast: think about all the opportunities in a college town, you could go back to school if you wanted. As they prepared dinner: you'd have a regular job with benefits, not this crappy jigsaw work life you have to piece together. While they were brushing their teeth at the permanently stained enamel sink: it's not that much further to see your grandfather and my parents (though the ability to visit Marco's parents was hardly a selling point for Claire).

She couldn't dispute the logic of his arguments, though she resented what she knew to be an accurate description of her career up to this point. But she was overwhelmed by all the changes she'd have to make: job, doctor, dentist, friends, home. She'd had too many changes in her life. That was one of the reasons she had resisted taking Marco's name when they got married, in spite of pressure from his mother who probably thought her rebellious daughter-in-law was going to spend eternity burning in hell because she was unwilling to become Mrs. Capobianco, let alone her refusal to convert and commit to raise any progeny in the True Faith. But Claire had held firm. "I won't know who I am if I turn into Claire Capobianco" she said. Abandoning her name felt disloyal to her parents, her grandmother, Zayde.

She knew that her resistance to the move lacked substance and that Marco was right about the need to accept the offer. After a week of restless nights and agonized days, she reluctantly agreed to go. When she visited her grandfather to tell him about the move, she repeated Marco's arguments about all the reasons it made sense for them to accept the offer. "And of course I'll come to see you just as often." Zayde was quiet for a moment, then said "Avekgayn mit mazel," (go with good luck) which was as close to a blessing he, still an unrepentant atheist, knew how to give.

In late July they loaded their small accumulation of furniture and clothing and a dozen cartons of books into a U-Haul and headed north. Marco drove all the way, singing Joni Mitchell songs in his baritone voice. She ignored his invitation to join him. When she offered to drive for a while, he said, "No, I feel like a million bucks!" Claire was quiet for most of the trip.

They spent two nights in a motel on an ugly downtown strip on the edge of town. The realtor with whom they were working tried to convince them of the wisdom of buying rather than renting, but Claire was unmovable; that felt too permanent. At the end of the second day they were shown a two-bedroom flat that was within their budget in a newly built apartment complex about ten minutes from campus. The landscape was still raw, but the apartment was luxurious compared to their minimalist digs in Philadelphia. It had a real kitchen with cabinets and Formica countertops and two big closets in the bedroom, picture windows that looked out over what might eventually become expansive lawn, but at the moment was a sea of mud. And no waterbugs.

The first people they met after unpacking were Jerry, the newly hired experimental psychologist with whom Marco shared an office, and his skinny wife Greta, who spent hours reciting Greek poetry to their infant daughter in their determination to get her into Harvard eighteen years in the future. "You won't believe what his dissertation was," Marco told Claire after he first met Jerry. "Get this: approach-avoidance conflicts in painted turtles."

"I think we've moved to Disneyland."

They went to a few deadly departmental parties, where everyone drank sherry and the conversation almost buckled under efforts at wittiness. "If I hear one more dry snotty joke I'm going to deck whoever tells it," Claire said after one party, as they lay in bed comparing notes on their tedious experiences on opposite sides of the room.

They were invited to dinner by Claire's new boss Hal and his wife Maria, a biochemist working on some arcane research project, whose major interests were science and science. She went to lunch several times with a few of her colleagues, but found that out-of-office conversation became strained after the first half hour, so on the wishful pretext of dieting she started to bring her lunch several days a week. The other people they saw socially those first few months were the young faculty families who lived in their apartment complex, most of them attached to the agricultural college, with whom she struggled to find some area of commonality.

"Why did you drag me here to the alien corn?" Claire whined after their first neighborhood gathering, a dish-to-pass supper and scavenger hunt in the common area of the apartment complex. "Come on," Marco said, "Don't you want to learn how to breed blotches out of tomatoes? How to produce the best chicken roll? Where's your intellectual curiosity?"

She was not going to let his humor deflect her barrage of complaints. "The big event in this place is the opening of hunting season! We're in a God-forsaken wilderness where people run around in camouflage pants and shoot Bambi. And what's more, you can't even get a decent bagel. Did you see that array of pasta salads swimming in mayonnaise?"

"You forgot to add that the Chinese food here tastes like it comes out of a can and gives you headaches." Then he added more seriously, "I never realized what a snob you are."

"Make something happen to stop me from feeling like's we've landed in an alternate universe," she said. "Take me back to the real world."

And then their first upstate winter hit. Smacked. Bludgeoned. They had never considered Philadelphia a southern city until that winter, when it seemed subtropical by comparison. It snowed every day for two months. The wind created whiteouts which made driving a cross between Blind Man's Bluff and the Ice Follies. Icicles hung menacingly like stalagtites. The sun was almost a distant memory.

"We have to learn to flow with the season, not fight it," Marco said, so one Sunday, when the wind died down to a low howl and the white-outs had stopped sweeping snow across the road like a sandstorm, they rented cross-country skis and drove to an area where a trail had been plowed through dense evergreen woods. But after her fourth fall Claire returned to the car, teeth chattering and fingers frozen inside her insulated gloves. She sat behind the wheel swearing that her winter sport would be drinking V.S.O.P, which they couldn't afford in front of the fireplace they didn't have. Marco, on the other hand, took to it immediately, gliding through the woods on the gently rolling trail, and returned to the car exhilarated, his cheeks glowing with health. "That was fabulous," he crooned. "You should have stayed with it."

"How many years will I get for homicide?" she asked and turned the car heater up to its highest level.

For the first few weeks on the job Claire accompanied Mary to lectures, where afterward she sat quietly while Mary interviewed the lecturer. She clipped articles about the faculty in the *Times* and other newspapers and helped to reorganize the information files. After a while she started to do her own interviews, mostly with guests from other universities who were visiting for a semester, or with writers who had come to campus to do a reading. Although she found most of them interesting and friendly, there was no opportunity to develop any kind of relationship.

Nonetheless, Claire knew she was lucky to have a job, even if she'd gotten it because the department wanted Marco. She soon learned that the town was filled with overqualified people, many of them supporting graduate student or low-wage junior faculty spouses. They were so desperate for any kind of work that when an ad appeared for a receptionist or a manager at the local food co-op, seventy-five men and woman would show up, half of them having completed graduate school. Wait staff at local restaurants were likely to have advanced degrees and comment on Kierkegaard or Ingmar Bergman as they delivered dinner.

Although she grudgingly admitted that she enjoyed the interviews, most of her job was a far cry from the high-powered investigative reporting she'd dreamed of when she majored in journalism. She'd had fantasies of uncovering a major political scandal or untangling a mysterious killing. Still, she'd arrived here daydreaming about writing stories that would blow open a scandal in the state education department or reveal a scheme to undermine a highly qualified woman's tenure hearing. Instead, a good chunk of her thirty-five hour work week involved putting a good face on the need for a new roof for the Geology building or a major overhaul in the plumbing system of one of buildings on the Arts Quad, probably ruined by years of being stuffed with discarded condoms.

The best part of Claire's job was that it led them to Harry and Maude Cohen. It was during their first February in Ithaca, a month for which she would have gladly pushed the delete button. The University was raising funds to buy a version of The Peaceable Kingdom for its art museum. In a search for angles that would attract donors Claire was assigned to interview Harry, then head of the art history department.

She dressed in the artiest outfit she could assemble: black turtleneck and slacks, long copper and ebony earrings she'd bought at a flea market in South Philadelphia, a black and tan scarf she struggled to tie rakishly at her throat. Looking in the mirror to check the effect, she registered her customary dissatisfaction, wishing she had longer legs, bigger breasts, a flatter belly. Maybe straight blond hair? She twisted her dark hair into a bun, grimaced at the results and shook it loose again, so that it fell to her shoulders in a disarray of curls.

After searching the dimly lit corridor of an old building on the main quad, Claire arrived at the open door of Harry Cohen's office.

"Professor Cohen? I'm Claire Goldstein from *Scholars*," she said, knocking on the open door.

Harry greeted her without getting up from behind his desk, and motioned her to a chair. He was somewhere in his late fifties, with the softened look of a man who had spent too many years hunched over books or at the typewriter that sat on a rickety stand near his desk.

"I know, you're here to get me to say something nice about the Peaceable Kingdom." He smiled in a way that made his face look suddenly younger. "Off the record, it's a piece of crap."

He tilted back and clamped his Birkenstocked feet on the desk. He was wearing khakis and a dark green pullover sweater, from which the frayed collar of a plaid flannel shirt was visible. "Trite. I hope none of our alumni are dumb enough to come up with the money for that one." He leaned forward to scratch his foot, then tilted back in his desk chair, which made a complaining squeak.

"I'm sure you don't want me to quote you."

"Crap, who cares? For years I've been trying to get the goddam selection committee to buy a Kathe Kollwitz or a Ben Shahn, but they're more interested in grinning lions and tomato soup cans," the latter a recent acquisition of which the museum was inordinately proud.

Claire laughed, shifting to a more comfortable position in the wooden chair. "You sound like my grandfather. He flies into a rage over most modern art. Shahn's his favorite painter. When I was a kid he gave me that wonderful clown poster—you know the one I mean? I still have it in our kitchen. But I have to admit that some of the boy-meets-girl-under-tractor stuff my grandfather used to like is a little over the top for me."

Harry laughed. "Boy meets girl under tractor. Haven't heard that one for a long time. What does your grandfather do?"

"Writes furious letters to the editor, reads *The Nation*, shouts at the TV. He was a union organizer. He still does some work for them."

"Which union?"

"He was vice president of the Bronx branch of the IFWU, the International Furrier Worker's Union."

"Oh yeah, Ben Gold's old hangout. One of my few heroes. You probably don't remember him."

"I've heard my grandfather talk about him. When my father was a kid, Zayde –that's what I call my grandfather—anyway, Zayde used to drag him to May Day parades in New York, and Gold always walked at the front of the Furrier's brigade. Hecklers used to throw things at the marchers. My father said it took a few days to get the rotten egg smell out of his hair."

"God, what memories that brings back!" Harry said, smiling. "It must have been scary as hell for a kid, but the feeling of that crowd was something else. We thought we were going to change the world. We thought we were stronger than all the big-money capitalists and FBI thugs and union busters combined. We even thought that one day we'd elect a Negro." He shook his head. "And now look at us:

fucking Reagan in the White House, Russia testing more nuclear bombs, people being spied on."

"My father used to tell me how freaked out he'd get when he was a kid and FBI agents would show up to question Zayde. But he'd fly into a rage and yell at them to get the hell off his porch. And then he was subpoenaed and he went to jail for a year because he wouldn't cooperate with HUAC. Dad said that when he got to be a teenager he was so burned out by Zayde's politics that he wouldn't even read a newspaper or watch the news. He said that for him the biggest event of those years was the release of a new Frankie Laine record."

Claire realized when she stopped chatting for a few seconds that the roles had been reversed: Harry was interviewing her. "My god, I don't think I've talked so much since we moved here!" she said.

"So what brought you to this remote corner of the globe?" Harry asked.

"My husband. He got a job in the psychology department and I followed him. Dutifully. Doesn't that sound like something straight out of the fifties?"

"How do you like it here?"

Without warning, Claire's eyes filled with tears. She lowered her head. "I'm sorry, it's just . . . I haven't . . .It's too . . ." She glanced at her watch. "I'd better do my job."

"All right," Harry said. "I'll give you a bullshit statement about the Kingdom painting on one condition: you and your husband come for dinner Friday, six o'clock. You have to come meet my wife, she'll change your mind about living here." He wrote an address on an index card and handed it to her. And that was how Maude came into Claire's life.

CHAPTER EIGHT

ON MONDAY, Maude took a long shower before her appointment with the neurosurgeon. Wrapped in a towel, she stood in front of her closet and pulled out one of the denim skirts in which she felt most comfortable, along with a plaid shirt, the sleeves already neatly folded to elbow length. She smiled, remembering the way her mother used to make sure that she and her sister were wearing clean underwear with no holes before every visit to the doctor.

Harry tapped the horn for the third time, the motor running as he waited in the driveway. Maude couldn't find her purse; it wasn't where she always kept it. She had a flash of fear that she was getting forgetful but reassured herself that it was just nerves. Although she had minimized her situation to Claire and Harry, she was worried about the appointment. The pain had been getting worse, pushing its way through her sleep and making it impossible to find a comfortable position.

What was the doctor's name, Glass? Gebhardt? She looked at the appointment card: Aaron Gelb. You'd' like that, mama, you old witch, she thought, hearing her mother's voice: "If you get sick find a Jew doctor, that's the only thing they're good at besides making money."

Gelb had been recommended by Sid Lorimer, their primary care doctor and a close friend. She and Harry had been invited to the Lorimers for dinner a few weeks ago. Taking her coat in the front hall, Sid had said, "I don't like the way you're moving, Maude," and insisted that she describe her pain. "I think you ought to see a neurosurgeon and figure out what's going on." Sid had seen them through years of minor bouts of flu, Harry's prostate scare, a case of pneumonia that had hospitalized Maude with IV drugs for four days. A few other crises, nothing major: a hernia operation for Harry, an infected gall bladder for Maude. When Alice was diagnosed, he had accompanied them through that agonizing journey, cutting through red tape whenever possible, finding the latest research on childhood leukemia, finally weeping with them at the quiet memorial service.

More recently Maude's heart had begun to beat irregularly, something that was being treated with medicine. Pretty much, though, she and Harry had been lucky with their health. They'd watched too many friends begin to spiral downward into dementia, or succumb to cancer, or tremble with Parkinson's. She was afraid that their luck was beginning to change.

When they reached the office in the medical arts building next to the hospital, a receptionist took her insurance cards and slid a clipboard across the desk with several pages of repetitive paper work. Maude began to fill them out, with Harry coaching over her shoulder. "No, don't you remember, you had the gall bladder surgery in 1989, not 1981." "We had tetanus shots in 2007." "You take 12.5 milligrams, not 25."

"I know, you don't have to tell me everything," she said, then regretted the irritation in her voice. Harry was as worried about this visit as she was. But at that moment she needed some space. He looked stung when she told him she didn't want him to come when a nurse opened the door to the inner chamber and called her name. "I'll have them come out for you when I talk to the doctor, after the examination," she said, relieved to move away from his palpable anxiety.

Dr. Gelb rose from behind his desk to shake her hand. He wore a slightly wrinkled white coat open over a stomach that pushed apart the buttonholes of his blue shirt. He was barely forty, she guessed. She was still not accustomed to such young people having so much responsibility. Even the president, though the longer he was in office, the older he'd begun to look.

As the doctor reviewed her health, she looked around the office. There were four framed diplomas and a photograph of two little girls on the wall behind his chair. Otherwise the usual neutral furnishings of most doctor's offices. She wondered if they all used the same decorator. His desk was stacked with files on one side, a small computer on the other. He tapped a pencil against his cheek as he read. Putting the file aside, he asked her a number of questions about the pain: sharp or a dull ache? Constant or intermittent? Affected by different positions? Interfering with sleep? Then he directed her next door to the examining room where she changed into a soft cotton gown. When he came in, he asked her sit on the edge of the examining table. The paper crackled beneath her as she gingerly shifted back, trying to avoid the motion that set off a chain reaction of pain. A middle-aged nurse entered, wearing a smock covered with a pattern of yellow smiley faces.

"Here, let me help you lie down," she said. Maude inched down on her side with the nurse's assistance, then rolled onto her stomach. If Alice had lived, this young doctor could almost be my grandson, she thought. His fingers probed, gently at first, then seemed to locate a core of pain that flashed all the way down her leg and made her moan.

"Sorry. I'll try not to let that happen again. Don't hesitate to yell if it hurts."

He continued to prod and explore the length of her spine. When he was finished, the nurse helped her dress and then Harry joined her in the doctor's office.

Gelb told them that he was concerned about what was causing her pain and wanted to run some tests to determine what was going on. He thought they shouldn't wait and had his secretary set up appointments for her in the hospital lab and the radiology department. Maude tried not to react to his insistence of acting immediately. Harry pushed: "You make it sound urgent. What do you think is wrong??"

"I don't have enough information yet. We'll know more when we get the results," Gelb said, not unkindly.

For the next two days Maude was poked, prodded, bled, observed, scanned, and most difficult of all, fed into a claustrophobic tube where she had to lie very still. The technician gave her earphones and a choice of music, but the jackhammer noise of the MRI machine overwhelmed the Goldberg Variations and made her think of the sound of Nazi boots coming up the stairway to the hiding place of the Frank family. In a flash of panic she almost rang the buzzer she was clutching, but toughed it out by counting backward from a thousand until the drumming stopped and she was slid back into the brightly lit room.

On Friday they were back in Gelb's office. He looked older than the first time they had been there. Maybe it was because he was delivering the news that she had been expecting, but which nonetheless left her breathless: you have cancer. He surrounded the announcement with other phrases—large mass, cell cluster, probably treatable. But what stayed in the air, hovering like a toxic insect, was the word: cancer

"I'm going to have my secretary set up an appointment with an oncologist. She's an excellent physician, came here from Sloan," he told Maude. Then he reached out and touched her arm, a gesture that brought unexpected tears to her eyes. "Cancer isn't a death sentence, Mrs. Cohen. These days there are lots of people for whom it's a chronic disease."

She was thrust back into another office long ago: seven year old Alice playing Chinese Checkers with a volunteer in the waiting room while she and Harry, their hands interlocked so tightly that their fingers were white, sat across from the pediatric oncologist. He had avoided their eyes as he told them their daughter had incurable leukemia. Maude had wanted to die right then, before she had to watch helplessly as the disease consumed the white cells of their little girl's body. All of their energies went into the façade they maintained with Alice, doing anything they could to buoy her spirits, deflect her attention from the pain they could not take away. Maude found herself whispering prayers to a god she didn't believe in.

They had moved like ghosts through the months after Alice's death. For two years she had wanted to die herself, but she couldn't bear to think what that would do to Harry. Eventually she had been lured back into life, primarily by her work with children in the school library, by Harry's needs, by friendships. Now death had invited itself into her world again, and she was surprised by the depth of her anxiety.

Maude had often thought, as she listened to grim prognostications on NPR or read in the *Times* about global warming, terrorist access to nuclear weapons, starvation in Africa and all the other horrors that were threatening the very existence of the world, that maybe it wouldn't be bad not to be around for what might well lie ahead. Not to bear witness to what seemed terrifyingly possible. She and Harry had talked vaguely about how nice it would be to lie down together and not wake up. But facing the reality of what was happening in her body, she was surprised to discover how much she wanted to live.

CLAIRE CALLED THURSDAY AFTERNOON. "I can't believe I forgot about your appointment," she said. "Dammit, I've been up to my ass in work and lost track of the time. I'm so sorry!"

"What are you working on?"

"Give me a break, Maude! I called to find out how your appointment with the neurosurgeon went, not to talk about my stupid job."

Maude didn't tell Claire about all the tests and the referral to the oncologist. She wasn't ready to talk about it to anyone, not even Claire. Especially not Claire, who maintained a special territory somewhere between daughter and friend. Claire had already lost one mother. It was hard enough trying not to see the expression on Harry's face during unguarded moments. And the effort he made to be cheerful and optimistic was even worse. She didn't have enough strength to comfort and reassure them both. She wondered if he had the same thought that had recently occurred to her: perhaps her genetic markings were responsible for Alice's cancer.

"I have another appointment next week," she told Claire. "A follow-up. I'll know more then."

Claire probed for more information. "Did he give you any idea? Anything to help you get more comfortable? A physical therapy referral?"

But Maude remained evasive. "Too soon, I have to have more tests. We'll know more after the results are back."

"Can I come see you after work tomorrow?"

"I have a lab appointment, I'm not sure when I'll be home. I'll call you."

Maude hung up, and looked around the living room. She was overwhelmed by the amount of stuff they had accumulated over the years. She should probably have pushed to move to The Meadows, a nearby life-care community, a few years ago, while she had the energy to downsize. Harry would never be able to manage all this by himself. She realized that she was already writing herself out of the picture, looking at her world as if she were no longer in it. She had to stop doing that.

But dear Jesus, look at all of this! If she started to give away things Harry would think she'd given up. But she had a longing now for lightness, for a sense of the Spartan. Maybe because her body was being crowded by so many cells. She looked around the living room. So many books—thousands of them. Well, that wouldn't be too difficult, they could all go to the Library book sale. Her clothes ---stop that, there you go again! She told herself. Wait until you have to face whatever you have to face. It was an old maxim of Harry's, one she had never managed to live by: if you worry about things and they happen, you pay a double price. If they don't, you've wasted a lot of energy worrying. From the way Harry had been looking lately, his faith in the maxim seemed to have weakened.

A slender Turkish vase caught her eye. She remembered the smoky shop where they had bargained for it. One of their many travel tchochkes, as Claire called them. Nothing museum quality, mostly folk art. Maybe Claire would want some of them. Or a craft shop might take and resell them. Stop it, Maude, she said aloud. She went into the study and carefully lowered herself into her reading chair. Picking up the volume of Bleak House she had decided to revisit, she withdrew gratefully into the world of Jarndyce vs. Jarndyce.

ON MONDAY, after filling out the same paperwork she had completed the week before in Gelb's office and trying to shush Harry's grumbling about "all this stupid goddam waste in the American medical system," they were shown into Dr. Mason's office. There were framed Monet water lily reproductions on the tan wall, a soft oriental carpet on the floor, a Victorian loveseat and two antique chairs that looked as if they had been recently reupholstered. The doctor sat behind a gleaming wooden table, with a neatly organized stack of files on one side, a glass vase of yellow roses on the other.

Dr. Mason was a woman in her early forties. When she rose to greet them she was surprisingly tall, and moved with the ease of someone who had learned to live comfortably in her body. She might be a runner, with her long arms and legs, her fluid movements. She wore an open white coat with a faded stain on the left front pocket, and under it tan slacks and a paisley shirt. Her dark blond hair was pulled into a low ponytail, held in place by a tortoise shell barrette.

"I'm Yvonne Mason," she said, shaking Maude's hand first, then Harry's and pointing them to leather-covered chairs across from her desk. "I know this is a stressful time, and you probably have lots of questions, so let me get right to it. I've looked over the test results, and I think we should explore a little further see how far the cancer has spread." Maude saw Harry wince at the word. They would have to find a way to decontaminate it; the word had invaded her vocabulary the way the cells were invading her body, but Harry would not say it. Years ago she had read Susan Sontag's book *Illness as Metaphor*. It had seemed very smart to strip away the loaded language surrounding cancer. She wondered if it would help Harry to find a metaphor.

"Once we have the full picture you'll be able to decide about treatment. We'll take all the time you want for questions, but if you don't mind, I'd like to examine you first." Maude found her directness reassuring.

The doctor led Maude to an examining room while a nurse guided Harry back to the waiting area. As she was changing into the short blue gown the doctor had handed her before she stepped out, Maude looked at her body. Old, sagging flesh. Spots all over her arms. She should have applied sunscreen more regularly when she was in the garden. Maybe she should have joined a gym when she was younger, or played tennis or taken up golf, but none of that had appealed to her. She'd never had a weight problem; in fact she'd been having trouble keeping her weight up in the last few months, and her pelvic bones seemed to jut out more sharply than usual. She used to be a strong swimmer; she loved the cold bite of the lake in early summer, unlike

Harry, a city kid who had never felt at ease in the water. He would stay behind on shore, watchful until she swam back to where he was waiting to wrap her in an oversize towel. And she had treasured hiking the gorge trails that left people younger than she panting, balancing herself with the walking stick Harry had carved for her birthday years ago. She would stop only to lift her binoculars to catch sight of a distant bird, and, if it was a rare species, record it in the bird book she kept in her backpack. But in the last two years the aching in her back and legs, which she had attributed to arthritis, had limited her activity to gardening. And that she had refused to give up. She knew that, even with Harry's best efforts, most of the garden would wither and go to seed without her care.

She sat carefully on the edge of the examining table, waiting for the doctor to return. Bodies. How little thought she'd given to her own, how much she'd taken it for granted. It had done her bidding for so long but now she felt estranged from it, alienated from its systems, from the heart that pumped its blood and the lungs that expanded and contracted with each breath.

Dr. Mason re-entered. As she checked Maude, she explained everything she was doing and why. "Your blood pressure is a little high, but we'll check it again before you leave. Stress can knock it out of the park," she said, "and there's probably nothing more stressful than your first visit to an oncologist." Maude watched her face carefully as she gently pressed into the soft flesh of her abdomen, but was unable to interpret her expression beneath its appearance of intense concentration.

When the examination was finished, the doctor left the room while Maude got dressed again, then walked back into the first office.

A few minutes later, the door opened and Mason came in with Harry following behind her.

"I'd like to run a few more tests, if you're agreeable, including a biopsy so we can determine the exact nature of the cancer cells. And I'm a little concerned about your pulse rate."

Harry started to say something, but Maude interrupted. "Okay, let's do whatever has to be done."

"Great, Mrs. --may I call you Maude?" The doctor asked.

"Please do."

"If you'll call me Yvonne. We might as well be on a first-name basis, we're going to be on this journey together for a while."

I'm old enough to be your mother, Maude thought, and here I am putting myself completely in your hands. How old would Alice be now? She pictured Alice when she was about six, a skinny little girl with long legs; Yvonne probably had legs like that when she was a kid. She remembered Alice stroking the wing of a bird that had flown into one of their windows and begging Maude to take it to the animal clinic at Cornell where Pansy, their dog, got her shots. Maybe Alice would have been a doctor, too.

The biopsy she had the next day was brief and painful, and for a few days Maude was unable to lean back against anything that put pressure on the area where a surgeon had extracted some cells. Claire called a couple of times but Maude was evasive.

"I'm coming right over, I don't think you're being straight with me," Claire said.

"Dearie, don't, please. I just had a minor procedure and they don't want me to risk infection," she lied, "so no visitors for a week."

"What kind of procedure?"

Maude told her only part of what she knew, minimizing the potential seriousness. She knew how vulnerable Claire was, in spite of the sardonic humor and shell of toughness she projected. There was something profoundly hurt, a child hiding from her own pain. She and Claire were important to each other in very different ways. Maude had lots of friends, many of them younger women who turned to her for advice and support. But the relationship with Claire ran deep, as if they were connected by blood.

A FEW DAYS LATER, on a bright morning at the beginning of October, Yvonne Mason came out from behind her desk and pulled over a chair so that she sat facing Harry and Maude as they sat holding hands on the sofa. She felt the chill coming off Harry's hand.

Yvonne spoke quietly. "I'm afraid the cancer has progressed throughout your spine. I'm sorry, Maude, it's not operable. And even if it were, your heart isn't strong enough for surgery. I've consulted with several colleagues, and they've come to the same conclusion." She paused; the silence filled the room like mustard gas. "I'm not throwing in the towel," she said. "We'll try to shrink the tumors with radiation. That should give you some relief and some time. But it's important to start right away. I'm going to give you something for pain. And something to help you sleep."

Harry escalated into a manic spiral of problem-solving. "We'll go somewhere else—maybe the medical center in New York, or Cleveland Clinic. How about the Mayo? I saw online that the Anderson Center is doing some innovative work with this kind of cancer." It was clear that he'd put his research skills to work.

"Of course you can go anywhere you like; I'll be happy to give you a referral," Yvonne said. "I do want you to know, though, that our hospital is connected to the cancer center at Roswell Park and we have access to their oncology staff as well as all the latest research." She told them that she had e-mailed the results of Maude's biopsy, the MRI and other tests to Roswell, and the specialists there agreed with the treatment plan Yvonne was recommending. If they decided to remain in town for treatment, she would be consulting Roswell all along the way, as well as checking any clinical trials that might be appropriate.

"There's no way I could travel," Maude said to Harry. "It's exhausting even to think about it. I'm not going anywhere else."

"What about the equipment here? I want her to have the newest generation of radiation." Harry's voice threw out a challenge, which made Maude cringe, but Yvonne was unfazed. "We've got a new radiation center with extremely well-trained technicians and state of the art equipment. We're very lucky."

Maude looked at Harry and could tell that he was thinking that nothing about this was lucky. After all these years, how well she knew the way his mind worked behind that dear craggy face. She'd been reading his expressions for more than fifty years. They had always expected Harry to die first because he was a few years older than she. Against her protestations he had insisted that they talk about their finances, their wills and how she would manage when he was gone, but never the reverse. A surge of relief had accompanied her realization that she wouldn't have to cope with life without him, followed by a guilty sense that she was abandoning him.

"Let's get started," she said to Yvonne "You're in charge, do whatever you think is best," Maude said, turning her palms outward, as if she were offering her life to this lanky, compassionate doctor.

MAUDE CALLED CLAIRE AT WORK THE NEXT DAY. She'd been putting her off with one excuse after another. It was time.

"Can you come by for a drink later?" she asked. "I have something I need to talk to you about."

"Of course. I was beginning to think you were pissed at me about something. I'll be there around 5. And I'll tell you about this mess I've gotten caught in at work, if you promise not to say anything. Not even to Harry."

Maude hung up and sat with her hand on the telephone. Dear Claire. If only your work problems were all that Harry had to think about.

CHAPTER NINE

AT A FEW MINUTES BEFORE FIVE O'CLOCK, Claire walked through the cluttered living room, into the kitchen and out the back door. It was unusually warm for this time of year. Maude was stretched out on a recliner under a hawthorn tree that was beginning to drop its soft yellow leave leaves. Some had floated into her hair and onto the plaid blanket tucked around her.

"Hi, don't get up." Claire leaned over and kissed Maude's forehead, then gently brushed some leaves out of her hair.

"Couldn't if I wanted to."

"Hurts that much?"

"Not for long, I took something a few minutes ago. Go into the kitchen and pour yourself a glass of whatever. And me too."

"Should you drink if you're taking pain medication?"

Maude frowned at her and pointed. "Go."

Claire poked around in the refrigerator and extracted an open bottle of Chardonnay. She liked knowing where to find everything in this kitchen, as if it were her own: glasses, dishes, cooking implements, the drawer in which Maude stored onions and garlic, sometimes forgetting them until their rotting stench was a reminder to throw them out. Old cast iron frying pans were stacked on the left side of the stove, with its right-side oven that never maintained its temperature and required repeated adjustment. Good old Harry, with his mantra of "What do we need it for?" That was his response to a microwave oven, a dishwasher, a new stove, updated plumbing. "Harry never quite recovered from the depression," Maude would say, laughing. She never pushed hard for things that Claire considered essential, and if she was resentful, she never allowed it to show.

Maude opened her eyes when Claire returned, the bottle tucked under her arm, two heavy Mexican glasses clanking against each other as she walked.

"Maybe you should wait a while, I mean, the pills . . ."

"Just pour me a little and stop hovering." Maude's uncharacteristic rebuke startled Claire. She meted out an inch of the pale liquid, handed the glass to Maude and then half-filled her own glass.

"So? Have you heard from the doctor yet?"

"We've been seeing an oncologist and having a whole battery of tests." Claire's breath stopped for a second. Oncologist. "I got the results yesterday," Maude continued, taking a sip, then setting the glass on the low table next to the chaise. "Funny thing, I realized it was the first Tuesday in October. Me and the Supreme Court," she said, in a transparent effort to lighten the news she was about to share.

Claire tried to keep the anxiety out of her voice. "What do you mean? What did he say? "

"She. My goodness, even your generation still assumes that doctors are men! "

"Stop it, Maude, I don't need a lesson in gender politics. What did she say?"

"I'm sorry. I'm trying to get used to the news. It's not good. I have cancer that has spread throughout my spine."

"But . . . but . . ." Claire heard herself stammering and took a deep breath. "What are they going to do? Surgery?"

"No, it's beyond that. There's not much to be done, other than radiation to shrink it for a while. It's not the kind of cancer that chemo would help. And even if it were, I'm not sure I'd go through all that." She patted her white hair and smiled. "You know how attached I am to these gorgeous tresses. If I were bald it might send Harry right off into the arms of some long-haired beauty."

"Not now, Maude. Please, be serious. You are going to do the radiation treatments, aren't you? And what about after that?"

Maude sighed. "I don't think I have any choice. My doctor—I hope you'll get to meet her, she's a lovely woman. Even younger than you, dearie. Anyway, she's looking for any possible clinical trials, but I doubt I'll be eligible. Anyway, she thinks I'll get some pain relief from radiation. And I have to do it for Harry; he'd wouldn't countenance my not doing something that makes him feel I'm fighting this damned thing. Even though it's a battle I can't win."

Claire sat with her hand over her mouth. What she wanted to do was shout: How could you let this happen? Why did you wait so long? You've been having back pain for two years, goddam it! And most of all, she wanted to say how could you do this to me? Me me me. She felt as if everything inside her was crumpling. This isn't about me, she reminded herself. And yet she knew that in profound ways it was.

"When do you start?"

"In two days. Monday through Friday for four weeks. There go my mornings of tennis and jogging."

"Stop it. I can get some time off and take you. At least a couple of days a week."

"No, dearie, Harry has it all set up. He wanted to take me every time but I said no, we'd get bored with each other. Truth is, this is harder on him than it is on me. So he set up a schedule—a spread sheet, do you believe it!—with friends who are retired, or who freelance and can work out their own times. Like Shelby and Carolynne. I said he could drive me twice a week but that's all. So he's doing the first shift with me tomorrow and then I'm laying him off for a few days. Truth is, I never thought much of Harry's driving, anyway. Remember when he took off our mailbox?"

Claire had a deep flash of jealousy. Shelby and Carolynne were friends of hers, too, a few years older than she but still much younger than Maude. They used to call themselves Maude's Claque, like the adoring fans of an opera singer. Why did they get to drive her at a critical time like this? Claire had always been certain that she was the favorite, with special rewards as well as responsibilities. After all, it was her house Maude and Harry came to for Thanksgiving dinners; it was her family they joined for secular Chanukah/Christmas celebrations and Seders where they mostly talked about freedom and sang spirituals and union songs. And she knew that her kids were Maude's favorites, practically her own grandchildren, weren't they?

"Well, I don't care what you say or how it screws up Harry's spread sheet, I'm going to call him tonight and tell him to put me on that schedule." Claire struggled unsuccessfully to hold back her tears. "I can't . . . I can't bear it," she said.

"You don't have a choice, dearie." Maude said quietly and patted her shoulder.

"I'm sorry, I should be comforting you, and here I'm the one who's falling apart." Claire said, wiping her eyes with the back of her hand."

"I can't afford to fall apart. Not yet," Maude said. "I have to hold it together for Harry. I'm sorry, Claire, I know this is hard for you. I dreaded telling you." Maude smiled sadly. "But I also dreaded not telling you. We'll both need you, whatever is down the road. And I know you'll be there for us. Now tell me about this work secret you mentioned. I need some distraction."

Maude chuckled as Claire described her summons to Jasper's office, but her expression shifted to a critical frown when she heard about the assignment. "How in heaven's name are you supposed to be neutral about fracking? You should tell him to take his neutrality and stuff it."

"Maude, it's my job. I'm hoping I can do it responsibly, in a way that makes it possible for the university to come out against it without losing a huge amount of financial support."

"Careful, dearie, you're walking on shifting sands," Maude said. She yawned.

"You need a nap. Anyway, none of this seems very important now," Claire said, pulling herself out of the lawn chair.

Maude turned her cheek to receive Claire's kiss and patted her cheeks. "Oh yes it is. It will be important long after I'm gone, Claire. But I'm sure you'll do the right thing."

WHEN CLAIRE TOLD MARCO ABOUT MAUDE that night he put his arms around her and rested his chin on her head. "Goddam lousy break," he said in a husky voice. "Hard to believe. Shit." After a minute he pulled back and said, "But she's a strong woman, who knows, maybe she can beat it. Or at least. . ."

"Stop it," Claire said. "That doesn't help."

Marco looked abject. "I don't know what else to say. I don't know how to deal with this." He shook his head. "I wish I knew how to help you."

"Just be there for me." Claire pulled away from him and went into the living room to lie down on the sofa. Marco came and covered her with the afghan his mother had crocheted for them years ago, then walked to the telephone in the hallway. He was talking to Harry, stammering slightly as he searched for words of support. He offered to be one of the drivers, and they arranged to get together for a drink on a day when someone else was handling the transportation. Then Marco called the florist and ordered a bunch of red roses to be delivered to Maude.

When he came back into the room Claire shifted so that he could perch next to her on the sofa. He put his head in his hands, and Claire felt the comfort of shared sorrow.

CHAPTER TEN

MAUDE LAY FACE DOWN on the radiation table while people in light blue shirts and pants moved efficiently around her. "Have you ever wanted a tattoo, because you're getting one now, sort of," the young man said.

"Do I get to choose the design? Maybe something a little smutty?"

The technician laughed. "Sorry, we have our limitations. I'm just graphing where we need to aim the beam so we zap right on the tumor. We try to leave the rest of you unzapped as much as possible."

Maude thought about another time she had lain in this position, when a few years ago she had used the gift certificate for a massage that Claire had given her. "You'll love it!" Claire had insisted. "It's the most relaxing thing in the world!" But she hadn't loved it. She didn't like the feeling of a stranger's hands on her body, even though the young woman avoided touching any of her private parts, including her breasts. It had taken her most of their first year together to ease out of her brain and into her body as Harry's hands and tongue explored her. At first she would lie still with her eyes closed, thinking about what he was going to do next, aware of his impatient erection against her hip.

Sometimes in those early months when she sensed his frustration at being unable to arouse her, she would fake her readiness and her orgasm, to get it over with. She occasionally wondered whether she'd missed anything, marrying so young and being faithful for so many years, while people around them were experimenting with all kinds of sexual activities, psychedelic drugs and open marriage. She was such a novice in the beginning, shy about telling him what she needed, unsure of herself and unable to dispatch the observer who took up residence in her mind as Harry worked to arouse her senses. She thought about kids today, watching movies and television with people making love, or just having sex, no love involved. Was all that graphic information instructional? Were they less inhibited, more honest with each other? Claire had told her Sara's comment about sexual activity among her fifteen-year old peers. "It's, like, they don't think blow jobs are sex." Maude had been appalled, but who knows, maybe it would all be easier for them.

"Okay, Mrs. Cohen," the technician said, "I think we're ready to start. This will only take a few minutes, so please try to lie very still." She couldn't see what he was doing, but heard something being moved above her body; then he left the room.

Maude lay without moving, trying to keep her breathing as shallow as possible. Even so, the antiseptic smell of the chamber filled her nostrils. The small space was overwhelmed by its huge, steely equipment. That smell. The breathing. "Just breathe into the contractions," the doctor had said when she was in labor with Alice. That was the era of natural childbirth; she would have been ashamed to ask for the sedation she desperately wanted. She had struggled to engage the Lamaze panting she had practiced weekly in a circle of other pregnant women. They were not allowed to use the word "pain" in the group; it was all "discomfort" or "pressure." In the delivery room the nurse had told her, "You won't remember how much it hurt as soon as the baby is born." And she was right.

This was the first time in all these years she'd thought about the pain of bringing Alice into the world. So much less than watching her leave it, for which the only sedation had been the sleeping pills which left her thickheaded the next morning, her anguish untouched.

Her mother had never talked about childbirth or any of the activities that led up to it. She was an angry, pragmatic Kansas farmwoman who worked hard and rarely smiled at her husband or either of her daughters. It was hard to imagine her having sexual feelings. Harry used to say that she'd probably only let Maude's father near her twice, and then only because her god had instructed her to be fruitful and multiply.

Maude and Harry had met in December 1952, when she was a sophomore at the University of Chicago and he was a 24-year-old graduate student. Ambitious throughout high school, Maude had won a scholarship so generous that her parents couldn't prevent her from leaving, though they thought it was a waste of time and urged her to go to the local business school instead. They also feared for her safety in the city, their symbol of perdition. "Niggers and Jews, that's what cities are full of now," her mother cautioned. But Maude persisted, with the steady encouragement of her freshman literature teacher, the woman who had seeded her love for poetry.

Maude spent much of her first year trying to disguise her sense of not belonging. She couldn't grasp the mores of this new environment, in spite of her pleasure in the intellectual life that was spread before her like an overloaded table, making selection almost unbearable: Romantic poetry, anthropology, Italian. The work was compelling, difficult but manageable, and her first English class was so exhilarating that she knew very soon that her future somehow had to be involved with books. She tried unsuccessfully to explain why she was majoring in English when she was home for spring break. "What in the Lord's name are you going to do with a degree in English?" her mother demanded, walking out of the kitchen before Maude could answer.

Her first roommate, Lola, was a girl from the suburbs of New York City, who had spent the summer working on the Stevenson campaign against Eisenhower. Lola was a curvy blond who wore twin sets and tight skirts and smoked Marlboros one after the other. Maude became aware of her own angular, awkward body: big hands and feet, broad shoulders. Her breasts were okay, though the plain white cotton bras she wore tended to flatten them. In fact all her clothes were wrong: pleated plaid skirts and white blouses, dark slacks, penny loafers. She didn't own a single cashmere sweater, let alone a twin set.

That first year she had a few dates with smart, eager boys from the Midwest; they were drawn by each other's accents as well as a shared sense of strangeness in this big city. Even when she was pushing their hands out from under her starched blouses, she felt somehow at home with them. And bored.

She met Harry at the cafeteria near campus where she used to study, an escape from the endless 45's of Johnny Rae and Nat King Cole her roommate played at high volume on her portable phonograph. The place was crowded, and a young man asked if she'd mind sharing her table. He had a notebook pressed against his side with one arm and was balancing a tray with the other. The tray was at a dangerous angle and Maude jumped up to help him before it could fall.

"I haven't even met you and you already know what a klutz I am," he said, and laughed. He had a big loud laugh. She noted his dark wavy hair, deep brown eyes and uneven front teeth that had never seen the inside of an orthodontist's office. Different looking than most of the guys she knew.

He introduced himself, Harry Cohen, and between bites of his ham and cheese sandwich he told her he had done his undergraduate work at City College, and was working on his Ph.D. in art history. He was writing his dissertation on mural paintings of the Great Depression. He lived in a rented room a few blocks from the main library when he wasn't traveling to Michigan, Nebraska and throughout Illinois to spend hours decoding and analyzing murals, most of which had been done under Roosevelt's WPA.

What he wanted most of all was to spend time in Mexico and really dig into the murals of painters she'd never heard of: Rivera, Siqueiros, Orozco.

Maude told him that she was studying English literature, and that she had become passionate about modern poetry. He asked about her favorite poet, and she answered without hesitating that it was Yeats. "But I change favorites about once a week, depending on who I'm reading."

"Yeats was a great Irish nationalist," Harry said. "Good man."

"That's what Auden thought. Did you ever read his poem about Yeats? 'He disappeared in the dead of winter,'" she recited. "The streets were frozen, the airports almost deserted.'" When she reached the line "Mad Ireland hurt you into poetry." Harry burst out "Jesus! That is the greatest poem!"

She would learn that he lived in superlatives: this was the most delicious fish he'd ever eaten, that was the most beautiful painting he'd ever seen, Dostoevsky was the greatest writer he'd ever read. It didn't matter if within the same conversation he later said that something or someone else was the most. His immoderate enthusiasms both embarrassed and excited her. Conversely, things or people could be the worst he'd ever encountered: Eisenhower was the stupidest president, the University had the most racist housing policy, Chicago had the most corrupt political system. But what most elicited his rage was McCarthy and the House Un-American Activities Committee. "They're the worst bastards we've ever had in this country. They'd burn the Constitution if they could." She didn't admit that not only hadn't she paid attention to what the committee was up to, she didn't even know what it was.

They agreed to go out for pizza the next evening. She stood in front of her closet trying to decide what to wear, and settled on a black skirt and a fake angora sweater, bright pink, a birthday gift from her mother. She pulled off the sweater. Too kittenish. Makes me look liked a colt wearing an Easter rabbit. She replaced it with a black cardigan, leaving the top two buttons open, and added her longest pair of earrings. There, she thought, wishing her cheeks were more sculpted, less rosy. She wanted to look older than her nineteen years.

Harry arrived at her dormitory wearing jeans and a navy down jacket with bits of feather sticking out around the zipper. His dark looks were so different from the flaxen-haired boys she was used to, with their neatly pressed chinos and blue oxford shirts, sleeves crisply folded back to the elbow. And he looked more like a man than a boy; she was a little intimidated by their age difference, though intrigued by it as well.

As they walked to the pizza parlor, they talked—or more accurately, Harry talked and she listened to his passionate opinions about politics, art, social class. He told her that his parents had belonged to the Communist Party until Russia signed the non-aggression pact with Germany, but that they were still active in left-wing causes. She tried to hide her shock. Communists! She imagined her parents' open-mouthed reaction and the burst of hostility that would follow. "We should ship them all out to Russia, every last one of them! Goddam Jews." It made him all the more attractive.

Over a large pie with anchovies and mushrooms, Harry's monologue continued. He was an only child, and had been raised with an intense awareness of how lucky he was to have enough to eat while war was raging through Europe and Hitler and his henchmen were trying to annihilate every Jew they could find. "With the cooperation of all the anti-Semites in Europe," he said. He talked about things she hadn't given much thought to in her nineteen years: racial discrimination, economic inequity, intransigent politicians. She would later wonder if part of her appeal to him was that he saw himself as a guide to the perplexed.

"Jesus, listen to me, I haven't stopped talking. Maybe I spend too much time alone. I can't shut up when I'm with someone who's a good listener. So tell me about yourself."

Maude's history was embarrassingly tame in comparison to his. She didn't want to tell him about her bigoted parents. That would come later. She described the farm, what it was like to have her own horse and how she'd felt when it had to be put down; what the earth smelled like in the spring after it had been plowed. She wondered if she was boring him, but he never took his eyes off her as she talked, and occasionally said "Yeah!" as if she were telling him something wonderful.

He asked how she'd gotten interested in poetry, and she told him about Mrs. Duke, her junior-year English teacher. "Thanks to her I can recite a bunch of poems, from Shakespeare sonnets to Prufrock."

Harry frowned. "What's Prufrock?"

She recited a few lines, stopping to catch her breath after "In the room the women come and go talking of Michelangelo," but before she could continue Harry reached across the table and took her hand. "You are the most amazing girl. I've never met anyone with so many poems in her head. And you say them like you really feel them."

No one had ever called her amazing before.

He didn't kiss her until their third date. They had spent half an hour at the Art Museum in front of Edward Hopper's "Nighthawks," their fingers interlaced. He pointed out the icy light, the cold steel of the coffee maker, the lack of connection between the people in the painting, and how it all contributed to the feeling of loneliness and isolation. She told him that the painting made her think of some of the novels she'd read about the Great Depression. After hamburgers at the White Tower, they went to a movie at a nearby art house—a special showing of "Citizen Kane", which Harry proclaimed the finest movie ever made; he had seen it a dozen times. "Look at the next camera angle," he whispered, "the way it makes Kane loom." When Kane stormed through his castle after Marian's departure, she felt Harry's arm slip around her shoulders.

After the movie they went to his apartment. She had never been to a man's apartment. She put her coat down on an overstuffed chair that had probably been salvaged from Goodwill and looked around. Harry's sofa had threadbare cushions and looked as if its springs were about to pop. Two walls were lined with bookshelves made out of cinder blocks and unpainted boards. The walls had one framed picture of a dark-skinned woman with a heavy basket of calla lilies, and several posters put up with masking tape, one of someone named Pete Seeger holding a banjo and singing, another a picture of a Negro named Paul Robeson playing the role of Othello.

They were sitting on the sofa drinking cheap red wine as he talked about the destructive force of excessive wealth and power, when, mid-sentence, he took the glass out of her hand and put in on the table made of a piece of glass set on bricks. He pulled her close and pressed his lips to hers, a soft, almost tentative kiss. There was a sweetness to it she would always remember. When he moved back, she rested her head on his chest, listening to the beat of his heart.

Later that night, after a more urgent kiss when his tongue tried to push into her mouth, she pulled back and told him she was a virgin. "Jeez, I didn't think there were any still around," he said. "Okay, we'll take this at your speed." But her speed was slow, and over the next weeks his frustration escalated until one night, after he had tried to move her resisting hand to the bulge in jeans, he said "Listen, honey, I don't want to make you uncomfortable, but you have to help me out here." He unzipped his pants and released his penis, which sprung out as if it were an entity separate from him. She had never seen an adult penis before, let alone a circumcised one, and was surprised by its neat collar of skin. "Just rub it a little," he said, leaning back with his eyes closed. But almost as soon as her fingers touched the smooth surface, he came in a flood of stickiness. "Whew, sorry, I didn't think it would be that fast. That's been building up ever since I met you." She wiped her hands and skirt with the tissue he handed her, then held it, not knowing what to do with it. The whole experience felt awkward and messy. But until she was ready to go further, she would have to go along with it. The following week she agreed to let him remove her bra, and was surprised when his lips, circling her nipple, stirred a feeling that seemed to come from her very center.

Why me, she sometimes wondered when he would tell her that she was the girl for him. Why this plain, bony girl with big feet and big hands and frizzy brown hair? Why someone who never thought much about anything but escaping the farm and reading poetry? Does he love me for the same reason that I love him, because we're so different from anyone we've ever known? And what would his parents think about the daughter of anti-Semitic Republicans?

Harry often launched into diatribes about the contradictions of capitalism. Before she met him she'd barely thought about the things that aroused such passion in him. Being with him was like learning to see for the first time. She began to notice homeless people living in stairwells, children begging, angry adolescents defacing brick walls with spray-painted messages. He took her to a Pete Seeger concert, and she joined in, tentative and self-conscious at first, then with full spirit, as the crowd sang out "Way up north, Wimoweh, Wimoweh."

"You're the best part of my education," she said to him one night, after they'd spent an hour talking about the tragedy of the Joad family in *The Grapes of Wrath*. "I've been stumbling through my life in blinders until I met you." They were lying on top of the quilt on his bed, she naked from the waist up, though she was still not ready to go all the way.

"And you're teaching me about a world I never paid much attention to," he responded. "I mean, I look at trees and birds and flowers, all the stuff I never noticed before. I can even tell a robin from a sparrow because of you," he said, and leaned down to kiss her throat and moving down to circle her breast with his tongue. "This one's the robin," he said, and moved to the other breast, "and this one's the sparrow."

"Just lie still for a few minutes," the technician interrupted her reverie. "Don't want you to get up too fast, you could get dizzy. I'll be back in a few minutes and help you off the table."

Maude closed her eyes and went back to her memories. She pictured Harry's face as it was during those early days together. She remembered how his intensity had sometimes frightened her. When he told her about the anti-communist hysteria that was raging through the country, and the framing of Julius and Ethel Rosenberg, who were scheduled to be executed as atomic spies that June, he spoke with such rage that she didn't know how to respond.

As the end of the spring semester approached, Maude was determined not to return home for the summer. She found a job working as a clerk in one of the university offices and, declining Harry's invitation to live with him for the summer, sublet a small apartment near the campus with a friend. She felt very adult, and loved the sense of independence.

One Thursday morning in the middle of June her phone rang as she was getting ready to go to work. "You've got to come to New York with me." Harry's voice was urgent. "The Rosenbergs are going to be executed tomorrow night, but there's a huge crowd organizing to protest. I have to be there and I want you with me. I need you, honey. My parents have been out petitioning, raising money, doing everything they can. I feel like shit sitting here like some dumb jerk-off while this is going on. That goddam attorney general and that fucking Hoover--" She tried to ignore her unease with his language. Sometimes she would try using some of the words herself, but they came out of her mouth as if they were in quotation marks.

"Come with me, please, honey. I'll pay for your train ticket and we'll stay with my parents, so it won't cost anything. I don't want to go through this without you. Anyway, I want my parents to meet you."

She made an excuse to her boss about having to miss work the next day. They left late at night, pushing their suitcases onto the slanted metal rack over their heads and settling into comfortable plush seats. It was a sixteen-hour trip, and Harry said they should try to get as much sleep as possible because he didn't know how long the demonstration would go on. But he was too agitated to settle down, and spent the first few hours filling her in on the details of the case, especially on what had been happening in the last couple of days. "People all over the world have been sending telegrams and letters begging to have the sentence commuted. The whole thing was a fix, they were framed. Her own goddam brother lied about her. There's a stay of execution, but it's tenuous."

They dozed fitfully as the train moved through the darkness zooming toward New York. Maude had almost gotten used to

Chicago, at least the area around the campus, but New York! What was it her mother called it, the devil's playground?

It was late afternoon when they arrived at Grand Central Station. Maude was awed by its palatial ceilings and the clock she'd seen in photographs. A newsboy hawking papers called out, "Court vacates Rosenberg stay of execution!"

"What does that mean?" she asked.

"It means they're going to kill them if the governor doesn't do something to stop it, probably tonight. Filthy sons . . . Let's go, we've got to get to Union Square."

It was almost rush hour and the subway was packed. Maude had a moment of terror; what if she and Harry were separated? She didn't even know his parents' address. She had brought some money with her, but not enough for a hotel. And he had the return train tickets. She clung to his arm as their bodies swerved with the motion of the train.

Union Square was filled with people holding signs or standing hand in hand. Every few minutes a rumor would ripple through the crowd, but it would be denied by the people speaking into a microphone on the platform at one end of the square. A voice announced that the execution had been set for eleven p.m. but that in a last desperate move to buy more time, their attorney Manny Bloch, had said that since it was Friday, that would violate the Rosenberg's Jewish heritage. But instead of further delay, the execution was moved up to eight o'clock, before sunset on the Sabbath. There was a loud wail from thousands of voices. Harry held tight to her arm. She heard bits of conversation: "Who's next? Who are they coming for next?" "Fucking government, they never had a chance." "Jew haters." There were speeches and chants and prayers, but at 8:00 p.m. a hush came over the crowd, followed by a howl of pain, then weeping and angry outcries.

When the crowd began to disperse they took a subway to the Bronx, then walked three blocks to the apartment where Harry had grown up. He was silent all the way, and when she tried to talk to him, he didn't answer, leaving her confused about how to connect to what he was feeling. His parents hadn't yet returned from the vigil, so they sat at the kitchen table of the small apartment without speaking. They hadn't eaten since the cheese sandwiches they'd packed for the train ride, but Maude didn't feel entitled to the hunger that was grumbling in her stomach.

The apartment was filled with books, mostly about history and psychology, his mother's profession. She worked with retarded children, as they were labeled then. His father taught social studies in a liberal private school in Riverdale. The furniture was old but comfortable: overstuffed chairs and a sofa, lots of reading lamps. There were framed reproductions of paintings by Kathe Kollwitz and Ben Shahn, a photograph signed "Warm regards, Paul Robeson." Ashtrays full of butts were on every table, and the house reeked of smoke. Maude thought of her mother's stricture to her father: you want to smoke your filthy cigarettes, go do it in the barn, not in my house.

THE DOOR OPENED AND HIS PARENTS CAME IN. Harry rose to greet them, and his mother leaned into him and began to weep. His father's eyes were red. He was handsome in a way that was so like Harry, though a little taller and heavier. His mother wore no make-up, not even lipstick. Her hair, wound into a loose bun low on her was neck, was streaked with grey. Her high cheekbones gave her a Slavic look. Her body, though not fat, suggested roundness and comfort

"It's over," his father said, shaking his head. "It's all over."

His mother clung to Harry. "I can't believe they went ahead with it," she said into his shoulder, then pulled back and reached both hands out to Maude. "I'm sorry, you must be Maude. What a way to meet you, with something like this happening. But I'm glad you're here. Harry's written us about you."

She set out supper for them, things Maude had never eaten before: borscht, smoked meats, lox, some kind of pudding made of noodles. Before they ate Harry's father filled small shot glasses with Seagrams.

"One day there will be justice in this county. We can only hope," he said, downing the whiskey in one swallow.

His mother said, "I think we should say Kaddish."

"Rose, what for? You don't believe in any of that."

"I think we should say Kaddish," she repeated firmly, and began, lowering her head. "*Yis kaddal, v'yis kadash...*" Harry and Maude followed her lead, but David sat and sipped a second whisky. Maude listened to the strange words, a chant that sounded as if it carried a thousand years of grief.

When they'd finished eating, Harry's mother, seeing their fatigue, handed them towels and walked with them into Harry's room, so narrow that the maple bunk beds almost filled the room. There was the same poster of Pete Seeger Harry had in his apartment, and a framed picture of a Negro in a Brooklyn Dodgers baseball uniform.

"I changed the sheets this morning, you're all set." Maude tried to hide her surprise; she had assumed one of them would sleep on the sofa, since there were only two bedrooms. She could only imagine what her mother would say about these arrangements.

"Why don't you change in the bathroom, I'll do it here," Harry said. "I'll take the top bunk."

It was almost the first thing he'd said to her since they'd arrived at the apartment. She had been wondering all night if he wanted out, if being back in his old life, with his parents, with this ugly thing that had happened, made him realize how enormous their differences were. She was a stranger in his world, an uncomprehending outsider who knew something about poetry and nothing about how the world worked. But she longed to be part of it, part of this family, to be swept up by the intensity of their passions, to feel as if she could, with her small life, make a difference.

When she had replaced her wrinkled clothes with a nightgown and brushed her teeth, she got under the faded quilt on the lower bunk. Harry came out of the bathroom in his tee shirt and boxer shorts, closed the door and sat on the edge of her bed. He stroked her arm but his eyes were on the wall above her head.

"This is the worst night I can ever remember," he said. "I'm ashamed to be part of this country." He began to cry, deep choking sounds. Maude had never heard a man cry. She pulled him down so that he was lying in her arms, soaking the top of her nightgown with his tears. And without quite realizing how, it just happened: he was under the quilt with her, he was touching her and rubbing and then he was inside her moving, moving and she bit her lip to keep from crying out from the stabbing pain that his steady motion provoked. It would always be a strange juxtaposition for her: the death of the Rosenbergs and what she thought of as the beginning of her adult life.

"WE'RE FINISHED FOR TODAY, you can get up, Mrs. Cohen." The technician's voice startled her back into the present. She held tightly to his arm as he pulled her into a sitting position. "Just let your legs dangle for a couple of minutes so you won't get dizzy," he said. She sat at the age of the table, her feet above the floor like a child whose legs were too short to reach.

CHAPTER ELEVEN

H ARRY STILL HAD AN OFFICE AT THE UNIVERSITY, though after his retirement he had to leave the spacious corner room he'd occupied for more than thirty years. He'd been consigned a small space with a window so high he'd have to stand on his desk to get a glimpse of anything but sky. He missed his former office with its smell of old books, its large window overlooking the quad, its closeness to the museum. But he still biked to campus when Maude felt well enough to be left alone for a couple of hours, or when a friend was visiting her. Being at the University reminded him who used to be, the life he used to live. His graduate students were long gone, many of them teaching in universities and colleges throughout the country, a few curating small museums in places like Wilkes Barre, Canton, Jefferson City. A couple of them had even made the big time, managing departments at MOMA and the Chicago Institute. Every Christmas, cards and letters arrived, though in decreasing numbers as the years went by, with updates of career development, marriages and families. Occasionally former students would call to say they were bringing a kid to see the university, and could they have lunch? But these visits had tapered off. His students' children were adults by now, some with their own children old enough for college. He still had a couple of friends on campus, though too many had died and a few, as their health declined, had moved away to be near their families, or gone south to escape the harsh winters of the Finger Lakes. He didn't know many of the young faculty, beyond a friendly nod. When they were introduced, some were familiar with the work on Hopper and Jacob Lawrence he'd done years before, but instead of being deferential, they treated him like a not very valuable antique. Mostly he sat is his small office fending off a sense of anonymity in this alien space, where most of his books were still in cartons and framed paintings leaned against the wall, waiting to be hung. Sometimes he tried to write, but the words felt trite and meaningless. The field had moved on, left him in the dust. The chair of the department was someone whose critical approach to art history was meaningless to him, but it had influenced the selection of new hires as well as course offerings. It was a way of looking at art that removed it from its social context. Harry wondered how you could think about, let's say Hopper, without understanding the thirties, the depression, the lives of women.

Today he was having lunch with Burnham Walsh, an old friend who had taught sociology until he retired. He spotted Burnham walking spryly a hundred yards ahead of him. Burnham was aging well, Harry noted: his posture was erect, and his weight probably hadn't changed in thirty years, thanks to what Harry had sneeringly called compulsive exercise. Harry's hand went to the small bulge at his beltline; gotta do something about that, he thought. Then he said aloud, startling a baby-faced coed passing him, "What for?"

"How's Maude?" Burnham asked when they were seated at one of the polished oak tables of the faculty club dining room.

"She's holding up pretty well, though she's tired most of the time. Radiation wears you out."

"I know, remember Harris Green, he was in geology . . ." Burnham's voice trailed off, and Harry understood that his friend was embarrassed about fumbling into a story of someone who had died during treatment.

The arrival of the waitress was a welcome interruption. "Hi, Professor Walsh, Professor Cohen. Anything to start?"

Burnham ordered lemonade, and Harry asked for a glass of Cabernet. He didn't usually drink before late afternoon, but he needed something to soften the edges today. He hadn't been sleeping well. Too often he lay awake working to push away thoughts of what was ahead: what it would be like to lie in that bed alone, to come home to the empty house. What would he do about the garden? Would he start talking out loud to himself? He stopped himself: take it as it comes, not before it gets here.

"Have you heard about the history guy who's coming in next semester?" Burnham asked. "Name's Wilson, from Yale. He's giving a course on Vietnam. I thought I might sit in, at least try it out for a couple of lectures. See what the young Turks are saying these days. Interested?"

"I read his last book. He's good on the protest movement and the restriction of civil rights. A little soft on Kennedy, though. Anyway, I'll have to see how Maude's doing."

"He was very friendly when I emailed. Said he likes to have people in class who actually remember the war, told me to speak out, either to back him up or tell him where he's off base."

A few sips of the wine gave Harry a light buzz. I used to be able to down a bottle without feeling a thing, he thought. Fucking old age.

Burnham put down the menu he had been studying and asked Harry if he knew anything about a demonstration that might be coming up. "You always seem to know about those things," he said.

Harry raised his thick eyebrows and shook his head.

Burnham continued. "One of my former students who's on faculty now stopped by and let something slip, then made me promise to keep it quiet, not say anything. But I figured you'd know."

There was a time when Harry was the recipient of every rumor about political activities on the campus. There were years when he was asked by students to be the advisor for progressive organizations, or to enlist other faculty to join him in campus demonstrations. He felt out of sorts being in the dark about this one. "So who's protesting what this time?"

"Fracking. Apparently they're planning to demonstrate because the university hasn't taken a position; the administration is insisting that the facts are still unclear. I've heard rumors that they may lease some of the land they own out in the county. But I don't know how reliable that is, you know how things fly around a place like this."

"There've been some pretty damned convincing arguments against it. What's his name, in ecology –damn, you notice how the nouns are disappearing? I never lose a verb or an adjective, it's always the names of things—people, places, books, it doesn't matter."

"Yeah, tell me about it," Burnham said, "Apparently there's a study by someone in environmental science, I can't remember his name, shows the risks are still less than coal mining."

"Shit, that's like saying that cigar smoking is safer than cigarettes. They both give you goddam cancer."

They ordered lunch, corned beef on rye for Harry and a Caesar salad, dressing on the side for Burnham.

"You eat like a goddam woman," Harry said.

Burnham grinned without taking offense. "Believe it or not I've gotten to like eating this way. All Sally's Moosewood cooking has gotten through to me. You ought to try it, you're going to jack your blood pressure into the clouds."

And if I do? What does it matter if Maude isn't around? I wish... I wish I could go with her. He bit his lip. Stop thinking like that. But he had a flash of panic and realized that he wanted to be home with her, that he needed to spend whatever time was left with her, seeing her, touching her age-spotted hand, sniffing the familiar smell of her skin. And yet sometimes when he was with her he had an urge to flee. How do you rip away half of yourself and not get crazy?

After lunch he got on his bike and started the short ride home. I could steer into a bus, he thought. But I'd probably just break my bones. Don't like pain. Will Maude have pain? I can't watch her suffer.

Maude was dozing on the sofa when he came in, a wool lap robe covering her legs. Did they get that when they went to Scotland? He had a vague memory of arguing with her because he thought it cost too much. Shit, all that saving, all the times he said to her what do we need that for. He could hear her voice saying, "Harry, the depression is over. Relax."

She opened her eyes and smiled. "Hi dearie. Did you get any work done?"

"Nothing that's going to shake the art world out of its torpor. How you feeling?"

"Just fine. Do you know how many times a day you ask me that?"

"Sorry, I . . ." He leaned down and kissed her forehead. The smell: Was he imagining it or was there something metallic mixed in with her usual lavender? He tried to perch at the edge of the sofa. Maude pulled her legs up to make room for him. "You'll fall and break your back, and then where will we be?"

He leaned into the worn cushion and put his hand on her feet. The skin around her ankles was stretched thin, the veins lacing upward on her legs. He thought of how they used to read at night, Maude stretched out on the sofa holding her book up, her feet on his lap, his book resting on them. She'd been proud of the arch in her foot, not for the beauty of its curve, but for what it enabled her to do: miles of walking, hours of gardening, square dancing, something Harry had never taken to. She used to have a certain awkward grace, but he clumped around like a circus bear.

"I had lunch with Burnham. There's talk about a demonstration against fracking, but he didn't know any of the details."

"You should find out and go," she said. "It would be good for you."

"They're not having it for my benefit," he said and wished he hadn't. He could see that his irritation stung her. He'd been short with her too often in these last weeks. Maybe because he'd been sleeping poorly, drinking more booze than usual. And then there was the whole business of feeling like an intruder on campus.

He hadn't talked to Maude about this growing feeling of displacement. When she'd retired, she'd organized an after-school book club in their living room, with lemonade and cookies as an added lure to the kids with whom she managed to cross what seemed to him an impassable communication barrier, except for Stephen and Sarah. Maude read constantly, keeping up with new work and revisiting favorite nineteenth century novels. She gardened, spent time with friends. She never seemed bored or restless. Was it the difference between men and women, or was it just Maude? Probably some of both.

The truth was, she'd manage better if she were the one left behind. She'd grieve for him, he knew that. But she'd still have a life, other widows her age, and all those younger women who were almost like daughters. Especially Claire. Claire would always be there for her. He should be the one to go first; he'd always thought he would.

When she had started the radiation treatments he'd been reluctant to leave her alone, but she'd told him "Bosh, I don't want you sitting around watching me. I'm just fine. I'll call you if I need you. Unless you're carousing with some young graduate student, in which case I'll see to it that you die first."

He'd never done that, fooled around, even though they'd lived through the swinging sixties. Not very swinging for him, nor, he was sure, for Maude. Yeah, there had been temptations along the way when he was in his forties and fifties: a couple of female colleagues whose signals had been unmistakable, the occasional graduate student who showed up in his office needing help with a problem for which she already had a solution; even the wife of a friend who had followed him into the pantry at a Christmas party and put her tongue in his mouth. It wasn't that she wasn't attractive, or that it was bourgeois morality, he'd said to her as he removed her hands from his shoulders; it was a matter of the trust he had with his wife, of not wanting to risk it. He didn't have any regrets; he'd played those games before he and Maude were married. And now, desire was more memory than anything else, except for an occasional stirring that he could satisfy by himself, though it took more work than it used to. Sex with Maude had been slow to develop; she'd been so naive when they met, so locked up by that crazy mother of hers. He was pretty sure that it was a few years before she had a real orgasm; he suspected that she had faked it a lot in their early days together. Why did women do that? To reassure their men that they were good lovers? He wondered if women still pretended to come, with all the sex information that was everywhere you turned these days.

After a while Maude seemed to relax and get pleasure from making love, even if she didn't always climax. And he remembered how happy he was the first time she initiated by putting her hand on him in a tentative gesture, as if she were afraid he would turn away. He never did.

If he were honest with himself, he had to admit that sex had stopped being very important to him a few years before Maude's illness. They hadn't made love for a year after Alice died, though they often clung to each other, she weeping quietly, he, in an effort to comfort her, swallowing back the sadness and rage that overwhelmed him.

They had gotten past that, but sex was different afterward, driven more like the need for release than by desire, dwindling gradually as they arrived at a friendship so deep that he couldn't imagine going on without her.

He forced himself to think about something else. Maybe he'd write an article about new directions in Mexican art, the way it had veered away from the lushly beautiful social criticism of Rivera and Orozco to the kind of claptrap bullshit that people like that kid, what was his name, was producing. A toilet in the middle of an empty room. That gets an exhibit in a museum? Fucking travesty, that's what it was. That would be a hoot to write about. But he knew he wouldn't bother to switch on the power button of his computer. No one would publish it. He was howling in the wilderness.

He turned his head to look at Maude, his hand still resting on her feet. Her hairband had slipped back, and her thinning hair was spread across the woven cushion on which she lay. Where did they pick that up? Ireland, maybe. Yeah, Donegal. That trip to Ireland, still the time of the troubles between north and south. They were maybe in their fifties then. He remembered when they'd stopped at the checkpoint between north and south, how the uniformed guard had asked, as he looked at their passports, "What do you do in the States, sir?" Harry had responded that he was a professor. "And what do you profess?" the guard had responded. How they'd laughed! They'd driven to a weaver's cottage overlooking the ocean; Harry recalled waiting in their rented car, a dinky little Morris it was, while Maude poked around looking at fabrics and getting the weaver to talk about his life. Maude was always good at that, getting people to open up about themselves. He remembered, and felt a pang of regret slash through him, that he'd

169

tapped the horn impatiently until she emerged with the cushion cover wrapped in brown paper and tied with household string, a smile of pleasure on her face.

"What do we need that for?" he'd asked.

"Never mind, you old skinflint," she'd said without anger. "What an incredible man that weaver is! The wool is from his own sheep and his wife spins and dyes it. And would you believe it, he has a nephew who's at the College? I promised we'd have him for dinner when we get back."

And they had. As they'd had hundreds of students from all over the country, all over the world. It wasn't that he didn't like people, enjoy the parties and the visits. It was that she was almost always the initiator. And she was the one who drew people to her, young people, old people. Throughout the year cards and letters appeared in their mailbox, some with exotic stamps from far-away places. She answered every one of them. Well, that would come to an end. It would all come to an end.

He lifted her feet and pulled himself out of the sofa. "I need a drink," he said, and walked into the kitchen.

CHAPTER TWELVE

JASPER HAD BEEN SATISFIED WITH THE LETTER. "I knew I'd picked the right person." Jesus, Claire thought, sitting across his gleaming desk, even his compliments manage to be self-congratulatory.

"Okay, now that you've got all that information under your belt, you've got the green light. I'm giving you more space. Same tone, but an article for the Alumni Magazine. With your own byline. But first we need a general email statement to go out to everyone, announcing the upcoming series, etcetera. The pressure cooker is starting to sizzle and we want to let our people know we're working on this, so whatever comes next won't be a total surprise."

Claire tried to demur. "But I've got to get the next issue of the newsletter out."

"That's why you have a staff," Jasper said. "Let me give you a little tip. Never turn down an opportunity to get your name out there in front of a lot of influential alumni. Especially on a hot button issue."

NOW, THINKING THAT WORK might be a way to keep her mind off Maude's declining health for a few hours, Claire made several starts on what she thought of as Jasper's article, but each effort made her grateful for the delete button on her Mac. What the hell was she going to do? She selected the trash file and extracted the most recent effort. "While recognizing the economic benefits of drilling for natural gas, the University remains cautious about the potential environmental and health hazards of hydrofracking. Therefore, we support a delay in further approvals for drilling leases until there is greater clarity about its impact." Christ, that is a lot of diddly-squat, she thought, using one of Maude's favorite words. Maude. What would she think about the latest development in this crappy project? What about their other friends, many of who were active in the anti-fracking movement? Claire had mostly observed Jasper's strictures about silence not so much because she thought it was a secret worth keeping, but because she was embarrassed by having a role in it.

She was staring at the two sentences on her computer screen she had managed to write in the last half hour. They sounded clumsy, apologetic, as if she were saying we regret to inform you that drilling may despoil your environment. What would she write if there were no constraints? Maybe that was the way to go, just let the words fly, then go back and wrap it in ways that softened the meaning, put a curtain up around the reality.

She started to type and found that, without restrictions the sentences were flowing. She looked up, irritated, when Marianne buzzed her on the intercom.

"Your son is here."

She hastily saved and closed the document on her computer just as Stephen came into the room, looking tired and disheveled. Claire was surprised to see him. Stephen had made a point of avoiding contact with either of his parents on campus. "Otherwise I'll feel like I'm still in high school," he'd told them when they asked why they didn't see him more often. Usually when he spotted them on the quad on his way to the library or to class, he waved with a barely perceptible gesture and walked faster.

"Well, this is an honor." Claire immediately regretted the sarcasm in her voice.

Either Stephen didn't notice or he decided not to react.

"Hey, mom. I need some advice. Well, help, really."

Claire experienced a rush of pleasure. She couldn't recall the last time Stephen had asked her for help with anything other than money.

"Sit down, sweetie. What's up?"

Stephen closed the door of her office and sat on the old oak chair next to her desk. She bit back the desire to ask why he had to wear jeans with his knees showing through.

"This has to be strictly confidential," he said. Claire's mind rushed through a list: Nora was pregnant, Stephen was dropping out of school, he had contracted a venereal disease...

"You can't say a word about this to anyone. I need your promise."

How like Stephen, she thought. She remembered how he would jump up and down as a little boy: Promise, mommy, you promise?

"I promise," she said. "Go ahead."

"It's about this fracking business. I don't know how much you've been following it, but if the state allows it to go through it's going to be a disaster. What are you smiling about, there's nothing funny."

She was smiling with relief that it wasn't a personal crisis. "What a coincidence," she said, pointing at the pile of papers. "You're not the only one with secrets. I'm working on an article about it."

"You are? For the paper? Cool! That's great, mom! It's about time someone around here took a stand. Can I see it?"

"I'm not done. And I can't talk about it yet, hon. It's complicated."

"You kidding? There's nothing complicated, it's all shit."

Oh to be young, Claire thought. Sweetie, there's nothing about anything that's not complicated. "Never mind my stuff, tell me what's up with you. And how I can help."

"Don't forget, this is top secret." "Stephen uncrossed his long legs and leaned forward, lowering his voice. "We're planning a big anti-fracking demonstration on the quad during Parent's weekend. Something to really get people's attention, get them to realize how dangerous all this shit is. And we're going to demand that the university get off its butt and come out with a strong position against it."

Claire shifted uneasily. "What are you going to do?"

"Something that will get a lot of attention, that's all I can say. But we need to get a lot of publicity. We can handle the Facebook and Twitter stuff, but we want this in the news. Not just the local paper, we want to take it out as far as we can go. TV, you know, Syracuse, Elmira, Binghamton. "He rubbed his chest, and his voice rose with excitement. "I don't know, maybe even people from, like, MSNBC, the *Times*, CNN. This could go viral, YouTube and all."

Claire tried to keep her voice calm. "Aren't you being a little grandiose? There are demonstrations about all kinds of things on half the campuses around the country."

"What's grandiose about trying to save the environment? Stopping something that could destroy our water supply, cause cancer, all the crap we know about? Jesus, mom." He shook his head, then softened his expression so that for a moment he reminded her of Stephen the little boy. "Look, this is really important. I need some leads, and I don't' know how to get through the door. I thought maybe I could use your name, some of your contacts."

Claire put her hand on his arm. "Honey, I can't do that. I wish I could, but it has to do with what I'm working on right now. I've got to appear neutral, even though I agree with you. It's a basic principle of journalism, you know that." She heard how defensive she sounded and added quietly, "Anyway I've got orders from above."

The little boy disappeared in a flash, replaced by an angry young man who looked at her with disdain. "I don't fucking believe it," he said. He pulled his arm away. "How the hell can anyone be neutral about this? What kind of chicken shit is that?"

"Look, I'll explain it in a couple of weeks. And if I were you, I'd think twice about creating a disturbance during Parents' Weekend. That could do your cause more harm than good."

Stephen's voice iced over with contempt. "You bucking for a promotion or something?"

"Stephen! Jesus . . ." Claire felt her cheeks burning. She took a deep breath. "Look, I'll do what I can for you, I'll give you some contacts and phone numbers. But keep my name out of it." She opened a file on her computer and wrote the information on a pad with the university crest at the top.

Stephen folded the paper carefully and put it in his backpack. "Thanks," he muttered without a trace of gratitude in his voice.

"And I don't think you should talk to me that way. You don't know anything about my world, damn it," Claire felt as if she was about to cry. She was relieved when Stephen turned and left without saying goodbye.

JASPER CALLED LATER THAT AFTERNOON. "Almost finished? The heat's on; there's a rumor that the students are cooking up something, but we haven't been able to confirm it." Jasper always used the royal we.

"Getting close," Claire lied.

"We need you to have something emailed to me Thursday by noon. Oh, and I want hard copy on my desk at the same time."

So hit the print button, you asshole.

"This is going to be big if the kids get involved. I want your piece in everyone's—and I mean EVERYONE'S—email Friday morning and in the Friday editions of the student paper and the staff bulletin." She heard him sigh. "Sometimes I long for the good old days when I was a reporter. Hands on, you know, right down there in the mud with the troops."

You asshole, Claire thought. If you had a speck of mud on your shoe you'd find a serf to wipe it off. "I'll do my best," she said. "Good," he replied, and hung up.

She looked again at the last piece. Maybe that was as good as it was going to get. This piece was only a promissory note, anyway.

Later she'd cite some of the studies, include the few contradictory ones that supported fracking. Or were at least some of the conclusions premature, too tentative for a definitive statement? Maybe that should be the angle, focus on prematurity.

For the next few hours, Claire dug in. She called Marco and told him to have dinner without her, she didn't know when she'd finish, then turned the phone off and forced herself to stay at the computer. At 7 o'clock she gave up. She couldn't think of a way to end it. Rereading what she'd written, she was reasonably satisfied; it was, at least, articulate in the way it straddled the fence. She decided to let it simmer and finish the next morning, have Marianne review it, then send it off to Jasper. He could print out his own fucking hard copy. Claire yearned to be finished with the damned project and get back to her own work.

CHAPTER THIRTEEN

A FEW DAYS LATER, THE HOUSE WAS QUIET when Claire got home from work early after a visit to the dentist. Marco was probably in his office wrestling with his latest grant proposal to NIMH. Sarah hadn't left a note, which usually meant she could be found at Joline's. The silence was soothing. Claire poured herself a glass of wine, settled into her favorite chair and opened the *Times* to the editorial page. Before she could take the first sip, the telephone rang. There was a strange noise on the other end of the line; it took a few seconds for Claire to realize that the choked sounds were coming from Sarah. She was sobbing.

"What happened? Are you all right? "

The weeping continued. Her words were garbled and hard to understand.

"Stop it!" Claire shouted into the phone. "Stop it and tell me what happened!"

"Stephen," was all Sarah could manage.

"Put him on."

There was a shuffling noise, then Nora's shaky voice came through the telephone. Her words tumbled into each other.

"He's going to be okay, but there was an accident. The ambulance got there fast and he's in the hospital.

"Oh my god. What happened? How is he?"

"He's going to be all right, he's not dying or anything, but something went wrong, the wind or something, and he got some pretty bad burns on his arms and the ambulance came and I'm at the hospital." She caught her breath and continued. "He's sleeping now, they gave him something because he was in a lot of pain. "

"Pain from what? What happened? Calm down and tell me what happened."

"We were getting ready for the demonstration. The one on the quad for Parents Weekend. About fracking. You know how he's been all involved with it, heading up the committee and everything and we were doing a trial run out in the back yard of Alison's co-op and something went wrong." She began to sob, then must have handed the phone to Sarah, who had pulled herself together but was still speaking faster than usual.

"Come right away, mom. He's sleeping, but he's still in the Emergency Room in this, like, little cubicle with curtains around it. They're waiting for a room to open up."

"Sarah, are you okay? Did you get hurt?"

"I'm okay, they had a doctor check me out. All I got was a tiny singe."

"Have you called dad?"

"There's no answer at his office, just the answering machine. I didn't know if I should leave such a scary message on it. And he's not picking up on his cell phone. You know how he always forgets to turn it on."

"I'm on my way. I'll be there in fifteen minutes. Stay right next to your brother until I get there."

Claire tried to reach Marco several times as she drove, foot heavy on the accelerator. Let a cop pull me over, I'll ask for a police escort. Where the hell is he, she said aloud. The third time she left a message on his answering machine. "I don't know where you are, but Stephen's been hurt. I'm on my way to the hospital."

THE SLEEK WHITE HOSPITAL ACROSS THE LAKE was the pride of the community. It had won awards for its low infection rate, its number of specialists, its nursing care. But when Claire arrived at the front desk, no one seemed to know where Stephen was. He'd been moved out of the Emergency Room, but the volunteer in the salmon-colored smock had not yet received word about which room he had been taken to. Claire heard herself shouting, in a voice that sounded like it belonged to someone else, "Find out, goddam it!" to the startled and apologetic woman. In a moment a man in a formal dark suit came over and told her that Stephen had been moved to a private room in the medical/surgical unit and that he would escort her there. Probably afraid I'm going to shoot someone, she thought.

Stephen lay in a bed with the sheets carefully arranged beneath his bandaged arms. One eye was covered with gauze and adhesive tape. The top of his hair was blackened, as was the brow barely visible above the bandage. His other eye was closed, and he was breathing noisily. Sarah sat in a straight chair next to the bed, an ice pack strapped to one wrist. As soon as she saw Claire she rose and burst into tears in her mother's arms.

"It was so scary, mom, he was screaming and they couldn't get the fire out and we threw him on the ground and we rolled him around and . . . "

Claire didn't want to hear the details yet. "But now, how is he now?"

"I don't know. The nurse said she'd talk to you."

Claire leaned over and spoke quietly near his ear. "Stevie, it's mom, I'm here, honey." No reaction. She repeated her words.

"They gave him a lot of stuff for pain," Sarah said. "He's really doped up."

"Stay here, I'm going to find someone who can tell me what's going on," Claire said.

The nurse was tapping notes into a computer behind the high counter. "I'm Claire Goldstein." There was no recognition in the nurse's face. "Stephen Capobianco's mother. What can you tell me?"

She stopped typing and came to Claire's side of the glossy white counter. "He's lucky, it could have been a lot worse. He was in a lot of pain, so the E.R. doctor gave him a shot to knock him out. I don't think he'll wake up until tomorrow morning."

"Will his arms be all right? What about his eye, will he be able to see? Will he need surgery?"

The nurse put her hand on Claire's arm. "I know you're upset, but please try to calm down. His life isn't in danger, I can tell you that much. The doctor will be here at seven tomorrow morning for rounds, so come back early and you can ask all your questions."

Claire pulled her arm away and tried to control the sense of helpless rage that was about to explode. "I'm not going anywhere. I want to be here in case my son wakes up. But can't you tell me . . ."

The nurse shrugged. "All I can tell you is that he's not in danger. You'll have to talk to the doctor. Why don't you go stay for a while, then go home and get some sleep?"

Claire had an impulse to shake her. She said coldly "I already told you, I'm not going anywhere."

The nurse shrugged. "Your call. The cafeteria's open until eight, then it's closed until six in the morning. But I can get you some juice and coffee anytime you want."

Claire checked the status of her cell phone battery—good, fully charged—and tried Marco's office. He answered on the third ring.

"Where the hell were you?" she demanded.

"I was just running some errands. What's up?" He hadn't checked his messages.

"Stephen's in the hospital. He had an accident."

"Shit, is he okay?"

Claire filled him in on what little she knew about Stephen's condition.

"I'll be right over."

When she turned the phone off Claire felt a surge of relief; Marco would be here soon. This was too big to handle alone. Although she sometimes complained that he was laconic about ordinary life, Marco was good in a crisis, especially if it was about the kids. She remembered him telling knock-knock jokes to Stephen after he was hit in the head with a hockey puck, as she drove frantically to the emergency room; the way he calmed a frightened eight year old Sarah before her appendectomy. And when Sarah had fallen just as she was starting to walk, knocking her front teeth up into her gum, Marco had rushed home. Don't freak when she smiles at you, her front teeth are gone, Claire had warned him, her voice shaky. He hadn't freaked; he had picked Sarah up and sat her on his lap, singing, "This old man, he plays one . . ."

On the way back to Stephen's room Claire walked past the visitors' lounge. Nora was leaning against the wall, a stunned look on her face. Several other young people tipped back in the few available chairs, their legs stretched out. They looked up when Claire stopped at the doorway.

"We're sorry, Mrs. Capobianco," one young man said.

"I need to know how this happened," Claire demanded.

"Something went wrong. We had this thing all worked out, down to the last details. We were just doing a run-through, you know, a rehearsal sort of. Stephen was supposed to go close to it with one of those lighter things and back away fast without letting the flame touch it, but I guess some of the fluid had spilled on his jacket and I don't know, he had this mask on to look like the governor, and maybe he couldn't see so well, and it was windy, and like. . ."

Nora sucked in some air and continued. "A bunch of us started batting at the flames and it was so scary, and then police and the ambulance came and. . ."

"Why don't you all go home? There's nothing you can do right now. You too, Nora," Claire said. "Maybe you should take Sarah with you. She looks wiped out."

"She won't go, I told her we'd take her home when you got here but she said no. And anyway I want stay too. I'll wait out here until I can see him. I told them that I was his girlfriend, but they wouldn't let me in. Only immediate family. Stupid hospital rules."

"Why don't the rest of you leave? You can check back tomorrow," Claire said. She wanted to blame them, to blame someone, but they looked so anxious and filled with remorse that she was disarmed. She walked out as they were surrounding Nora with hugs and reassurances.

Back in Stephen's room tubes connecting him to screens mounted on the wall were charting things Claire didn't understand. The green lines were hypnotic and oddly reassuring, though occasionally there was a beep that sounded like an alarm. The first time it happened she sent Sarah out to get the nurse, who told them it was routine, nothing to be concerned about, and that they were monitoring everything at the nursing station.

"Can I sit there, honey?" Sarah was in the chair next to Stephen's bed, close to his head.

Sarah touched her brother's shoulder with her cheek, and then collapsed into a plastic recliner on the other side of the room. Her clothes were rumpled; her hair was sticking up in uneven spikes.

"Are you really okay?" Claire asked.

"Yeah, it's not a burn, just a scrape. They said I can take the bandage off in a couple of days."

Claire sat very still in the straight aluminum chair, as if any movement might cause Stephen additional pain. When Marco came in a few minutes later, he didn't glance at either of them, but went right to Stephen's bedside.

"Jesus, Steve. Sweet Jesus," he whispered, bending over to kiss Stephen's forehead. "What do we know?" he asked Claire without turning.

"Not a lot. They're acting like his condition is a national security issue. Wait for the doctor, wait for the doctor, it's like a Gregorian chant." Claire sighed. "Maybe you'll have better luck with Nurse Ratchett."

He returned fifteen minutes later. "I just spoke to the doctor on the phone, he says he's stable, second degree burns on his arms, but he was damned lucky. His eye will be okay, the bandage is just—I forgot what he said. Anyway, no vital organs involved. He says we should go home, come back and he'll talk to us in the morning. Seven."

"You take Sarah home, I'm staying."

"I don't want to leave, either."

"I'll insist that Nora take her home and spend the night with her," Claire said.

NORA SEEMED RELIEVED to have something useful to do. Sarah agreed reluctantly to go. She hugged her parents, kissed Stephen's good hand, and left, turning at the door to look at her sleeping brother.

"By the way, where were you?" Claire asked Marco when they were alone with Stephen. "You didn't answer your phone."

Marco shrugged. "I must have forgotten to put it on vibrate. I was just doing some work with old files in the office," he said. Claire would remember that later and wonder why she hadn't asked more questions.

Stephen moaned several times during the night but didn't awaken. Each time Claire jumped up and put her face close to his, then sank back in the chair and dozed. She was asleep with her head on Stephen's bed, a light blanket over her shoulders, when the morning noises of the hospital woke her. Marco was sleeping soundly in the recliner.

"Hope you don't mind, I covered you when I came on shift. You never actually woke up," a nurse said. "I'm Velda, I'm on until three this afternoon."

Marco stirred, and joined Claire at the bedside. Claire felt as if every muscle in her body was protesting the folded-over position in which she had slept. They watched anxiously as Velda checked Stephen's vital signs. He opened his eyes and tried to smile at them.

"Hi sweetie, we're here," Claire said. Stephen tried to lift his head as the nurse straightened the pillow, but grimaced. "Time for another pain injection," Velda said. "But otherwise all good. These young guys, I'm telling you, they can come through anything."

Outside the sky was beginning to lighten in pink streaks. The hospital was waking up; trays rattled on a cart, cleaning people were sweeping and mopping floors, nurses were taking blood pressures, temperatures, checking pulses.

"We look like we're the ones who should be in the hospital," Claire said.

"The joys of parenthood." Marco stretched, and Claire noticed that he was wearing jeans. He never wore jeans to campus.

"I'll see if I can scare up some coffee," he said. "You stay here in case the doctor shows up early."

HE DIDN'T. IN FACT HE WAS TWO HOURS LATE. He arrived without an apology and introduced himself in a voice as crisp as his starchy white coat. Stephen opened his eyes at the sound of a strange voice.

"Well, young man, I guess you won't be playing with fire again."

Claire thought it would feel good to smack him.

Stephen started to say something, but Marco, on the other side of the bed, put his finger to his lips.

The doctor unwrapped the bandages from Stephen's arms. Claire had to steel herself not to look away. She felt nausea rise in her gut when she saw the raw flesh on her son's arms.

"Looks worse than it is, though it will be pretty painful for a while. We'll keep him on medication to help while it's healing. The big thing is to prevent infection, because we want to keep the bandage off from now on; the air facilitates new skin growth."

Marco asked how long Stephen would be in the hospital.

"A few more days, at least."

Claire was relieved. She'd never been good with illness; Marco had been the one who nursed the kids through high fevers, dressed wounds from playground falls, held their heads while they vomited. She felt inadequate and cowardly in the face of sickness and disease. She remembered listening outside her parents' bedroom door while her mother threw up into a basin when she was being treated with chemo, and later the stench of sickness that pervaded the house. When she was a kid, if she felt nauseated she would run to the front door and stand outside, gulping in fresh air in the hope that it would push whatever was trying to work its way up back down into her stomach.

THEY DISCUSSED SHIFTS. "Aren't you working with a deadline?" Marco asked.

Claire had forgotten about the fracking assignment. "I'll call Jasper, get more time. Even he can't object to that, he's got kids."

She stepped into the hallway with her cell phone. There was a quiet lounge at the end of the hall, and fortunately it was empty.

Jasper's voice was cool. "I just heard about the accident. I'm sorry about your son's injury." He paused, then asked, "Did you know what they were planning?"

Claire hesitated.

"It would have been a major embarrassment. And on Parents' Weekend! Did you know anything about this?"

"Look, Jasper, my son has second degree burns on his arms. He's in a lot of pain, has to stay in the hospital at least until the end of the week. Frankly, that's what matters to me right now."

"Too bad," he said. Claire wasn't sure how he meant it.

"I'm going to need a little more time on the assignment. I have to be here with Stephen."

Silence. "How much more? Can't you bring a laptop in and work from there?"

That was the moment when Claire lost it. "Jasper, my son is lying in a goddam hospital bed with raw flesh on his arms and a bandage over his eye, and all you can think about is why I can't write a bunch of half-truths because you're afraid someone won't write a big check. Give me a fucking break!"

Silence. Now she'd done it. She'd probably blown her job, but she felt a surprising sense of lightness.

"Never mind," he said coldly. "I'll send someone over to your office for the files. I'll find someone else to take over." He hung up without saying goodbye.

Claire marched into Stephen's room and told Marco what had happened. She was disappointed in his response.

"You think this was the time to tell him off? I mean, your job . . . hell, you're upset, you're exhausted, maybe you're not thinking as clearly as . . ."

"Thanks for your support. I don't want to talk about it," she said, and went to the window overlooking the lake. She watched a small huddle of hospital employees standing in a pergola, the one place where they were allowed to smoke.

MARCO LEFT AT NOON TO TEACH A SEMINAR; he'd be back around five. Claire paced the room as Stephen slipped in and out of wakefulness. She wanted the comfort of Maude, but how could she make any demands on her? Maude was failing; she could see it, week by week. She'd call a little later to tell her what had happened.

At three Claire's cell phone rang. It was Maude. "Why didn't you call me?" she demanded. "I had to hear about Stephen from Carolynne." Periodically Claire forgot what a small town it was; news flashed from house to house, building to building, like Tinkerbell.

"I figured you had enough on your mind."

"Well you figured wrong," Maude scolded. "Harry and I will be there in half an hour."

Claire almost wept with gratitude. Then she remembered the stricture on family-only visitors. She went out to the nurse's station. "His grandparents are on their way," she said.

MAUDE'S WEIGHT WAS BALANCED between Harry and her cane; her face showed the strain of walking down the long hospital corridor, but she had refused a wheelchair. Claire rose and hugged her carefully, and kissed Harry on his stubbly cheek. He looked exhausted. Clearly, caring for Maude was wearing him out.

Maude sank into the chair next to the bed. "Well, little man, what trouble have you been making?" No one else could have gotten away with saying that to six-foot Stephen. He opened his unbandaged eye and waved two fingers at them, then closed the eye again.

"What does the doctor say?"

Claire filled them in. "Damn fool kids," Harry said, but she heard the affection in his words. "I remember when we were trying to think up something like that, fake napalm. But we never pulled it off. You've got to give these kids credit, they almost made it work."

"Not now, Harry," Maude said. "This isn't the time to talk about your exploits."

They spoke in the quiet voices people use in hospital rooms. Harry went downstairs to the cafeteria to bring back cups of herbal tea.

"How are you holding up, dearie?" Maude asked.

"I go between wanting to scream at him and wanting to hug him, sometimes at the same time. Anyway, I may have lost my job."

Maude looked alarmed. "What happened?"

"Jasper was pushing me on a deadline about the fracking articles and I sort of told him to shove it."

Maude grinned. "Well, that's been a long time coming!" Then, more seriously, she said, "He won't do anything, this is a medical crisis."

"Oh Maude, you don't know Jasper. For him a crisis is a negative sentence about the university in any newspaper."

Harry returned balancing a cardboard tray with the tea and some blueberry muffins. Maude filled him in on Claire's conversation with Jasper.

"Don't you worry. You have any trouble about this, we'll take it to the ombudsman. That's what he's there for."

They left after half an hour; Claire could see the fatigue in Maude's eyes. "I can't even begin to tell you how grateful . . ."

"Bosh. You didn't think I wouldn't come, did you?" Maude patted her shoulder. "You've got too much on your plate, dearie. I'll call you tomorrow." She turned to Harry. "Maybe I'll take that wheelchair back to the car, after all."

CLAIRE AND MARCO SPELLED EACH OTHER in the hospital for the next few days. Maude called several times a day, but Harry wouldn't let her visit again. "He's such an old fusspot, he's afraid I'll pick up an infection. If he hovers any more, I swear I may have to overcome my feelings about gun control."

Harry came by himself, bringing Stephen a graphic novel which would have been exactly right for a hospital stay, except that Stephen couldn't use his arms to hold it. The television, projecting out of the pale green wall, was on most of the day, even when his friends stopped in, an endless repetition of MSNBC with an occasional few minutes of FOX news. "Have to keep track of what the enemy is saying," he told them.

Nora came every day at noon between Claire and Marco's shifts. On the fourth day in the hospital, she arrived with her face flushed with excitement. "You won't believe this, Stephen! You did it! It's amazing! It's wild, everyone's getting on board about the fracking movement!"

"What do you mean? We missed Parents Weekend."

"Yeah, but listen. There was an article in the paper last night about what we were planning and why and what happened to you, and some quotes from the flyer Sarah did, and the campus just about exploded! It's incredible! The committee went into emergency action and they're printing a thousand copies of the flyer, and there's going to be a demonstration tonight—without fire, but with speakers on the quad and signs, the works! It's unbelievable! Suddenly everyone's pissed about fracking. This is going to be really big!"

Stephen grinned, then grimaced. "Shit, I want to be there."

"Oh sweetie, I wish. . . it's so not fair."

"You guys are doing just fine without me. I'm really proud of all of you." He looked away. "It's just that . . . ah, shit, I'd give anything to be there."

Claire stood up. "Forget it. No way. Anyway, I'll leave you together and go to work. By the way, Stephen, I thought you'd like to know, I'm off the fracking article." He looked vague for a moment, and then smiled.

"Hey, mom." He raised his thumb and grinned.

IN THE NEXT FEW DAYS there was a buzz of anti-fracking activity. The committee set up an information booth in the quad, there were posters on every campus bulletin board, and rumors were circulating about an impending sit-in in the administration building if the University didn't come out with a clear anti-fracking position. A large group of students, joined by some members of the faculty, arrived at meetings of the city's common council and the county legislature. The local newspaper featured a lengthy article about the anti-fracking activism, including an interview with Stephen that included a photograph of him in his hospital bed. "Atta boy, Steve-o!" Harry shouted into the phone when he read the article. Claire was proud to see how articulate and knowledgeable Stephen was about the technical aspects of fracking. Someone from his group had provided the paper with preliminary evidence of a new study of the dangers of underground gas escaping into local aquifers, and another about the probability of cracks developing in some of the concrete wells. In five days the University issued a statement: in view of the overwhelming weight of evidence, the university has decided to refrain from any possibility of leasing its land for the purposes of hydrofracking. And a wealthy environmentalist alumnus wrote a check for two million dollars in support of the decision.

CLAIRE RECEIVED A WARM WELCOME from her staff when she returned to work, especially from Marianne, who had been peering at her computer screen which was dotted with red "track changes" marks. "God, this interview Carla did is almost unreadable! Do I ever I miss your writing! I hope you're finished with your Jasper project soon. This newsletter is getting more illiterate by the minute."

"Not to worry. I quit it. Who knows, I may have done in a not-so-beautiful career."

Marianne looked upset. "You're kidding. Just when my life seems to be calming down—oh, I haven't told you. Chet agreed to contact that writing coach, and she's already got him doing some exercises, and she's sure she can get him back on track with the dissertation. She's really terrific! And he seems so much more hopeful."

"That's great. I'm really glad for both of you." She remembered what a depressed bear Marco had been when he hadn't been able to write; she had compared it to a severe and extended bout of constipation.

Claire sat down at her desk and looked around the office. Twenty-five years of her life. She'd had several promotions since she started here. Finally, the editorship of the newsletter. More responsibility, more inside connections, more money. Was she happy with what she was doing? Sometimes. She supposed she was content. Did any of it make a difference? Probably not. No one thumbed through a course catalogue and decided to come to the university because of the faculty newsletter. No one gave money or awards, though she did have a framed certificate on the wall, presented a few months ago, to congratulate her for her twenty-five years of employment. "Not even a goddam watch from the noble institution," Stephen had said. This fracking project, Stephen's accusations, the accident, her telling Jasper off—all had jarred the way she thought about her job.

Well, she said to herself, this is no time to think Big Thoughts. If Jasper wanted to get rid of her, she'd take Harry's advice and go to the Ombudsman. She had to get through these next weeks while Stephen recovered, see Maude as often as possible, visit Zayde, get back to work on the newsletter, find some time to be with Marco. They'd seen each other mostly passing in the hospital corridor, and at night exchanged a few words before collapsing into sleep. Maybe they'd take in a movie;

she'd noticed that there was a new Woody Allen at Cinemapolis. Yes, a funny movie would be just right.

CHAPTER FOURTEEN

AUDE WAS SLUMPED ON THE PORCH SWING thinking about her shrinking world. There were things she'd already had to give up: The Farmer's Market on Saturdays to buy crusty bread and free-range chicken; walks through the winding paths of the Plantations with Capsule, their aging dachshund, circling the pond as he barked half-heartedly at the unflappable ducks; her afternoon drink, which made her dizzy because of the pain medication she took with increasing frequency. This morning she had tried to pick the last of the tomatoes, but stopped when a flame of pain knifed through her spine and along the front of her leg. It had eased only slightly.

Damn, damn, damn. Digging beneath crumpled tissues in her skirt pocket she took out a small white pill.

"Okay, dearie," she said to herself, "time to get stupid."

The ice had melted in the glass of iced tea she had been drinking; she put one of the pain pills Yvonne had prescribed on her tongue and swigged the sweet liquid quickly to get rid of the pill's bitter taste. When Yvonne had handed her the prescription, Maude had looked at it with surprise and said, "That's a pretty powerful narcotic. Isn't it what kids are using to get high these days?"

"You could make a fortune selling it on the street," Yvonne said, smiling. "But keep it for yourself, you may need it."

Maude tucked the prescription into her pocket. "I suppose at this late date I don't need to worry about getting addicted, "she said. "It might be nice to get high."

She had waited to use the medication until the pain became a palpable and aggressive presence, asserting itself in her back, her legs, sometimes her neck and shoulders. Although she didn't like the haze that created a curtain of fuzz around her mind soon after she took a pill, she found it did provide a barrier between her and what she had come to think of as the enemy that had taken over her body. Along with the relief it delivered, the medication played havoc with her digestion, but even worse, it made her brain loopy: verbs bumped into adjectives and nouns were as evanescent as soap bubbles. "Rate your pain, one to ten, one being the lowest," Yvonne had said when she finished looking at the results of the latest scan. Although Maude had become very fond of her, she had barely contained her irritation. "One to ten when? When I'm sitting still? Walking? Pulling weeds? Making love? Ah, there's a pretty memory." Then she said, "I'm sorry, dearie, that wasn't necessary. Five."

The glider creaked back and forth as she waited for the pill to take effect. The late October sun was surprisingly hot. Why do they call it Indian summer, she wondered. So many things she still didn't know, didn't have time to learn. All the books she'd meant to read, some she'd wanted to re-read. She'd promised herself years ago to go back and read the whaling chapters of Moby Dick she'd barely skimmed in her haste to discover the meaning of the white whale. There were letters she hadn't answered. Why do we always believe that there will be time for everything, all the things we want to do or need to do? As if the time we have were some infinitely elastic commodity rather than a shrinking pile of hours. She hitched her denim skirt up high and tucked it under her, noticing again the random brown spots sprinkled around her hands and arms, the spidery blue veins on her legs. Knobby old lady legs, she thought as she swung back and forth, back and forth.

"Maybe you should start to think about a walker," the radiologist had said after the last treatment, helping her get down from the table. "Just to be sure you don't fall." Dear God, she thought, but reminded herself that there was no God, and if there was, he or she was certainly not dear. What's next, a wheelchair? There was no way to maneuver a wheelchair around their old house with its narrow doorways and odd corners.

She was grateful for the few outings she could still manage. Claire or other friends would pick her up and drive through the countryside to see the changing leaves floating down or clinging to thinning branches, achingly beautiful against the autumn sky. She and Harry would sit on their porch and watch the late afternoon clouds deepen from gold to pink to almost blood red before darkness set in. She occasionally went to a film at Cinemapolis—how grateful she was that the new theater had no steps, something she'd never paid attention to in the past. She was careful to sit on the aisle so that if she needed to, she could get out of her seat and move around in a search of a more comfortable way to live in her body. But even these expeditions were coming to an end. She knew that she was coming to an end, and she was frightened that it would come too soon. She was also frightened that it would come too late.

Maude knew what she wanted to do when the last stage approached, but she might need to enlist help. The problem was timing: acting while she still able, but not too soon. She didn't want to abbreviate whatever good time remained. Yet if something happened, or if she waited too long, she needed a backup plan so that she could maintain control. She had spent hours at the computer, her bony bottom uncomfortably propped on a pillow. Some of the sites were fanatic rants; others were sponsored by organizations to which she'd written checks over the years, like Compassion and Choices, because she believed in what they were trying to accomplish, not because she thought she'd be in need of their assistance so soon. A few weeks ago she had ordered copies of *Final Exit* and *The Peaceful Pill* from Amazon. Although she'd always purchased books at the independent bookstore downtown, she didn't want anyone to know about these. They lay hidden in her underwear drawer, like a teenage boy's secret copy of *Hustler*. She couldn't let Harry know what she was planning; in spite of everything they'd talked about before it became real, she suspected that he would find a way to stop her. She'd been stashing away pills, everything she could find that might be useful, including some of Harry's sleeping medication. He could get more afterward. She worried about causing him embarrassment and additional anguish. Unattended deaths might require an autopsy, or at least an investigation.

She needed more information about how it would play out. Yvonne. She phoned for an appointment and asked Claire to drive her there. "Let's tell Harry we're going out for a ride," she said. "I would like to be able to have at least one private talk with my doctor without him interrupting every other sentence."

"Sure. Can I ask what it's about?"

"Birth control pills. None of your beeswax."

YVONNE GREETED HER WITH A CAREFUL HUG. "I'm glad to see you. But aren't you due in next week? Is something wrong?"

Maude eased herself into a chair. "Nothing a new body wouldn't take care of." She paused and looked pointedly at Yvonne. "I want to know how things will go. At the end, I mean."

Yvonne was obviously uncomfortable, and paused before answering.

"Come on, the reason you're my doctor is that I trust you to be straight with me."

"Okay. Given where the largest tumor is located, you might become paralyzed. But I can't be sure."

Maude took a deep breath. "You mean I won't be able to . . . make my own decisions. About the end, I mean. I don't want to get you in trouble, but is there any way you could . . . you know?"

Yvonne's face softened. "Maude, you know I'd do anything I could to help you. You've become very important to me. But assisted suicide is illegal in New York State."

Suicide. The word was so hard-edged, judgmental. Self-deliverance? Maude mused. Self-euthanasia?

Yvonne appeared to be struggling for words. "I can't risk losing my license."

"Forget I even mentioned it, dearie, I don't want you to take any risk. I was just wondering, that's all. And if I were to . . . well, you know, I don't want to put Harry through any more than he'll have to cope with anyway. I don't want police coming and asking him questions and putting those yellow tapes around the house as if he'd done me in."

Yvonne put her hand on Maude's. "I wish I had met you years ago, and that we could have been friends, not doctor and patient."

Maude patted her arm. "We are friends, dearie. I feel as if I've known you for a long time." Someone else she would be losing. Who would be losing her.

MAUDE LAY IN THE HAMMOCK waiting for Claire to come, thinking about a conversation they had had a few months ago, before the diagnosis, when what she was dealing with had seemed liked uncomplicated pain—was it possible that it was just a few months ago, not another lifetime?

"I've been thinking," Claire had said. "Maybe it's time for you and Harry to move. To the Meadows, you know."

"The Meadows!" she had snorted. "Good name for a place where people are put out to pasture."

"You know that's not true. It's a life care community, that's all. Most people manage to live independently. You have lots of friends who live there."

Maude told Claire that it simply wasn't right for her. She didn't want to be in a place where there were no children, where so many of the residents moved around on wheeled walkers and others scooted in electric carts like beetles. "I don't want to spend the rest of my years surrounded by sick and dying people. Or by people doing things for me that I'm perfectly capable of doing myself."

"You forgot to say 'harumph'," Claire had said. "You don't have to use the services, you and Harry can live completely independently, but if you need help, like if you fall, you just pull a cord. And there's a lot to do that you'd enjoy, talks and a book club and chamber music. Even an Olympic swimming pool. Maybe swimming would feel good."

"I'd have to get a new bikini, "Maude had said. "There's a pretty picture."

She remembered the exasperation in Claire's voice. "Will you for once be reasonable about this? You don't have to do paint by numbers or crochet toilet paper covers. And you know what? You sound like a snob."

"I'm not being a snob. I've been there to visit friends many times. What I dislike is the frenzy of activity. It's ridiculous, the way they're all running to lectures they have trouble hearing and seeing films they've already seen. You go into the art studio and they're learning how to throw pots they don't need, they're taking yoga classes and twisting themselves into pretzels and writing poetry no one wants to read. Not for me, thank you very much. And Harry would probably hate it. Either that or he'd organize a strike against the administration for something or other and get us thrown out." She paused, and then said, "Everyone is running around so they won't have to think about what they all know is coming."

"You make me crazy!" Claire had said. "You're as bad as Sarah!"

"I consider that a compliment."

BUT CLAIRE HAD BEEN RIGHT. They should have gotten rid of most of their stuff, packed the rest and moved. It would be good for Harry after she was gone. Now she didn't have the energy to face the overwhelming work of downsizing and relocating.

She had blamed her unwillingness to move on Harry, but in truth she was the one who loved this house, even with its faltering plumbing, its uneven heating system, the scratched oak floors in need of refinishing. That was why she pulled herself upstairs to the bedroom in the evening, and inched down in the morning, sometimes on her butt. Both left her exhausted and breathless. She cursed the tumor that zigzagged its way through her spinal column like a violent and disobedient child, following its own rules, thumbing its nose at the rays that left the skin on her back glossy as red satin.

Even through the haze of the opioid she was tormented by her concern about Harry. If something happened to her-- what was she saying? When something happened, what would he do? Would he become a hermit and exist on scrambled eggs and cans of tuna? There was no child to watch over him, move him to an apartment close to her, call him daily to make sure he was all right. That would have been Alice's responsibility. She would have been almost Claire's age. Claire would do what she could, but she had her own life and her own problems. Was it really too late to move? If they could get in to the Meadows, at least when she was gone he would eat one meal a day with other people in the cafeteria. Harry liked being with people, but, as in most of the couples they knew, she was the one who organized their social lives, invited friends, planned dinner parties. Besides, so many of their friends were gone, died or retired to someplace warm or nearer their kids. Would he meet another woman, possibly even marry again? He was in pretty good shape for a man his age. And now there was Viagra. There were probably lots of widows and divorcees who would be happy to take care of him. She remembered how they used to lie in bed laughing over whom each would select as a next partner.

"Helena? You're kidding! The last book she read was *Gone with the Wind*! And that was when it first came out."

"And you'd pick Art?" he'd countered. "He hasn't smiled in fourteen years. You'd make one of your funny remarks and he'd sit there like a stone."

"Louise? You're not serious! She's a vegetarian. You'd have to eat cauliflower and broccoli all the time. You'd fart her right out of the house."

"Bill? No, he has too much money. You wouldn't know how to live like a rich woman, I've trained you too well."

Since her illness that conversation had stopped. In fact they didn't talk about the future, real or pretend, at all. When they were both healthy they'd sat at the dining room table one Sunday afternoon filling out health care proxy forms and living wills and medical directives. "If I'm in a coma and I get pneumonia, don't let them give me antibiotics," she'd instructed. "And if my heart stops and I don't breathe for more than a couple of minutes, no machines, you hear?" he'd said. They'd completed the forms, filed them with their doctors and lawyer and placed copies in the safe deposit box and the glove compartment of the car. They'd arranged for a number of charitable bequests to come out of their IRAs, the money carefully invested in socially responsible mutual funds that had ridden the waves of bear and bull markets. She'd insisted that they leave some money for Sarah and Stephen. They'd updated their wills periodically. Now whenever she tried to talk about anything that circled around the subject of dying,

Harry would say that there was plenty of time for that, and change the subject or leave the room.

HER CELL PHONE RANG. Harry had bought it for her and insisted that she carry it at all times. "I hate the damned thing," she'd told him. "It feels like an intrusion, like it's watching me."

Yvonne was on the phone.

"When you were in last time I explained what I couldn't do. But there is something we can do. I can have someone from hospice get in touch with you."

Maude grimaced. "Forget it, I don't want people chanting around my bed and putting crystals on my eyes."

Yvonne laughed. "I can't believe that someone of your intelligence thinks that's what they do. They've got a very competent staff of highly trained people. Good people, people you'd like."

"It's not exactly the right time of life to start making new friends," Maude said. "It's hard enough to think about saying goodbye to the old ones. Besides, I've got you."

"You know I'm here for you, no matter what. But I wish you'd consider it. My specialty is oncology, but they're experts in working with people with advanced disease."

"You mean people who are dying," Maude said. "Please don't start getting euphemistic with me this late in the game."

Yvonne started to explain how the hospice staff could be helpful, then added "Maybe I shouldn't tell you this, but I will. When a hospice patient dies in this state, there's no investigation or autopsy, unless there's some suspicion of foul play. That's all I can say."

"Thank you, my dear," she said. "Harry will hate this, but he'll go along if I insist."

"What the hell do we need them for? I can take perfectly good care of you," Harry said when she approached the subject that night. "And I don't want a bunch of strangers marching all over the house. Especially not now."

"Yvonne thinks it's a good idea. She says they won't be intrusive, but they know a lot about managing pain and we can call them any time, day or night, if anything comes up. That way we won't have to rush to the hospital." She grinned at him. "You know what a rotten driver you are in the dark, anyway. You'd probably do me in on the way there." They argued for a few more minutes before he acquiesced.

GINGER WAS THE HOSPICE NURSE in charge of her case. She was about fifty, dressed in slacks and a heavy sweater—no uniform, Maude noted gratefully. Solidly built, with short graying hair and remnants of a New England accent. She introduced herself crisply, easing Maude's fear that she would be drowned in dewy-eyed sentimentality.

"Where are you from?" Maude asked.

"Small town way up in the north of Maine. Makes winters here seem like Florida. But I haven't lived there for years. And I wouldn't go back if they paid me. Which they've offered to do—not many hospice nurses hanging around out in the north woods."

Ginger sat in the living room with them and reviewed the services that were available. When she mentioned the hospice chaplain Maude said quickly "No thank you, I'm not going out of this world with a minister tugging at my soul trying to get me to redeem myself. I'm a female Christopher Hitchens."

Ginger looked blank.

"He was a smart old reprobate who was religious about his atheism. Everyone waited around at the end hoping for him to recant, but he never did. Here's to him, I say," Maude said, holding up an imaginary wine glass. "Anyway, it's too late for salvation. My mother has already set me up for an eternity of damnation for marrying this guy," she said, pointing to Harry.

Harry didn't smile; he was scowling over the brochure Ginger had given them. "No volunteers," he said. "I don't need anyone cooking or shopping or reading aloud to her, for Chrisssake. That's what she's got me for. And all her friends. You just keep her out of pain, that's all."

Ginger didn't appear to take offense. "You're in charge, we'll provide what you want. And you can always change your mind. The only other person who has to come one time is the social worker; it's a requirement of Medicare if we want to get paid." She asked if Harry could show her through the house so that she could figure out what might be needed in the way of equipment and check for safety issues. When she came back into the room she said, "We've moved a couple of the small rugs to prevent tripping. You don't need a broken hip now. And since there's a bathroom down here, with a little rearranging I think we could fit a hospital bed in the living room. It'll save you from dealing with the steps and let you be as social as you want."

Maude raised her hand and started to object.

"Why don't you try it for a few days? It will make getting in and out of bed much easier, and you can adjust it to sit up."

"Not yet, maybe later. I can still get up the steps if I take my time and use a cane."

The idea of not sleeping in her own bed felt like another death. She needed the warmth that came off Harry's body under their old heirloom quilt, the one she'd picked up at a garage sale years ago. She needed to know that she could still touch him, hear his soft snoring. She remembered that when they were first married, she sometimes woke up and put her hand on his stomach as he slept to make sure he was still breathing.

Ginger shrugged. "Like I said, you're in charge. We're just here to make things work the way you want them to. As much as possible." She gave them a thick packet of information, got a dozen signatures on that many forms—"keeps the Health Department busy"-- and shook hands. "Don't forget, you can call twenty-four hours a day about anything. No question is dumb or unimportant."

When she left, Harry harrumphed a little before acknowledging that it was, in fact, reassuring to know they could get help if they needed it, even in the middle of the night, and that Ginger wasn't as bad as he expected.

Benjamin, the social worker, arrived the next morning. He was in his early fifties, with an owlish look that became puckish when he smiled, which he did often. Harry stood in the doorway to the hall, as if he were prepared to flee if he didn't like what he heard. "We're not into that touchy-feely stuff," he said.

"Neither am I, so we should be fine," Benjamin said. "I bet you're wondering what do I need this guy for?" Benjamin asked.

"You got it right," Harry said.

Maude said. "It's a little late in the game for therapy."

"No therapy, I promise. What I'm supposed to do today is an assessment of your psychosocial needs. Don't you love words like that? Mostly it's to keep the bureaucrats in Albany happy." When he grinned, he reminded Maude of the leprechaun in "Finian's Rainbow".

"Fire away. At least I'll know I've contributed to a data bank that will live on after I'm gone. Like organ donation."

Benjamin laughed and opened his laptop computer. "Sorry about this. Another glorious requirement of the state. Actually, it's good for me, because I was always way behind in my paper work. I have this problem: I like people more than I like paper." He asked questions about her family, tapping her responses onto an electronic form. When she mentioned a deceased daughter he simply said "I'm sorry," It was then that Harry slipped back into the kitchen.

"Important friends? Religious affiliation? Have you completed your advance directives? Made out a will? Made burial decisions?" Tap tap tap.

When the form was complete Benjamin turned off the laptop and closed it. "Enough, that will keep the state health department busy for a while." He looked around the room. "You've got wonderful things in here, looks like they're from all over the world."

"Harry and I used to travel some every summer. We'd rent a flat in a country we hadn't visited, and take day trips to explore. We'd get to know people, shop in local markets, picnic in the parks, invite neighbors in. It was a great way to get a sense of how other people live. And of course we did every museum within a hundred miles. Harry never got tired, he could spend ten hours a day in the museums."

"I wish I knew more about art. You brought back wonderful mementos." He stroked the smooth surface of a small stone vase, a replica of a pre-Columbian drinking vessel.

"Memories more than mementos. Harry, that old Grinch, has never been keen on souvenir shopping. I had to sneak things into my suitcase if I wanted to bring something home." She laughed. "My friend Claire used to say that Harry was the only person who came back from a trip with more money than when he left."

After half an hour Benjamin stood up. "I have to leave now, but I hope you'll let me come back. No therapy, no social work—I would just like to spend some time with you. For my sake."

She reached out and patted his hand. "Where have you been all my life?" she said.

THE NEXT DAY CLAIRE CALLED to say she was bringing over a pot of soup. "It's what I do at night when I can't sleep, I cook gallons of soup. Porridge therapy. You have to help me out and eat some of it."

Maude was lying on the sofa propped up on several pillows when Claire arrived. She went into the kitchen and returned a few minutes later with a bowl of steaming pea soup on a tray. It smelled wonderful as Maude lifted the spoon to her mouth, but she stopped eating after a few sips. The pills did in her appetite, she explained to Claire.

Settling back on the sofa, Maude took a deep breath. "Do you remember the young woman who was in a coma but kept alive on machines even though she had stated that she didn't want to be?" she asked.

"Why are you talking about this, Maude?"

"What was that movie about shooting horses? We should be able to help people who want to die," Maude said. "And that's the perfect lead-in to something I want to talk to you about."

She put it out in as straightforward and unemotional a way as she could. "If this thing drags on I might need your help getting out of here. There's no one else I can ask. Harry won't be able to do it, I know that. I don't think he could."

It was a difficult conversation, but Maude had been rehearsing it all week. "If I were your dog you would get me out of a life that wasn't working any more. And I'm only asking you as a backup, in case I can't get the medication in by myself. "

"Maude, I can't . . ."

"Claire, I'm asking you to help me let go if I can't do it myself. I'll figure out a way so that you can't get into any legal trouble. I've been reading a lot about how to do it."

Now Claire was crying. "I can't believe we're talking about this."

Maude was surprised by her own lack of emotion as she continued. "I have to talk about it. I have to be able to tell someone that I'm afraid. That I'm a coward and I don't want to watch my life seep away inch by inch."

"You, a coward? After what you've been through, not just now but your whole life? I mean, your crazy mother, losing Alice? And still being so full of love for kids and for people. You're the bravest person I know."

"Take my word for it, I'm a coward about dying. It's not the pain; I know they can keep that under control, but I'd probably have to take so much medicine that I'd be a zombie toward the end. What's the point of it? Why should Harry and you and anyone else who cares about me have to watch me go out drop by drop? Living in diapers, having to be turned so I don't get bedsores, having to be fed. Seeing Harry's face grow darker day by day. That's what terrifies me." Maude felt her composure slip and turned her face to the wall. Her hands had begun to tremble.

"Don't answer yet," Maude said when she had regained control. "Think about it. All I'm asking is that you help me get some medication down, if I can't manage it by myself."

"How would I live with that? Harry would never forgive me if he knew, and I'd feel guilty for the rest of my life."

"Take a few days to consider it. I don't know how much time I have before it becomes an issue. If it even does."

CLAIRE CALLED THE NEXT DAY to say that she'd been agonizing about Maude's request. She wanted to come over and talk more with Maude about her concerns. When she arrived an hour later, she came upstairs to the bedroom where Maude was lying down, talking to a man sitting in the small upholstered chair next to the bed.

"Hi, dearie, what a nice surprise! You're just in time to meet Benjamin. He's the social worker from the hospice." Maude grinned. "He's my new shrink."

"It's about time someone helped you get your head together. I'm sorry, I didn't know you had company," Claire said.

"It's okay, this is hardly a professional visit. I just stopped in to drop off a book I thought Maude might like." The slender volume was on the bed next to her: a collection of poems by Mary Oliver.

"He's cheering me up by not being too cheerful," Maude said. "Not a word of Freud, either."

"I understand you've had the privilege of knowing this lady for many years," Benjamin said.

"She's made my life possible," Claire responded. "I think I would have fled this town kicking and screaming if I hadn't met her our first year here. She introduced me to all the good stuff."

Benjamin stayed for another half hour. When Claire asked how he'd gotten into this work, he explained that he'd been a tax lawyer for several years before he awoke one morning and asked himself if this was really the way he wanted to spend his life. The answer was clearly no.

"Unfortunately for my wife it was clearly yes. She liked the perks—Fifth Avenue apartment, maid, charge accounts. She wasn't about to support her husband through a master's program in social work and go live on a reservation, which is what I did when I graduated at the age of thirty-five."

"What a huge life change! That must have taken courage," Maude said.

"It would have taken more courage to stay with what I was doing; in reality it scared the hell out of me to think about what I was contributing to. Helping corporations move money offshore so they could avoid taxes. And now they buy our elections."

As they continued to talk Maude drifted off to sleep, their words weaving in and out of her hazy awareness. Sometime, when she'd increased the pain meds, she was unable to separate scenes from the past from the reality of her bedroom. People who had disappeared from her present life reappeared, drifting across the room, and though she called out to them to stay, they obeyed their own ghostly rules. Her mother and father, still scornful and distrusting, "Don't ever bring him here again," her mother shouted, as Harry was proclaiming about the exploitation of migrant farm labor. "But this is his house, he lives here," Maude said, and her parents faded away. Old friends whom she hadn't seen for years, friends who had died, stopped by her bed. Renata and Warren, who never spoke to them again after the crisis on campus because she and Harry took the side of the armed African American students in their Civil Rights protest. A lover, Gregory---go quickly before Harry comes in, she whispered, he never knew about you. But Gregory, who had enjoyed taking risks, lingered, grinned that sexy grin of his. He looked so young—what was he, thirty? It was the sixties and she was the last woman in her consciousness-raising group to take a lover. She remembered their late afternoon meetings in his office, after she'd left the school library. Harry was still at work, Alice at a piano lesson or playing at a friend's house. The patterns of the oriental rug on his floor—she could see the maroon and blue designs— not quite wide enough so that they would sometimes roll onto the hard concrete and land on the tangle of clothes they had removed in their haste to be skin to skin—yes, here, no there, mmmm yes, that's it. She felt something stir; no, that isn't possible any more. Go away, Gregory. Go back to your wife. And probably to your grandchildren by now. Is that why Alice died, to punish me? Is there in fact some punitive deity out there in spite of what I've believed all my life?

Her sister Helena appeared at the foot of her bed. Helena who never left Kansas, stayed and took care of their parents until they died, then married a widower with one of the biggest farms in the county. There she stood, still with the rugged look of a pioneer: broad shoulders, big hands, a body that said no nonsense here, thank you very much. Maude remembered how enraged Helena was when JFK was elected—a Catholic running the country; we'll all be in the Pope's pocket. I was lucky, I went away to school, met Harry, he saved me from that life. Opened my eyes to the world. But Helena never forgave me because she wound up taking care of mama.

Chanting sounds seemed to be coming from outside. Hell no we won't go. Hey hey LBJ, how many kids did you kill today? She remembered the flames of a monk burning himself to death in a village square. And that child—Alice's age?—fleeing naked, the terror on her face never to be erased. Maude squeezed her eyes shut, put her hands over her ears. Even so, she saw the helicopter readying to pull out of Saigon, people desperately clinging to anything they could grab onto. Saw the image of Nixon on the steps of his helicopter as he left DC for the last time, his fingers raised in a fake victory sign.

There was a light tapping on the door. No, no, Alice don't come unless you're going to stay. I can't lose you again. Oh baby, look at you, you're so little. Remember how you used to cry when I brushed the tangles out of your hair? No matter how hard I tried to hold them away from your scalp you screamed and once I got so mad I threw the brush at you. It was such fine golden hair. You're so thin, my little Alice. I'll buy you ice cream. Wait . . .

"Maude? Maude!" Claire's voice was something real, something to cling to. She opened her eyes. She looked around. Benjamin had left.

"I was up all night thinking. I even did some reading about the laws in Washington and Oregon. Okay, I'll do it if you still want me to."

It took Maude a moment to register Claire's meaning, then she held her hand out. "If I believed in God I'd ask her to bless you," she said. "What a comfort you are to me, my dear."

"And now let's agree never to talk about it again, unless we absolutely have to. I'm not even going to tell Marco."

CHAPTER FIFTEEN

ITHIN A WEEK AFTER LEAVING THE HOSPITAL Stephen was well enough to return to his apartment. He announced that he and Nora thought it was a perfect time for her to move in with him, and although Claire wondered if they were ready for something that approximated commitment, she admitted to herself that she was relieved. Nora would make sure Stephen was careful, took his meds and ate regularly. And Claire was ready to be finished with the flow of Stephen's buddies checking in, bringing with them the news of the latest anti-fracking activity, strumming guitars and blowing into recorders, and staying too long. Stephen seemed to groove on all the activity, but Claire was frazzled.

She hadn't heard from Jasper, not even a whisper, though of course Jasper rarely whispered. When she had returned to the office she'd expected a command to appear and be taken to the woodshed, but there was an eerie silence from the administration building. She resumed her after-work visits to Maude, bringing meals she'd cooked the previous night, soups stews, applesauce, which Maude barely ate but Harry consumed gratefully. Maude didn't seem to be in pain, though she drowsed off in the middle of conversations. Claire would return from these visits around seven, drained; she and Marco would exchange a few words, then share sections of the paper while they ate dinner. Sarah would have eaten earlier so that she could spend the evening doing homework.

On a rarely shared supper on Saturday Sarah announced that she was going to spend the night at Joline's. When Claire insisted on calling Joline's mother to make sure she was going to be home, Sarah shouted that she was tired of being treated like a baby. Marco chimed in with one of his least helpful statements, a vaguely uttered "Listen to your mother." When Sarah banged out of the house, the call having produced a satisfactory answer, Claire experienced a wash of relief. She was exhausted.

They cleared the table in what felt to Claire like a companionable silence broken only by the quiet clatter of dishes. When they were finished, Marco took her hand and led her into the living room. It was the way he used to take her hand when he wanted to make love. And sometimes, when they knew both kids were out and not due back for a while, they liked to do it in different parts of the house and to make the lusty noises which as parents they had learned to tamp down. "The living room? Hon, I'm too tired, and we don't both fit on the sofa anymore." But that didn't appear to be what Marco had in mind. He seated her on the couch and sat on the chair directly across from her.

"We need to talk," he said.

"Oh, she'll get over it. She always does. Teen trauma. But I wish I didn't always have to be the bad cop."

"No, it's not about Sarah." His fingers were doing fiddly things with each other. "It's about us, about you and me. I don't know where to begin." He took a deep breath.

"Just begin." While he struggled for words Claire's mind raced through the possibilities: He couldn't have lost his job, he had tenure. The grant? Maybe it had been rejected already? Did he have blood in his urine? Had he found a lump in her breast the last time they made love, what was it, about two weeks ago? But he would have said something sooner. Was Stephen in some kind of trouble? Sarah couldn't be pregnant, she would have turned to Claire first, and besides, she didn't have a boyfriend. At least not that she knew about.

His voice was shaky and sounded like he might cry. "I . . . don't know how to say this, Claire. I, I just . . ."

"What is it, Marco? Just tell me!"

Marco's words tumbled into each other, like a former stutterer who was losing his grip. "I need some time to myself."

"What do you mean, time to yourself? What the hell do you call all those hours you're on campus, or in your study?"

"No, I mean really to myself. I need some time to figure things out."

"What are you saying? Are you having an affair?"

Marco didn't answer. His mouth twitched slightly, and his eyes were fixed on the wall past Claire's shoulder.

"Tell me, damn it, are you sleeping with someone?"

"It just happened."

"Nothing JUST happens. You let things happen, you make them happen," she said.

"I don't think it means anything. I know that sounds like some kind of cop-out, but . . ." He hesitated and took a deep breath. "It's more than whether I slept with someone else, let's be straight with each other. Something's been missing; you have to have known it. I, Jesus, I, I'm sorry. I know this is, I mean, it's a hard time for you, you've got a plateful, what with Stephen and Maude and your grandfather."

"So this is your way of helping me?"

He started to say something, then stopped. "Go on." Claire's voice was as icy as her hands had suddenly become.

Marco took a deep breath. "I need to move out for a while. A few months, to figure things out." They both stared at his long fingers that were twisting a rubber band he'd picked up somewhere. "Maybe we could see someone and try to work it out."

This was not possible. This could not be happening. Claire felt the blood pulsing through her veins as if it were trying to find an escape route from her body.

"So who is she?" Claire asked. "Some young graduate student? Are you going to turn my life into a cliché?"

"No, she's not a graduate student. It's not even really about her. It's about me, it's about my work, it's about my whole fucking life." He took a deep breath and sighed. "I don't even know where it's going, if it's going anywhere. I need time away, time to think."

"Goddam it, you could at least have enough guts to tell me who she is. I'm not going to take out a contract on her."

Marco lowered his head and spoke very quietly. "She's the woman who worked with me when I had the writing block."

Shit. The woman whose name she'd given to Marianne.

"My god, Marco, she's not much older that Stephen."

"That's not true, she's almost your age."

"So what is it? Bigger boobs? A better ass? Maybe she's smarter, more degrees?"

"Don't do this, Claire. You're demeaning yourself."

She wanted to scream at him. She wanted to shout every obscenity she'd ever heard, and to make up new ones when those ran out. What she didn't want to do was what happened next: she started to cry, her tears turning Marco into a blur across the space between them.

"Don't, baby, don't," he said, coming to sit next to her. "I know this is hard, it's crazy. I don't even know if it has anything to do with her. I'm going through something that's eating me up, and I need time and space to figure it out. It's not you, it's something in me that's screwed up. A fucking midlife crisis, I suppose."

"You were my best friend," she sobbed, not quite sure it was true. Still, it was effective. Marco began to cry with her.

"You've had to realize that something's gone missing," he said when he'd regained some composure. "We don't talk any more, except about the kids or how we need a new roof or if we're putting away enough for retirement. Not the way we used to talk. We hardly ever make love. And we don't laugh any more. Remember how we used to laugh? Nobody could make me laugh the way you did."

"Life is not fucking funny right now. I don't have any laughter left in me," Claire said. "And if we don't make love it's because you stay up for hours after I go to bed." She glared at him through watery eyes. "But you don't need to sleep with me any more, now you're getting it from – what's her name again? No, don't tell me, I don't want to know."

"Don't lay it at her doorstop. If you're going to hate anyone it should be me. What can I say? These things . . . just happen."

Now the tears stopped. "Will you for one goddam moment stop saying it just happened, you didn't mean for it to happen? You let it happen. You could have stopped as soon as you felt something begin. That would have been the end of it."

"And then where would we be? We're not what we used to be, something got lost, I don't know how. It was great when it was there, but we've both changed. And we both deserve better than what we've had the last couple of years."

Claire put her hand on her mouth. "Oh my god, I just realized. That's where you were when Stephen went to the hospital. No one could find you, and then you showed up in jeans. You never wear jeans to campus. You were there, you were fucking her while your son . . . You bastard."

She rose from the sofa and looked at him, his thinning hair combed to hide a bald spot, his body, once solid enough so that she felt she could lean on him without knocking him over, now softened from too many years in front of a computer.

"You need time to think? Go ahead, go stay in one of those apartments all your divorced friends move into. Eat frozen dinners—or will your lady cook for you? Wash your socks? Maybe she'll iron your underwear. Maybe she can even get you to put it in the hamper. Why don't you just pack your goddam things and leave?" She caught her breath and said coldly "But wait. Before you go, you have to tell the kids."

Marco's eyes filled again.

"Yeah, you have to be the one to tell them," she said. "And I want to be there to make sure you tell them the truth."

Marco blew his nose. "I don't even know what the truth is," he said.

"Just tell them hey, I'm walking out on twenty years of marriage, my family, my home. Tell them that in middle age you've turned into a horny adolescent. I wouldn't be surprised if you tuck copies of *Hustler* under your side of the mattress."

There was a certain pleasure in firing words at Marco, who looked like a partially deflated balloon.

"You really don't understand what I'm trying to say, do you? Anyway I 'm not making any final decisions, I just need some time to think about things," he said.

"Don't think I'm going to sit here like some sixteenth century wife and wait for you to make up your mind about whether or not you want to be with me." She stalked upstairs to their bedroom, threw his pajamas and toothbrush in a sad pile outside the bedroom door, which she locked. They hadn't used the lock for years, not since Sarah had gotten old enough to understand that her parents' closed door truly meant keep out.

Claire wanted desperately to call Maude, but couldn't allow herself to add to the burdens Maude was already carrying. There were other friends she could talk to, even two friends whose husbands had left for younger women. But not yet. She felt humiliated as well as enraged. But why should she be embarrassed? Marco was the one who should be hanging his head, hiding from friends, maybe getting out of town, though he was unlikely to leave a tenured job. Leaving town was out of the question for her; it would mean moving Sarah before she finished high school. Most of all, it would mean leaving Maude, who would, Claire knew, be leaving her before too long. She felt as if her life were lying in tatters around her feet.

THE NEXT MORNING she heard Marco on the phone with Stephen, asking him to come home. "Something important we have to talk about." Silence, and then Marco said with uncharacteristic firmness, "I don't care if you have a lot going on, you've got to come. We'll see you at six." He hung up the phone. "He's granting us a one hour audience."

"It won't take that long," Claire said, and went into her study.

That evening the four of them sat in the dining room, a mushroom pizza set in front of them. Marco served out slices, then, after a few minutes of small talk, took a deep breath and told them that he and Claire were having some difficulties and he was moving out for a while to think things over. "It has nothing to do with you," he said. "It's nothing you've caused in any way."

"Isn't it wonderful? You dad's studied the literature on how to make sure the kids don't think their parents' problems are their fault," Claire said.

Marco ignored her and continued, his eyes focused on the congealing cheese on his slice of pizza. "It's no reflection on your mother, she's been a wonderful wife. It's my problem; I need to be on my own for a while to figure things out. My problem."

"Mea culpa, mea maxima culpa." Claire made the sign of the cross.

Sarah pushed her plate away.

"Mom's right, you sound like a page out of some book you read about how to tell the kids," Sarah said. "You have another woman, don't you." It was a statement.

"That's not the issue. It's . . . difficult to talk about."

"What bullshit, what total bullshit," Sarah said. "I don't believe this. I don't fucking believe this." Marco winced as she hurled names at him, but he sat and absorbed her rage until she ran out of insults and stormed out of the room in tears. Claire was touched by Sarah's demonstration of empathy, if that's what it was. Someone had once told her that daughters don't know where they start and their mothers stop, but this was the first evidence of that claim that Sarah had ever shown since she was a toddler.

Stephen, on the other hand, was trying to be philosophical. "It's really sad, but what can you do? People change," he said. "Half of my friends have divorced parents."

"We're not there yet, Stephen," Marco said. "It's not clear where this is going. Don't get ahead of the process."

"Maybe you'll both wind up happier, who knows?"

Claire wanted to reach across the room and shake him, but when a few minutes later he rose and said, his voice husky, "I . . . I have to go. I'm sorry. I'm sorry for all of us," she felt an impulse to cradle him in her arms the way she did when he was a child.

Claire and Marco sat across from each other, the uneaten pizza lying on their plates with chunks of tomato like blood clots.

"I'll go upstairs and pack," Marco said after an uncomfortable few minutes. Claire remained at the table, tearing small shreds out of the pizza box and piling the scraps on her plate.

Half an hour later he came downstairs, carrying a large suitcase. "I'll call you tomorrow and let you know where you can reach me. You have my cell if you need me. I'll probably stay in my office until I get an apartment or a room somewhere," Marco said. He started to move toward her, but changed his mind. "I'm sorry, Claire. I'm really sorry."

"Just go." She got up and started to pile the leftover food in the tattered box. While she was scraping it into the disposal she heard the door close. She climbed the stairs, which seemed unusually steep, and sat on their bed staring at the empty spaces in their closet. As usual Marco had left his underwear drawer open, something else that always annoyed her, but it no longer held a jumble of boxer shorts and tee shirts.

That night she lay on her side of the bed; the other half stretched out like an empty coffin. She felt as if she were living someone else's life. She was overwhelmed by the hovering need to make decisions but she wasn't sure what they were. Money? She'd probably be okay. Marco wasn't irresponsible, not in that way. And there was the money left when her father died, which Marco had insisted they not use, even during the lean graduate student days. Not a fortune, but enough to assure that she wouldn't ever be a bag lady. Someone had told her that even highly educated women lived with a distant fear of one day becoming bag ladies.

TWO DAYS AFTER HE MOVED OUT, Marco called to tell her he had found an apartment to sublet. She hoped it was one of those colorless places, everything beige with plastic glasses and melamine dishes, a toilet that didn't always flush, water that ran cold half way through a shower.

"I'll come by while you're at work to get the rest of my things."

"We need to talk about arrangements," Claire said. "Money and the kids and stuff."

"You don't have to worry about anything, it's all in both of our names."

"I'm calling Laura," she said. Laura was their lawyer and a friend. She had walked them through writing a will, appointing guardians for the kids, buying their house.

"Just give me some time," he pleaded. "I'm not ready for a formal separation."

"Too bad. I have to protect myself."

"You know I'd never do anything to hurt you," Marco said. She wondered if he realized how ridiculous that sounded. "But okay, if you think you need to do that, go ahead."

Laura suggested marriage counseling when Claire called her later that day and told her what was going on. "Sometimes it can help people get back in touch with each other," she said. But Claire wasn't willing. "He says he has to figure things out, let him see a goddam therapist. I don't see the point in wasting money and time on a futile process."

"All right, but if you're going to get a legal separation, one of you needs to get another lawyer to represent you."

"Dibs on you," Claire said. "He can get his own goddam attorney."

CLAIRE KNEW THAT SHE WOULD NOT BE ABLE TO HIDE the separation from Maude, and in truth she ached for Maude's comfort. She was also concerned about Marianne: had she turned Marianne's husband over to a femme fatale? Sarah was spending most of her time at Joline's, and even though she was grateful that Sarah was taking her side, it was a relief not to listen to her unending rant against her father. But in the last couple of days she had sensed Sarah shifting: did you really try, mom? Didn't you see this coming?

Claire called Rivka, who had moved to Eugene, Oregon several years ago where she was chairing the Women's Studies department and was living with, of all things, an Israeli specialist in Biblical history. "What comes around . . ." Rivka had said when she had told Claire about him in one of their monthly phone conversations. "Would you believe it? My parents would have adored him, even though he's not religious."

Now Rivka said, "Oh sweetie, I'm so sorry. I thought he was too conventional to pull a stunt like this. But maybe adultery is the conventional thing these days. I'm sad you're going through this. But watch, he'll come back—if you want to take him back. Remember, I told you years ago these Catholics never get it out of their system. Somewhere in there is a little priest telling him that divorce is against the will of God."

They talked for half an hour. Rivka offered to come during winter break, but Claire held her off. She wasn't sure she could handle Rivka's energy.

When she hung up she drove to Maude's. Maude was sitting on the sofa, her feet on the coffee table, her lap covered with a faded Mexican quilt. Claire sat down next to her and took her hand as she spoke. She tried to control her anger when she told Maude about the separation, because she knew that Maude and Harry cared about Marco.

Maude shook her head sadly.

"You don't seem all that surprised," Claire said.

"Dearie, you've been complaining about Marco for at least the last year. Problems in a marriage are like plants: they grow over time. I've had a feeling that something was wrong for both of you."

"I want you to know right now that I'm not looking for neutrality from you," Claire said. "I claim you. I need your support to get through this."

"I don't like to give advice, but I will, anyway. Don't burn all your bridges. Things like this can pass or get worked out. It hasn't always been roses for Harry and me, either. I don't think any marriage is uncomplicated."

"I don't know how he could he do this to the kids, let alone me. Sarah will hardly mention his name."

Maude held her arms out, and Claire moved into them, her anger replaced by a deep-rooted sense of loss. She felt as if someone uncovered her heart and ironed it flat and crisp.

CHAPTER SIXTEEN

THE DAYS AFTER MARCO LEFT passed with agonizing slowness. But after a while Claire's anger began to drain like a wound. She felt sapped, as empty inside as her bed was each night. She couldn't concentrate enough to read, and lay in bed watching YouTube videos on her iPad until the effect of a sleeping pill eased her into unconsciousness.

She was overdue for a visit with her grandfather, so on a Saturday morning she checked the weather forecast and started the drive to Scranton. As she drove she rehearsed how to tell him about the separation. She smiled when she thought of him saying "son of a bitch" and said aloud, "You betcha."

When she got upstairs only Abe was in the room. After a prune-scented hug he told her that Zayde was in the game room, "with his sweetie, you should know," he said, winking. "I'll just leave this here and we'll open it later," Claire said, aware that Abe's eyes had wandered to the shopping bag she had brought.

Zayde was sitting at a card table with Bessie and two other people. He looked better than he had for months, even though he was wearing a cheesy-looking shirt with brightly colored baseball players all over it. She kissed him; his aftershave lotion smelled like a gingersnap. Bessie stood up and, holding the back of the chair with one hand, pulled her into an embrace against her tightly corseted body.

"This is David's granddaughter, a joy to him all his life," she told the two women who remained sitting at the table. "She comes from far away to visit, everyone here should only be so lucky."

Claire urged them to continue their game, but the seated women rose. "You should have some private time with your grandpa," one said. Bessie didn't budge. Claire was irritated, though in a few minutes she realized how much easier conversation was with her participation.

"I'm sorry I haven't been here for a while, Zayde. Stephen had an accident." She hastily added that he was fine now, and described what had happened. Zayde looked at her questioningly and pointed to his arm.

"The burn is healing beautifully, he's going to be fine. A little scar, and I hope a little wiser. But the kids were successful. The university has agreed not to lease any land, and busloads of people are going to Albany to demonstrate against fracking."

"Just like his grandfather, no?" Bessie said, and continued without a transition. "You like the shirt? I had my daughter pick it up for him. He says since the Dodgers moved he don't care for baseball, but I seen him taking peeks when the Mets are on the television. You want some tea, darling? They'll bring it if we ask them." Claire demurred, and Bessie rattled on about the Buster Keaton movie they had seen the night before, the birthday party for someone who had turned one hundred, the new cook who had been hired after months of complaints from residents and their families. She talked about Stephen and Sarah, about Claire's job and Marco's teaching. Mostly she had it right, though there were a few factual errors.

Claire was astonished. "How do you know so much about our family? Zayde can't talk."

"We look at pictures and I ask him questions and he shakes yes or no, or he makes signs with his good hand—what do you call them—charades? And I guess what he's trying to tell me, and when I'm wrong we have a good laugh. It takes time, but what else have we got? You'd be surprised how much I get right." She smiled at Claire and reached across to pat her hand.

"We have a good time, the two of us. Don't worry, darling, I'm not asking he should change his will. I'm only asking we should have a little happiness, whatever time we got left. "

"Son of a bitch," from Zayde, who was smiling again. Claire hadn't seen him smile this much since the stroke. She decided not to tell him about the separation. Maybe next visit.

IT WAS CLEAR THAT MAUDE WAS FAILING. Claire now visited every day after leaving the office. Each time she approached the house she wondered with dread if this was the day Maude would ask for her help in taking the pills she had managed to stash away. But Maude was usually drifting in and out of a morphine-induced sleep on the hospital bed the hospice people had finally persuaded her to let them set up in the living room. She had been awake enough to tell Claire a few days ago that the pills were under a pile of papers in the coffee table drawer.

"But I'm not ready yet, dearie, not yet," she had said. "The hospice people are taking such good care of me."

Though Claire hadn't told her co-workers at the office, they knew about Marco. Most made a brief comment of empathy, except Marianne who closed the door and hugged her. "I am so, so sorry, Claire. I wish there were something I could do." Claire resisted saying "Put a leash on your husband," and shrugged out of the embrace. "You know the bumper sticker, shit happens."

Finally the call she had been expecting came from Jasper's office. "He wants to see you right away," Marianne said.

To the woodshed. Or the unemployment office. Claire took a few calming breaths, combed her hair, checked her lipstick and pulled on the down coat that made her feel like a Pillsbury doughboy. It was too much trouble to put on boots, though there was a thin layer of frost on the ground. She walked carefully, filled with dread at what lay ahead. When she arrived, Jasper's secretary buzzed her in, smiling as if she possessed a nasty secret.

Jasper was standing at the window looking out over the quad, his hands folded behind his back. Without turning to look at her he said, "Well."

"Hello, Jasper."

"I'm going to miss this place."

Claire heard it as "You're going to miss this place." Her heartbeat accelerated.

"Yes, but who could say no to Stanford?" he continued, turning to face her.

Wait a minute. "What do you mean?"

"Don't tell me you didn't know. I thought your office had the bead on everything that goes on around here. Including demonstrations."

"No, I . . .I didn't know."

"They made an offer I couldn't refuse. Money, a huge staff, a gorgeous office." He was actually smiling without a hint of smirk.

Claire tried to piece together what he was saying.

"You mean you . . ."

"Well, aren't you going to congratulate me? Not every day someone gets an offer from Stanford."

If firing was going to be his last act before moving on, he was taking sadistic pleasure in drawing it out.

"When do you go?"

"Two months. We have to sell the house, find one out there, pick the best school for the boys. You know the drill."

Actually, she didn't. They had simply stayed in Ithaca, even through Marco's sabbaticals. The challenge of settling the kids in a new school and finding another job when they returned had been overwhelming.

"Anyway, there's something we have to deal with." He nodded her to a seat and moved to the throne-like chair behind his desk. She edged forward on the soft leather. Here it comes.

"I know I came down hard on you when your son was in the hospital. But dammit, you should have stopped him before he got that far with that stupid plan of his. That little incident could have cost us a shitload of money, I can tell you." He paused, and then continued with a self-congratulatory smile. "But we have our contacts, and your boy's little whoop-de-doo brought in some big gifts from new donors who are heavy into environmentalism. So it's pretty much a wash. You were lucky."

Jasper leaned back and looked out the window.

"Anyway, the President's appointed a search committee to find someone for my job. It's going to take time to find the right person. If all this hadn't happened you would have been in the running. But now I want to spare you the embarrassment. Don't apply."

Claire started to laugh, partly with relief, partly with a sense of the absurdity of it all.

"Jasper, what in hell makes you think I would want your job?"

He was startled. "Money, prestige, the president's ear. It's a damned good job. If you and your kid hadn't screwed things up you might have had a shot at it. But now it's all in your personnel file."

Claire stood up. "I appreciate the warning. But let me tell you something. I know this is a great institution filled with brilliant scholars, but I have absolutely no desire to be a mouthpiece for it. It would never have occurred to me to apply for your job. I happen to like my job and the people I work with." She smiled. "I'm not Big League, like you. Good luck at Stanford." She turned and left without waiting for him to say anything further.

On the way back to her office she felt like skipping and singing "Hi Ho the witch is dead." And what she'd said was true. She did like her job; she valued her connections to the people in the office, knew that they trusted and respected her. Even though she would always know that initially she'd gotten her first position because of Marco, for the first time she acknowledged that she'd earned her way up to the editorship, made it on her own merits.

Marianne looked at Claire with concern when she came in. Claire grinned. "I survived my whuppin'. It's going to be okay. In fact it's going to be more than okay. Did you know that Jasper is leaving for Stanford? "

Marianne clapped her hands and rose to give Claire a hug. "Let's go tell the rest of the staff. We've all been worried about you."

CHAPTER SEVENTEEN

I
N THE MIDDLE OF THE NIGHT Maude, disoriented, tried to get out of bed but fell. She bumped her head on the floor and was unable to get up. Harry panicked and called 911, even though Ginger had told him to call the twenty-four hour hospice number for any emergency. An ambulance was there in ten minutes, its siren wailing, followed by a police car. Two young men carefully loaded Maude onto a stretcher and took her to the hospital, Harry riding alongside her and holding her hand as they sped through the night, quiet except for the anxious howl of their vehicle. After a few tests, she was moved into in a small space in the Emergency Room for observation. In the morning, Ginger, scolding gently, showed up to drive them home. They were both exhausted.

Now she swallowed the small white pill Ginger placed on the back of her tongue, then waited for the relief she hoped would come quickly. She was immeasurably happy to be home, not in the hospital. She wondered why they paint hospital walls light green—puke color, Harry called it. It was so lovely and quiet here. She remembered how amplified the sounds of the hospital had seemed: a machine in the next cubicle beeping reassurance to the anxious, uncomprehending family at the bedside of their dying father. They were from – where? Indonesia? Thailand? Malaysia? She remembered the loudspeaker chanting "Paging Dr. Griswold." A buzzer. An alarm followed by rapid footsteps. Someone's heart must have stopped. Yes, so good to be home.

Maude tried to shift her position but a thunderclap of pain ordered her to lie still. She could turn her head without much discomfort, but the rest of her body had to wait for the pills to take command. She no longer cared that they soften the edges of her mind and gave her a sensation of drifting underwater through barely recognizable landscapes.

Maude had always prided herself on being stoic about pain. Stupid arrogant woman, she said aloud, and was startled by the sound of her words. She closed her eyes and started to count slowly backward from one hundred. Each time she did this she made a bet about when the relief would begin. The first time it was at eighty-six. Yesterday it took until thirty-five. Would she reach zero today?

At twenty-seven she felt the tension easing, her body loosening. She sensed that if she could touch her forehead the lines would have begun to smooth to simple old-age wrinkles. Her shoulders unclenched and sunk down into the bed as if someone had put weights on them.

"Hi, mama."

Maude opened her eyes and saw Alice.

"Hello, my darling girl. How grown up you look!"

Then she noticed that only Alice's clothing was grown up. She wore a tailored blue suit and low-heeled pumps, as if she were going to an office. An architect's office, I bet, Maude thought, that's what she said she wanted to be as she built elaborate castles out of Legos. But her face was that of seven-year-old Alice, and her hair was in golden braids, the way she'd worn it before the chemo stripped her scalp. Maude remembered how, before her illness, Alice would scream when Maude would try to brush nests of snarls out of her hair.

"What are you doing here?" Maude asked, and then wondered if her words seem unwelcoming. "I mean, I'm so happy to see you, but how did you get here? Where have you been?"

"That doesn't matter. I just stopped by to say I forgive you, mama."

Maude felt tears pushing toward the front of her eyes. She had made herself forget Alice's pleas from her bed in the children's ward of this same hospital: "Don't let them do this to me, mama. I want to go home NOW."

"You did what you had to do, I understand that now, mama." Alice paused and leaned over the bed. Her fingers brushed Maude's cheek.

"You're so old, mama," she said. "Maybe it's time."

Maude tried to reach up to touch Alice's face, but her arm would not obey the instructions her mind was struggling to convey. She closed her eyes and when she opened them a few seconds later, Alice was gone.

CLAIRE WAS SITTING AT THE KITCHEN TABLE reading Frank Bruni's column, but she was having trouble concentrating. It was eleven on Sunday morning and Sarah was still sleeping; must have been a big night last night.

When the phone rang her heart sped up, as it had many times in these last weeks. She'd tried to prepare for the call that would inevitably come.

Benjamin's voice was quietly urgent. "I think you'd better come soon, she's getting close. She's asked for you a couple of times."

Claire rushed into the first clothing she could grab and left a note for Sarah, then drove the few miles to Maude and Harry's house. "The streets were empty, the airports almost deserted." Auden's poem about the death of Yeats, ran through her mind like a mantra as she drove. The late February air was white with cold; she would hate this month even more now. The most recent pileup of snow lined the street and sidewalks with its sullen gray; the bare branches of trees looked vulnerable.

Benjamin opened the door for her and took her coat. "How long have you been here?" she asked.

"Harry called a couple of hours ago. Her breathing changed, and her feet were beginning to mottle."

Harry was sitting at Maude's bedside, holding her hand. When he looked up at Claire, his eyes were lined with red. She moved behind him and put her hand on his shoulder; he covered it with his own and she noticed the darkened age spots, the prominent veins, his wrists that were almost delicate. She wondered: how soon will he follow her, then forced the thought from her mind.

Maude's eyes were closed; her breathing was loud, but she didn't appear to be in pain. Ginger came out of the kitchen drying her hands on a paper towel.

"Claire. I'm glad you're here. It won't be long now. She's not in any pain. In fact, a few minutes ago she opened her eyes and told

Harry that she'd had a wonderful life with him. And then she asked for you."

Claire moved to the other side of the bed and wrapped Maude's chilled hand between her own. Someone, probably Ginger, had combed Maude's wavy hair back and held it in place with a red hairband, which looked oddly jolly. She appeared peaceful, her mouth relaxed, no frown of pain distorting her face, though her uneven raspy breathing was unnerving. Benjamin had given Claire a booklet detailing what to expect at the end; she had forced herself to read it and now she was glad she had. She thought about her mother's death, how different it had been. She'd been kept out of the hospital room, not allowed to see her. In those days, in that place, it wasn't considered advisable for an eleven year old to see a dead body. For the first few years after her mother died she'd dreamed herself into that room, and upon awakening had struggled to banish images of her mother lying in a blood-soaked bed, or sitting up howling with pain before she dropped back into lifelessness. The scene in Maude's living room could not have been more different from that recurring nightmare.

Benjamin and Ginger left the room. "We're right here in the kitchen if you need us, or if anything changes," Ginger said.

Claire thought about these last weeks. Maude had been spared paralysis, but she hadn't chosen to use the stockpile of pills hidden beneath old Christmas cards in the coffee table drawer. "I'm glad that they're available," she had told Claire, "like an insurance policy. It makes everything more bearable, knowing there's a way out if I choose to take it." Claire was grateful that she hadn't been faced with a decision to help Maude get the pills down; she still wasn't sure she could have done it, in spite of the promise.

Benjamin had told her that people live right up to the end, can hear, and even find pleasure in looking back at their lives. "Especially a life as rich as Maude's," he'd said. He was right; so much had happened in the weeks leading to this moment. Maude and Harry had included her as they talked about their life together, about how they met, about the night in Union Square when the Rosenbergs were executed. About the Freedom March and how Harry had almost gotten arrested for hitting a racist heckler. For the first time they told her the details of Alice's illness, the agony of the treatments and the courage with which she had tolerated them. They laughed about Maude's mother, who right to the end called Planned Parenthood a Nazi organization and thought Nixon had been framed. 'Lived a bitch, died a bitch," Harry said, and Maude had poked him but laughed in agreement. Until a couple of weeks ago, when Maude had said it was too tiring, there had been lots of visitors, many of them former students who had known her as the school librarian. They spoke about how much she'd influenced them, about how she'd inspired them to read and how it had enriched their lives. There were friends, some who came from long distances to see her and say goodbye. Marco came frequently, and if their visits overlapped he sometimes left when she did. Twice he'd invited her to have a drink, but she'd refused.

Maude opened her eyes and murmured "Claire."

"I'm here. I'm right here."

"Hello, dearie." Her eyes closed again, but she murmured "Take care of Harry. Make sure he moves to the Meadows. He promised me."

"I will, Maude. You hear that, Harry?"

Harry leaned close to Maude. "Don't worry about me, sweetheart, I'll be all right. Do you need anything?"

Claire had never heard him use that endearment, yet the word sat comfortably in the space between them.

Maude shook her head slightly. "I'm ready," and closed her eyes.

But I'm not, I never will be. I can't lose another person I love, Claire said without speaking. I cannot bear this.

Ginger brought them steaming cups of mint tea and some biscuits, then checked Maude before she returned to the kitchen.

They sat quietly for the next hour, murmuring to each other from time to time. The sound of Maude's slowing, raspy breaths filled the room. At one in the afternoon she uttered a loud gasp, and then her breathing stopped altogether. It was over.

That can't be it, Claire thought. That breath can't mean that she's gone, that can't be all there is between here and nothing. Harry rested his head on the bed, his shoulders trembling. She moved around and dropped to the floor next to him, her head on his knee and they wept quietly together.

Benjamin and Ginger came into the room. She put her stethoscope to Maude's sunken chest, then nodded and smoothed the sheet around her. She began quietly to pack her nursing supplies as well as the residue of medications Maude had been taking.

Benjamin's voice was barely audible. "Ginger has to leave now, but I'll stay. You let me know when you want me to phone the funeral home," he said to Harry. "Take all the time you want. There's no rush. Is there anyone you want me to call?"

Harry shook his head. "Friends. A couple of cousins. I'll do it later, Claire will help me." Claire realized that she should call Sarah and Stephen, and yes, even Marco. She didn't want to say the words "Maude has died," because they made her death more real, more — forever. Yet she would not dishonor her friend by sinking into metaphors: she hadn't lost a battle, hadn't warred against the disease. Nor was she "finally at rest," nor "on to the next world." She was dead, had died.

Ginger put on her down jacket and wrapped a scarf around her head. When she hugged Harry Claire noticed tears in her eyes. "That was one great lady," she said. "I'm so grateful we had these months with her. Thank you for sharing her." She reached for Claire's hand. "You were lucky to have her in your life for so many years. She told me you were as close to a daughter as anyone could be."

Claire turned away, afraid her weeping would turn into a primitive howl, a deluge in which she would drown. Her life was a life of losses: two mothers, one her best friend; her father, who may or may not have chosen to leave her. Her marriage. A grandfather who would probably die before too much time went by. At least Maude had died in her own sweetly cluttered living room, in a house she loved, with its familiar smells, stains, noises. She thought about where Zayde was, and wondered if, when the time came, she would have the courage to help him, if somehow he could communicate that it was what he wanted.

In half an hour Harry rose and went into the kitchen. "You can call now," he said to Benjamin.

Claire and Harry sat in the kitchen when the funeral director and his assistant came in to remove Maude's body. They heard the sound of the gurney being wheeled to the front door, then the door closing. It was over.

CLAIRE MOVED THROUGH THE DAYS that followed without being fully aware of what she was doing. There would be no funeral; Maude was to be cremated. But Harry agreed to a memorial service to be held in the spring so friends from distant places would be able to come without worrying about road conditions. That would give Claire time to work on the eulogy Harry had asked her to give. Claire agonized as she wrote and rewrote what she would say, wondering how you could summarize a life like Maude's in a brief talk. On paper: no great credentials. A Bachelor's degree in literature. One child, deceased. A long good marriage. Hundreds, if not thousands, of children encouraged to read, to love books and stories and poetry. She could say that that Maude had overcome a confining, conservative childhood and blossomed into an open-minded, progressive and loving adult. That she had, in spite of the loss of her own child, been open and loving to so many children. That she had earned, in this community of credential-conscious achievers, a Ph.D. in the art of friendship. Truly, the whole was so much greater than the sum of its parts.

CHAPTER EIGHTEEN

TWO MONTHS AFTER MAUDE'S MEMORIAL SERVICE, Claire sat at her desk staring at the phone. Twice she lifted the receiver, then returned it to its cradle. Finally, she punched in the phone number on the card she had taken from Maude's bedside table.

"This is Hospice," a voice said, with studied kindness.

"Is Mr. Carson available?" She identified herself to the receptionist and waited in the quiet space where callers were put on hold. At least no rock and roll, she thought.

Benjamin's voice came on the line. "Claire! How nice to hear from you! I've been thinking about you, wondering how you're doing. This must be a hard time."

Her eyes filled, grateful to have her sadness acknowledged. So many people seemed to hint that she should pull up her socks and get on with it. She also heard loud and clear his words: I've been thinking about you.

"I was wondering if you might have time . . ." she said. "I've been wanting to talk to you."

"Of course. Why don't we meet tomorrow morning for coffee at Dewitt? It's pretty quiet there before lunch. Say about eleven?"

"Thank you," she said.

This is bizarre, Claire said to herself, feeling felt like a teenager as she stood in front of her closet. What to wear. My husband left, what was it, six months ago, my best friend died four months ago, and here I am thinking about a man who's practically a stranger. Yet he didn't seem like a stranger, the way he tuned into her needs. She started talking aloud to Maude: look at me, this is crazy, isn't it? I'm fifty years old, and I'm all fluttery about sitting in a café drinking coffee with a man I hardly know. You'd have a good laugh about it, wouldn't you!

She dressed carefully in a way she hoped appeared casual. Long sleeve blue tee shirt, good color for her. She tied, retied then rejected a scarf, pulled over her head a string of African beads. Yes. Pants or skirt? Pants. Hair, oh Christ, this hair. Streaked with grey, too curly. Stop it, dearie, Maude's voice instructed her reflection. Act your age.

Benjamin was at the counter talking to one of the owners of the café when she arrived. She smiled and tried to look at ease. He gave her a brief hug.

"Hope it's okay, I ordered two lattes," he said. She didn't tell him that she always had hers with skim milk.

They settled into a corner table, away from half a dozen people who were drinking coffee and staring at their laptops.

"How are you doing?" he asked. "These first few months can be so tough."

"I'm okay, but I keep thinking of things I want to tell her, and then I remember that I can't and I fall apart."

"Maude was an amazing listener. I think she got me to tell her more about myself than anyone I've ever worked with. How did you get to know her?"

She took a sip of her coffee, and told him about her first encounter with Harry about The Peaceable Kingdom and his insistence that she and Marco come to dinner. She talked about how Maude had rescued her from a very bad start when they first moved here, about their hikes exploring remote and beautiful trails around the lakes, about the friends she'd made through Maude. Soon she was talking not just about how much Maude had meant to her, but about Stephen's accident, about the frustrations of her job, about her grandfather. "And I'm not sure you knew that in the middle of all this my husband and I separated."

Benjamin listened carefully. "What a lot you've been carrying," he said. He began to talk, a little academically, she thought, about the nature of grief, about stages people go through. "You've got to give yourself permission to feel whatever you feel at any given time."

Claire tried to ignore what sounded like canned comfort. Instead she watched the way his brow furrowed when he was trying to recall something, the slight gap between his front lower teeth, the dark hair on his arms when he sat back and rolled his sleeves to the elbow.

"Listen, it might be a good idea for you to talk to our bereavement counselor," he said. "She's terrific, very sensitive and knowledgeable. And you might want to consider a bereavement group, we always have several going on."

I'd rather talk to you.

He continued, apparently not noticing her lack of response. "And I'll give you the names of a couple of books that might be helpful."

He tore a page out of a small notebook and jotted down several titles.

"Thank you," she said, putting the page in her purse. 'Clearly I'm not as good a listener as Maude. I've been babbling away and I hardly know anything about you. Like, how long have you been doing hospice work? And how come you know so much about poetry and all those classic novels?"

He smiled that sweet gap-toothed smile and she noticed a slight dimple on the right side of his mouth. "Well, I told you that I was a money-grubbing corporate lawyer before I threw it over and went to social work school. After a couple of years on an Indian reservation I visited someone who was a hospice patient, and I felt like I'd come home. The rest is history. And the literature stuff? It wasn't my academic training. The truth is, it was someone I love who kind of opened me up to it."

"Was that your wife? The one who left when you quit law?"

He laughed. "She wouldn't have known a poem if she fell over it. No, my partner, Roger. He teaches literature at the university."

Claire sat perfectly still. You fool, you stupid idiotic fool, was all she could think as a litany of self-loathing swept over her. Sarah would have laughed: don't you have gaydar, mom?

"Are you all right?" Benjamin asked.

"I just . . . I didn't know . . ."

"That I'm gay? I didn't know either, or at least I didn't acknowledge it to myself until I was in my mid-thirties."

Claire struggled for composure and failed. 'Not that...it's just...I thought..."

Benjamin looked at her, and then reached across the table. "Oh Claire, I'm sorry. I hope I didn't mislead you. You're so vulnerable right now, it's not me, it's anyone who's kind to you. You've been through so much in such a short time."

"It's okay," she said. "I'm fine. But I've got to go, my daughter 's waiting for me to pick her up." She rose and held out her hand. "Goodbye, Benjamin. And thank you."

When she got home she was relieved to find Sarah's note saying she was going to soccer practice after school and wouldn't be home until six. Without taking her shoes off, Claire crept under the covers of her bed and fell into a thankfully dreamless sleep.

CHAPTER NINETEEN

CLAIRE WOULD NEVER BE SURE how she got through the next few months. Her desire to make changes in the newsletter waned. She and Marco had brief telephone conversations about the kids and finances. Sometimes he would perch on the sofa as he waited for Sarah and ask Claire about her work and what she had been doing with herself. Her responses were always short and unrevealing, and she never asked him anything.

In spite of the implicit threat, Claire never heard another word from Jasper. Finally, with a sense of dread, she checked her employment file to see how damaging his report was. She was stunned to find that he hadn't made any entries.

Stephen had been jubilant when the university finally took a firm position opposing fracking and supporting a permanent ban. The President's report had cited parts of Claire's original work, without credit, of course, referring to it as an "unbiased staff review of the current research." The movement had gained momentum; in many parts of the county, villages and towns had voted to ban fracking. But the state Department of Environmental Conservation, assigned to review the safety of the procedure, was under the thumb of the gas industry. Thousands of physicians, scientists and citizens were marching on Albany to demonstrate against the possibility of lifting the ban on drilling.

In early November Stephen, fully recovered except for the scarring on his arms and a barely visible line that divided one eyebrow, announced that he wanted to take a semester off to work in an orphanage in a mountain village in Guatemala. "I need time to figure things out," he said. He and Nora had mutually decided, as he put it, "to explore other options in relationships." Claire watched with concern his growing restlessness.

"I don't know what I'm doing, mom," he said over one of their rare lunches on campus. "I mean, the fracking stuff was great, but I don't have any sense of what's next. I don't want to waste your money and my time while I figure it out. Anyway, it'll be great for my Spanish."

He told her that when he called Marco that morning to tell him about the Guatemala plan, his father expressed fear that he would get involved in the political strife of the country. "I told him, hey, I'm just going to work with kids. And the orphanage is run by nuns—so how much trouble could I get in there?"

Maude put her fork down and frowned at him. "Do I think you're capable of keeping your views to yourself? No way am I that stupid. Have you read about Guatemalan prisons?"

But Stephen was adamant. He had been socking away money from his part-time and summer jobs, and he could live free at the orphanage. Claire was confronted with the limitations of her parental authority and her powerlessness to influence his decisions.

"Do you know what that son of yours wants to do?" Marco said over the phone that evening.

"As I recall, he was formed from my egg and one of your swimmers," she said.

Marco laughed. "Yeah, but you're the one with the crazy genes. All I brought was the revealed word. Anyway, do you approve of this Guatemala thing?"

"It's not a 'thing,' Marco." She sighed, knowing that she was pretending to be more positive than she felt. "Whether we approve or not, Stephen will be who he is and do what he does. He's twenty years old, he's not asking us for any money, he's simply informing us. There's no way we can change his mind. So we might as well be supportive."

Sarah had been reasonably friendly to Claire recently, though whether it was because her mother was an object of pity or Sarah was emerging from the hateful cocoon of adolescence was yet to be seen. She was letting her hair grow out of its spiky cut, and there were no visible new piercings. She played soccer after school, took clarinet lessons, babysat twice a week. There was a slightly nerdy boy who had begun to show up some evenings, supposedly to help her with trigonometry, but behind the closed door of Sarah's room Claire could hear the thump thump thump of blaring music. She listened as closely as she could to hear any other kind of thumping sounds, but the music was so loud she couldn't discern anything else. Sarah had begun to relinquish her anger toward Marco and had agreed to an occasional mostly monosyllabic lunch, about which Marco complained to Claire: "She just sits there, hardly says a word, just yes no yes no. I know she has a right to be mad at me, but I'm trying my damndest." Her angry outbursts at Claire over minor disagreements were less frequent, and life at home had taken on a relatively tranquil rhythm.

But Claire's sense of restlessness was unabated. Sarah would be looking at colleges next year; it was hard not to think about the emptiness that lay ahead. She needed to find something new to give her a sense of meaning, "Go online," her friend Carolynne said when Claire described her malaise. "Meet some hot guy who will take your mind off Marco."

"It's not Marco. I mean, of course it's Marco, but it's me, too. I feel so . . . I don't know, undefined. And I don't feel ready to start dating again. God, what an awful word that is!"

"What would Maude say?" That had become almost a mantra among the women who had loved and depended on Maude's wisdom and perspective. "Okay, if it's not a man, how about finding something new to do? Horseback riding? Swimming? Watercolors?"

Oh Carolynne, you're a dear friend, but you're no Maude, Claire thought.

A brief notice on the Planned Parenthood website mentioned a need for volunteers. With uncharacteristic decisiveness, Claire phoned the office and made an appointment with Madge Wilson, the volunteer coordinator.

"You can't know how great it is to have someone like you come in, someone who lives here year round and doesn't disappear at finals," Madge said.

THE VOLUNTEER WORK helped to fill some of the empty hours after work and on weekends. After a few hours of orientation she began as a Clinic escort on Saturdays, welcoming patients to Planned Parenthood and making sure that protesters stayed off Clinic property. The demonstrators continued their hostile vigils, but the staff and volunteers were ordered not to engage with them. There was nothing Claire would have liked more than shouting at them to fuck off. When a few weeks later she was asked to work inside helping with the monthly newsletter, she was relieved not to have to exercise all that self-restraint. And it was pleasant to get to know the staff, all of whom seemed inordinately grateful for any help she could provide. She enjoyed working on the newsletter, interviewing members of the staff and patients of varying ages.

On a Monday morning in June Libby Hatch, the Executive Director of Planned Parenthood, called Claire at her office and asked if they could get together, as soon as possible. "Can you give me some idea of what this is about?" Libby responded that she would prefer to talk in person. Claire immediately started her usual mental peregrinations: had Libby observed her give the finger to one of the demonstrators who was shouting "baby killers!" as people entered and left the building? Had she offended someone on the staff with her editing suggestions?

"I'd rather wait until we're face to face," Libby said. "Can you come over after work today?"

Claire agreed, but found it hard to concentrate for the rest of the day.

Libby had a small office on the second floor of the old building. As Claire walked toward it, she wound through a maze of staff desks crowded together; the walls were covered with clippings, pro-choice cartoons and inter-office communications. Staff members, busy at their desks, looked up and waved or smiled as she passed.

Libby wore her usual frazzled expression. The small computer on her desk was almost hidden by files and papers. She sighed as she rose to shake Claire's hand. "Look at this, it's a wonder I don't suffocate in it."

They talked for a moment about the demonstrations, and then Libby said, "Okay, we're both busy people, let's get down to it. I want to offer you a job." She paused. "You look surprised."

Claire nodded. "How about stunned? I spent the day wondering what I'd done wrong.""

Libby laughed. "You've been doing everything right. We have an opening and I think you'd be perfect for it. I would be thrilled not to have to do a search when we have the right person in front of our noses! It's a new position, Director of Communications. You'd be coming in at a critical time. I don't know if you've heard, but we're about to launch a capital campaign. You saw what it's like out there." She gestured toward the door. "If we don't get into a bigger building soon we're going to start eating each other for lunch."

Claire was speechless. This was the last thing she had expected. She'd never even thought about working here as anything other than a volunteer.

"I know it's going to be less money than you're making on the hill," Libby said. "That can't be helped. But we've got a pretty good benefit package. Of course we can't compete with the tuition freebie. Do you still have a kid going to college?"

"One who's about to wander Central America looking for himself; he has another year to go. And my daughter's sixteen. But her father is on the faculty so we'd still have the tuition break. Wow. I don't know what to say. This comes so out of the blue."

Libby reached into her drawer and handed Claire a job description. "You'd have a small staff. We're bringing in someone to run the actual campaign. You'll be working closely with her, but you both report to me. And I mean closely: we'll probably have to put your desks in the bathroom. She's great, lots of experience and real commitment. She's from Canada, worked at the Clinic where that doctor was shot." She tilted back in her chair back. "Who ever thought you'd have to bullet-proof a women's health clinic!"

Libby was right; the salary was eight thousand less than Claire was making.

"You'll need to meet with the Search Committee. The staff and I think you'd be perfect and you know half the people on the Board. Take a week to think about it, then if you're interested I'll get interviews organized at this end."

We all think you'd be perfect. She said the words aloud as she drove back to campus. We all think you'd be perfect. When had she ever heard that!

And yet Claire was overwhelmed by the possibility of such a huge change after all these years. Her job at the university was familiar, easy, occasionally interesting. She worked with good people. Planned Parenthood was under fire with crazies out there threatening its staff; some legislators in other parts of the country challenged its very existence. But was it any more dangerous than Stephen going to Guatemala? She longed to talk it over with Maude.

A FEW DAYS LATER MARCO CALLED. "Can we have dinner? I need to talk to you about Stephen," he said. "This thing about Guatemala is driving me nuts."

Claire found herself rising to Stephen's defense. "It's not so crazy, lots of kids take a year off."

"Let's talk about it over dinner," he said. "Please."

They agreed to meet at Madeline's. When she hung up she wished that she'd suggested someplace else. Madeline's had been their special occasion restaurant: birthdays, anniversaries. It was filled with memories: martinis in the room with the bar that looked as if it had been imported from a sophisticated Manhattan restaurant; desserts delivered with a birthday candle burning in the center of a decadent chocolate concoction.

They hadn't seen each other for a few weeks, though it seemed to her that Marco was finding reasons to call more frequently, to work out something about taxes or a repair he'd arranged to have done in the house if it was convenient for her.

Claire had gotten used to living without him, and sometimes realized that she enjoyed the freedom of it. If she awoke in the middle of the night she could turn her lamp on to read without his grumbling that the light was waking him. If Sarah was out and she didn't feel like cooking, she could eat a bowl of cereal. She didn't have to share the Sunday *Times*, and she could listen to Bach Partitas at top volume without anyone complaining, including Sarah, who, when she was home, was encased in earphones, her body moving to some inaudible rhythm. Claire had wearied of cautioning Sarah about destroying her hearing.

Claire showered and stood in front of the mirror, her hair wrapped in a towel. She looked at her reflection and saw a fifty-year-old woman. Not too bad for fifty. More lines around her eyes, the skin at her neck beginning to show signs of loosening. Breasts still firm. She'd recently overcome her aversion to exercise and had joined the Y, where twice a week after work and on Sunday afternoon she pedaled, lifted, climbed and sweated. Her body was beginning to show the effects, and she ran her hands with pleasure over her narrowed waistline. Belly, well, yeah, belly. She'd have to work harder on that. If she felt like it. She'd started to cover the grey in her hair, highlighting it with touches of auburn.

What does a spurned wife wear? She decided on a white silk blouse with black wool trousers, the black and white Kazuri beads Maude had given her years ago, and some long silver earrings. What am I fussing for, she asked herself aloud. I should show up in torn jeans and a stained tee shirt.

Marco was waiting at the bar when she intentionally arrived ten minutes late. He looked as if he'd also put some thought into his appearance; in fact, he looked damned good. He rose and was about to kiss her cheek when she pulled back and put out her hand to shake his.

"Hey," he said.

"Hey."

"You look great."

"Living alone agrees with me. I mean I live with Sarah, but in terms of communication I might as well live alone." They were shown to a table.

It was a weeknight and there were few customers. Tony Bennett was crooning "All of Me" on the speaker system.

"The usual for you?" he asked as the waiter approached. She nodded, wondering if he'd get it right.

"Two Sapphire martinis straight up with a twist, very dry," Marco said.

He'd remembered. "When did you start drinking martinis?" she asked.

"Tonight. So you wouldn't say anything about my 'girl' drinks." Marco's taste for whiskey sours had been a source of embarrassment when they were out with other people who were ordering single malt whisky or Malbec.

"You were never much for handling more than a glass of wine," she said. "You'd better be careful."

"Why, you going to seduce me if I get tanked?"

"Not funny,"

"You're right, I'm sorry." He was quiet for a moment.

"So. Here we are," he said.

"Yup, here we are. And if you think we're going to come up with a plan to change Stephen's mind we might as well cancel the drinks and call it a night."

"I know we're not. That damned kid, he's just like you. Makes up his mind and he forges straight ahead."

She looked at him and shook her head. "You've got the wrong woman. I'm the Queen of What-If. You must have me mixed up with Susannah or whatever her name is."

The waiter brought their drinks. Marco spilled a little as he raised his glass. "To you."

The drink was perfect: icy, served in a frosted glass, mostly gin with a hint of lemon.

"Susannah," he said. "That's a whole other story."

"I don't think I want to hear it." Claire dipped piece of focaccia in olive oil and leaned forward to avoid spilling any on her blouse.

"Let me give you the short version. It's over."

Claire was quiet for a moment. "Have you moved out?"

"I never moved in. I wasn't ready for that. She wasn't what it was all about, anyway."

"I really don't need to hear this."

"Yes you do, Claire." Marco reached across the table and took her hand. "This dinner—it's not about Stephen. I knew we weren't going to change his mind. It's about you. You and me."

"Marco, there is no you and me," she said, withdrawing her hand

He shook his head and bit his bottom lip. "I really fucked up. Leaving you was the biggest mistake I ever made in my life. I must have been crazy. I don't know what I was going through, some kind of midlife shit, I guess. My research had started to feel like I'd hit a wall, I was tired of chasing grants, you were all tied up with Maude—that's not a criticism, it's just – I was lonely, I guess." He pulled the twist of lemon out of his drink and twirled it. "I'm sorry, I know I hurt you. I don't know how to make it up."

Claire thought about how she used to imagine hearing Marco say something like this, usually when she was lying in bed with her vibrator. Now she thought of old movies where the waves break against the shore as the couple kisses. She surrendered to an impulse to laugh.

"I don't see what's funny about this," Marco said.

"We are. We're straight out of a B movie. Or a Sondheim musical. Me with my feet on the ground, you in the air, something like that."

The waiter came back to the table to tell them about the evening's specials. Claire decided on the striped bass; Marco ordered a steak.

After the waiter left with their order, Marco seemed unable to pick up where he had left off.

"How's your work going now?" Claire asked to fill the silence and give them both a change to regroup.

"Better. I got a grant, so I'll be spending some time in London next semester." He told her about the project that was being funded by the Anti-defamation League: an examination of peer pressure among British academics to ostracize Israeli scholars. "I guess they thought someone with a name like Capobianco would be objective. They don't know I have half-Jewish kids."

"Probably a good thing that you're separated from someone named Goldstein."

"No, it's not. It's not a good thing at all. It sucks. Claire." Marco reached for her hand again, but she pulled back and interrupted what he was about to say.

"Look, I'm not where you are, Marco. This has been a rotten year, a totally shitty rotten year. Stephen's injury, Maude's death. You walked out on me. My job is—but that's another story. The kids are pretty much grown and don't need me. At least not very much. Marco, I'm fifty years old and I still haven't figured out what I want in my life."

As she said it, she realized that it wasn't true. She wanted the Planned Parenthood job, wanted to believe in what she was doing, she wanted to work where her skill with words could make a difference. She wanted to work with people who were passionate about something. She wanted what she did to matter.

Marco took a sip of his drink and then said, "Claire, listen to me. Let's put this whole crazy time behind us. I want you to come to London with me, at least for part of the time. You can take a leave. And Sarah can stay with Joline."

Claire shook her head. "Not a chance."

"I won't go without you."

"Yes you will, Marco. We're not in our twenties any more. We're not beginners in life. Maybe Sarah and I will come visit you for Christmas and we'll have a little fling. We can stay in a hotel— remember how turned on we used to get by hotels? Or maybe the three of us can go to Guatemala to see Stephen being the Pied Piper with his orphan kids. I'd like that."

Marco's expression crumpled. "You're getting even with me. I guess I deserve it."

Claire smiled. "You can't begin to imagine all the ways I've thought about getting even with you. I could go to hell just for my fantasies. And now that there's a chance to get back at you, it doesn't matter anymore."

"What are you trying to say?"

The waiter appeared with their salads. Claire toyed at the arugula with her fork.

"I'm saying that I don't hate you. Who knows, I may even still love you. But I think I'm changing—or at least I'm trying to. I don't want to arrange my life around getting even with you or with pleasing you. I have a chance to take a job that really matters, and they want me, they think I can do it well on my own merits. You can't begin to imagine what that's like, after all these years. I need time, Marco, time to figure out if I still want to be your wife."

Marco drained his martini and ordered another.

"Am I going to have to carry you home?" she asked.

"You might. You might even have to put me to bed," he said.

"Now you're talking," she said, and they clinked glasses.

CPSIA information can be obtained at www.ICGtesting.com
Printed in the USA
BVOW02s2131250216

438128BV00001B/14/P